The Rise of Amphitrite

A Trident Trilogy

Savannah L. Zher

The Rise of Amphitrite

ISBN 9781088128114

Editor: Taylor Robinson

Cover Artist: Jaqueline Kropmanns

To my high school sophomore English teacher, Jessica Rewitz.
Thank you for believing in a girl who couldn't do the same for herself.
I did it.

Chapter One

THIRTEEN YEARS AGO

A loose strand of my raven-colored hair falls across my face. It tickles my nose as my body flows, with my bow in hand, against my cello. I ignore my hair and instead focus my attention on the musical notes placed in front of me. The notes are fast, precise and smooth. When Miss Justine first introduced this piece to me, my fingers fumbled up and down the neck of my cello. It was like I was a novice all over again. I practiced every day for months to get my finger work perfect.

Finishing the prelude, I take in a deep breath to steady and prepare myself to play it once more. Only this time I close my eyes, wanting to test if my body has memorized the music. Music that I've practiced so endlessly that I can see the sheet of notes even in my dreams. I want nothing more than for my mother and father to be proud of me. To see the look of pride shining upon their faces means everything to me. It's the only thing my childish mind focuses on. It would crush me if their pride was replaced by disappointment. I try every day to be the perfect daughter they wish me to be.

Releasing my breath, I relax my body and begin playing. I fall into a state of calm and obedience as my fingers work nimbly against the strings. The strings are coarse and have warmed from my recent playing. My body sways once more, and like it is second nature, I become one with the instrument, fused together like peanut butter is to jelly. The bow is merely an extension of my arm, an obedient partner while I maneuver it at different angles to catch the highs and lows of the melodious music. The back of the cello sits against my chest and its vibrations run through my body.

It whispers to my very soul. *Peace.*

And as I get lost in the waves of music, peace is what I find.

Ending the song with a flick of my wrist, I let out an audible sigh of contentment at being able to play the song from memory. My practice has paid off. I look over to Miss Justine, and her hazel eyes glow with approval as she leans over the gray chaise lounge that is placed strategically between myself and the wall of windows that overlook the ocean. Years prior, when she had become my instructor, she had placed the chair there because she noticed me often staring out, lost in my daydreams instead of the notes placed before me. Back then I didn't care to learn how to play, but now that I can actually create wonderful music, I find it to be a balancing experience. Whenever I am stressed by my studies, I get lost in my cello, where I can create music befitting my mood.

Unable to contain my energy, I tap my feet against the carpet and twirl my cello, waiting for her critique of my performance. Around and around the cello spins, at such a speed that I'm surprised Miss Justine hasn't scolded me yet. I can't wait till I get bigger, so that I can have an adult-sized cello like the one Miss Justine has. The notes are so much deeper that it has a prettier sound to it. It leaves you relaxed, so much so that at times it has lulled me into dreams of warm sunshine and soft waves against the sandy shore. The beach is the only other solace I have away from my endless studies.

Tomorrow night I will be playing this prelude at the event my parents are hosting. That is why I have been practicing relentlessly, because like always, my parents are expecting a perfect performance. I shall go above and beyond their expectations and achieve nothing less.

Every year, they host a charity auction to celebrate my birthday. Many people bring gifts, but the gifts they bring for me are actually what is going to be sold during the auction. The more expensive the gift, the more respect that person has for you. But in my case, since I am still a child, it is respect for my parents, or more so, my father. The guests are his clients and a few top employees that fly into Caracas from all across Europe and Asia, fully paid for by my father.

Bobbing my head, I tap my foot to a song that my mother often sings to me when she brushes my hair. Getting into the beat, I start to softly sing under my breath,

"Didada, dida dida.

Laoshu pashang da zhong.

Yi dian zhong.

Ta pao xialai.

Didada dida dida."

"Very good, Amy. I see that you've been practicing."

I look up at Miss Justine, who nods her head with a slight smile upon her lips. She doesn't comment on my restlessness as she watches me bounce around. Father has been very stern about me learning how to play. He believes that among the many necessary attributes of a lady, mastery of a musical instrument is essential. He has Miss Justine come over twice a week to teach me. I am forever grateful for that decision, for it has not only taught me patience but a love for classical music. Aside from practicing the cello when Miss Justine is not here, Father also has me learning French daily from Mister Gustavo, and he teaches me fencing himself.

My father is an outstanding fencer; his medals line the hallway that leads to the music and fencing room. Next to his case of medals are my mother's own medals and ribbons that she was awarded during her early years of dancing. My father and mother are both second generation Chinese—United Kingdom immigrants who just so happened to be in New York City at the same time. My father for business, my mother for dance. I was given the choice to learn ballet from my mother or fencing from my father for an extracurricular. I chose fencing because I found it more intriguing. Besides, fencing gives me an excuse to not be so lady-like, something that I'll never admit out loud, and I love the rush that sparring brings. Each session I am left drenched in sweat from the exertion of trying to lay a mark on my father. This past session with him I was finally able to mark him and it was exhilarating, to say the least, to outwit my father. In that moment he was nothing short of proud and my chest swelled with that approval. It was a day that has played on repeat through my mind. I don't think I'll ever forget the only true look of approval he has ever given me.

My eyes follow Miss Justine, her heels clicking as she gets up from the chaise lounge. She has a purple, ruffled blouse on, with plain black slacks to match. As she crosses the room to grab her bag, I focus my attention to my left, where the wall of windows is. With longing oozing from my pores, I stare out at the endless blue that glistens like diamonds in the sun's rays. The water crashes against the white shore and it makes me wish that I could hear the music of those waves. To me, each new day the beach sounds different. The clashing of wave against wave creates a different tune, and I swear the water itself sings to me.

A pelagic bird catches my eye as it swoops down and lands on the beach with its brothers. There's a group of them huddled together around some sort of mass. The mass is too far away for me to make out what it is. My mind springs to all sorts of possibilities. Maybe it's a mermaid basking in the rays the afternoon sun has to offer. Or maybe there were pirates who got caught in an earlier storm and the lone survivor got washed up on the shore. Whatever it is, I hope it'll be something interesting and not just a pile of seaweed and dead fish the birds could be feasting on.

The sound of Miss Justine's heels against the wood turns soft when she arrives in the carpeted area of the room where I am still seated, lost in my daydream. She clicks her tongue to grab my attention. "That was a wonderful Prelude 1 of Bach, and your parents will be very pleased," she says, and I beam up at her with a brilliant grin.

Miss Justine chuckles and gives my chin a little tug to close my slackened jaw. "I also see that you have finally lost your tooth."

"Yes, Mother says that the tooth fairy is sure to give me five dollars for it, but then father said that the tooth fairy isn't real." I furrow my eyebrows in disbelief, thinking about my father's comment and then ask earnestly, "Do you think the tooth fairy is real, Miss Justine?" With my front tooth gone, my words come out in a lisp.

My question makes her chuckle again. Or perhaps it is simply due to how I currently sound, but she replies, "Well, my dear, what do you think?"

I jump up with my bow in hand and arms flying in the air. "The tooth fairy has got to be real! It's the most logical explanation. Who else would want to collect teeth but the tooth fairy?" My mind is blown that my father is convinced that there is no such thing as a tooth fairy. I flail my arms around in indignation with my hands formed into defiant fists. Mister Gustavo recently mentioned the French Revolution, and with my fists in the air, I am reminded of the rights the French people fought for. Right now I feel like a Jacobin, but instead of fighting for the downfall of a crown, I am fighting for the tooth fairy's recognition in our society.

Miss Justine smiles as she takes my bow from me and places it on its stand. "I guess you have your answer, then. The tooth fairy is real. We are done for today—your rendition was flawless." She then brings out a small box I hadn't noticed from behind her back. My eyes light up in delight as she hands me a present wrapped in my favorite color. "Happy birthday, Amy."

I look at her tentatively as I carefully hold the box between my fingers. I've never received a birthday gift before, and I'm not even sure if this is alright. She nods her head in encouragement and I waste not a second more before I rip open the gift.

It's a box of assorted chocolates. I squeal in delight and jump into her opened arms. Giving her a giant hug, I say, "Thank you so much, Miss Justine. This is the best birthday ever. It's—" My words sputter over my tongue as emotion overwhelms me from the surprise. "It's perfect," I finally say.

She squeezes me back, a firm hug that is filled with so much tender softness. With our cheeks squished against each other, she whispers, "You are oh so welcome, sweet girl."

With my box of chocolates in tow, I walk down to the beach to inspect what the flock of pelagic birds have gathered around. Drawing nearer, I notice that they are Brown Noddies. Their foreheads are white that blends into a sliver of charcoal around their necks, and their bodies are a light brown. The blending of their coloring makes the birds look as soft as clouds.

I slow my pace so that I don't scare them off. They're completely silent as they stand around the mass on the sand. The silence is eerie and almost unnatural. They face outward, as if they are little soldiers on patrol duty lined up protecting whatever it is that their backs are turned to. I find it quite comical and give a giggle with the mental image of them dressed up in uniform with a metal hat placed upon each of their little bird heads, singing, *the Noddies go marching one by one hurrah, hurrah.*

Peering over the birds, at first all I notice is a pile of seaweed, but upon further inspection I see that there is a body under it. A pirate? I take in a deep, nervous breath as I notice the form is not moving. *Please don't be dead, please don't be dead.* I chant that mantra in my head like a prayer as I take slow, cautious steps closer. I am but two steps away from the body when the Noddies all turn to me at once and then fly off synchronously. The sudden flight of all the birds frightens me and I jump back, but I still keep my ground. During lessons with father, it's been always drilled into me to not turn your back on danger. The birds are no cause for alarm, but that didn't stop my heart from stuttering in trepidation. I have an odd feeling that this will be a crucial moment in my life.

Clutching the chocolates against my chest, my eyes follow the birds until they land on a nearby tree. I compose my erratic breathing before looking back down at the body, preparing myself for the worst. Did he drown at sea and get washed up? I hope he's not dead because I don't think I'm strong enough to carry him. I'd have to go get my father for assistance. But if this is a dead body, then Father might limit the amount I can go to the beach. Or worse, make it so my visits are supervised. I internally groan at that last thought. I enjoy my outings alone too much to let this person ruin it. I'd have to find someone else to haul this body off of the beach, but who? The gardener perhaps? He looks strong enough. But not as strong as my father. No, no ...

I tap my chin in thought about my dilemma and then see turquoise eyes staring up at me. They're the same color as my wrapping paper from Miss Justine. They swirl into different shades as they stare up at me and it's like the very ocean exists in them. Letting out a breath that I hadn't realized I'd been holding in, I loosen my grip on the chocolates. He's alive, and he's just a kid like me. *But he could still be a pirate,* the adventurous side of me quips.

"You're a strange boy," I state as I sit cross-legged next to him, not at all showing the hesitation and fear I felt earlier. He says nothing and continues to stare at me. Furrowing my eyebrows, I wonder where he came from. There are no children that live nearby and he clearly isn't a pirate, as he is dressed in normal clothing, although I kind of wish he was. It would be cool to be friends with a pirate. Maybe he's a grandkid of one of the neighbors who lives a few kilometers away? But I find it odd that he's covered himself with seaweed. Who does that? Maybe he was playing a game and was pretending he was a sea monster? That sounds more logical.

Thinking that I deserve to treat myself after experiencing the ordeal of maybe stumbling upon a dead person, I open my box of chocolates and pop one into my mouth. Oh, how I am so happy that he is alive and not a dead seaweed man.

My first bite of the sweet sends a moan of pure bliss through my lips. I haven't had chocolate this good in what seems like forever. I think this might be my new favorite brand. At the sound of my satisfaction the boy sits up, curiosity overtaking him as he stares between me and the chocolates in my lap.

"May I have one, please?" the seaweed boy asks. I am shocked by his voice; it's so deep that he sounds more like a man than a mere child. He also sounds a little funny, but I can't quite put my finger on why.

I raise my eyebrows in defiance. Still chewing, I say, "So he does speak."

"Of course I speak," he replies, a little dumbfounded.

"How come you didn't say anything, and just stared at me when I called you strange?" I didn't voice it, but my tone implied that by ignoring me he had caused offense. I was raised to always speak when spoken to, so his silence felt rude.

The seaweed boy rolls his eyes and in an annoyed tone says, "*You* insulted *me.*" He says it in such a way that it should've been obvious. At that, my cheeks tinged in embarrassment.

Touché.

Nodding my head, I place another chocolate in my mouth. "That makes sense, but you are strange. Why would you cover yourself in seaweed?" I still don't understand what would make a person do such a thing. He ignores my question and instead stares again at the chocolates.

"If you want the chocolate," I taunt, "then you must tell me why you are covered in seaweed."

He makes a tsk sound and says, "You wouldn't believe me even if I told you." Something about the way he tsked brings butterflies to my belly. It's an odd feeling that I've never felt before and for a moment, I'm confused at the torrent of fluttering.

"Try me." I wave the box of chocolates back and forth in front of his face and his eyes follow it with longing. He lets out a defeated sigh and then he straightens his shoulders. His face stiffens a little bit, and I am reminded of a king, one that is hardened from many years of experience. Which is weird because he's just a boy who looks around my age. With the straightening of his shoulders, he becomes taller, and he has a regal air and strength about him that I hadn't noticed before. I stop waving the chocolates and instead give one to him.

He looks at me in confusion but still takes the chocolate. "Why have you given me this? I have not done what you asked of me."

"I changed my mind, instead it shall be a gift to mark our friendship."

On the word friendship, his eyes stare into mine and I am again lost in their waves. The chocolate is long forgotten.

"Friendship?" My heart cries out at the ache that I hear in his voice.

"Yes, friendship. Will you be my friend?" My voice is hopeful. I myself am in need of a friend. It gets very lonely being homeschooled with no other children around. I have my parents, but it's not the same.

His face lights up at the idea of having a friend, and it immediately makes me happy that I had asked the question. He throws himself back onto the sand and puts the chocolate into his mouth. "Friendship," he says between a grin and chewing on the chocolate.

I lay next to him, copying his posture with my hands held behind my head, looking up at the clear sky. "My name is Amethyst, but I prefer to be called Amy. What is your name?"

His eyebrows squint together as if he's pondering his next words. It seems as if there is a war waging within his head. I wait patiently for his answer, but not for very long. "Percy." He rolls the name over his tongue like it's a new word, and maybe it is, but I don't care because I have finally made a friend.

"Percy. I like it," I say, and then put another chocolate in my mouth.

Chapter Two

PRESENT

After several months of training at the Bay of Biscay research facility, I'm assigned to a small group for some fieldwork at Port Du Betey in Arcachon Bay, France. Our main assignment is to tag the blue whales that showed up a couple days ago.

"It's weird that they're in this area," I muse to my team leader, Paul.

He bends over the safety railing with a pole in his hand. At the end of it is a tracking device that suctions to the whale. It's tricky to get the device on a whale properly, hence why Paul is doing it and not me. Practice makes perfect, but since this is an anomaly to the whales' routes during this time of year, I didn't want my many failed attempts at tagging to lead to no tags at all. Grunting, he says, "That's why we're here. Maybe the new tags will tell us if their route has changed altogether or if, for some odd reason, they took a detour."

The whale submerges just as Paul thrusts to apply the device. He leans back, waiting to see if the whale will reemerge. When it does, water shoots out of its blowhole. Ice cold water sprays over Paul and me. "Thank you for that!" Paul yells to the whale. I swear I hear the whale croon in playful laughter as it submerges itself again.

Annoyed as well, I say, "Maybe I should help? That way we can tag team. The sooner we're done the sooner we can get warm." Yes, we have insulated bibs and wetsuits on, but that doesn't change the fact that the whales keep spraying us. That was the *fifth* time within twenty minutes and I'm starting to think they've made a game out of it.

"Good idea," he agrees, turning his attention back to the open water.

I reach back to the storage box to grab a pole and then for the box between us for a tracker to apply at the end of it. Filled with jittering anticipation, I smile at him before readying myself for another whale. The female that had sprayed us earlier comes back around to play again. This time, we're prepared for her antics. I lean forward and in that moment, she sprays. Expecting this, I quickly back away while Paul goes full force into the geyser of water, tagging her on her side. I squeal at the victory and go to high five Paul. He chuckles as his hand smacks against mine. "I think I'd rather miss a couple times than be soaked in this frigid weather."

I crinkle my nose. "Yeah, sorry about that. Maybe this wasn't such a good idea." He nods his head with an apologetic look and with that, I put the pole and device back where they belong. Just then, a few meters ahead of us, a juvenile breaches. With its pectoral fins spread out, it twists in the air in a full circle. Both fins curl at the end right before it comes back down on its stomach. I've never seen a breach in person and it's nothing short of amazing. They're the gentle giants of the ocean and seeing them be so free and untouched by the world ... I can't even explain the feeling of tranquility that consumes my very being. It makes me want to jump in the water and dance alongside them.

"It's something else, isn't it?" Paul says quietly.

I wipe a lone tear from my cheek and close my astonished jaw. "It's magnificent. I feel like this is something everyone should experience."

Looking out, Paul says, "If they did, then everyone would fight for the ocean's rights." There's a slight frown at the corner of his lips and I know he's thinking the same thing as me. The ocean has no rights, meaning man will eventually destroy an ecosystem that they can't even comprehend.

Another juvenile breaches and I watch in wonder as it comes up, twists and lands back down on its stomach. All the while I dream of a day that will happen. How many of the ocean's problems would be solved if the mass human population understood what would be lost with their continued ignorance?

In silence, we glide through the open water, in the search of more whales that have risen to the surface. A female comes up to the left in greeting. Paul takes notice of her while I look to our right when we get bumped at the same time in the back end. An adult male glides over and raises his rostrum to me. With deep brown eyes, he stares at me with such intelligence that I know there's more to these mammals than what meets the eye. What stories of the sea would he tell me if only we could communicate?

I slowly reach out my hand until I'm touching his rostrum. At the contact, he gently huffs out of his blowhole. The water is warm as it mists over my face. It smells of salt, reminding me of Percy. With a smile, I spread out my fingers so that my palm is flat against his skin and I watch in awe as his eyes flutter close. Whales are known to never close their eyes, especially when humans are around. So *this,* this is the most bloody fantastic experience of my life. A warm feeling reverberates from my hand and up my arm, sending me signals of calm and trust.

Is this whale communicating with me?

My mouth drops open once again, but this time in a quiet gasp of shock. He opens his eyes and there I see full, undeserved trust. There's a shift in the boat and before Paul can tag him, he dives under the water. The end of Paul's pole finds nothing but liquid, missing its mark. Hissing in irritation through his teeth, he exclaims, "Ah Amy, you could've tagged that one yourself. He was so close you could've used your hands."

Still dumbfounded at what just occurred, all I can do in reply is nod my head. A whale just somehow sent me his feelings and I think I might be losing my mind. No, I am losing my mind because that is impossible.

Paul shakes his own head and turns in his seat to face forward. "Take us back to the others. I'm pretty sure that guy was the last one anyways, and it looks like they're done socializing."

Shaking out of my stupor, I raise my hand in a salute. "Aye, aye, Captain."

After being out on the water for over six hours with nothing in our stomachs, we were all starving and decided that the local seafood joint would be the perfect place to fill our grumbling bellies.

Sitting at the restaurant's outdoor patio that overlooks the bay, my teeth chatter from the wintery weather. It wasn't our first choice to be seated outside. Blimey, who would want to eat outside when it's so cold that you can't even fold your fingers? Unfortunately for us, the restaurant is bustling with today's lunch rush, making it packed like sardines within. No seating meant waiting for over an hour, time that we didn't feel like we could spare, given how hungry we are. Are the oysters that Les Tameris has to offer worth it, though?

Hell yes, they were.

Oysters on a regular day are my favorite. But give me a restaurant that is known for catching fresh daily oysters with an all you can eat option? It's a no brainer as to why we ended up here.

Alice, a tall lanky French woman on my team, sits next to me with a pint of ale in one hand and the other one clapping me on the back. Not only do the French enjoy their coffee, but they also greatly enjoy their beer. Every lunch I've had with her, she's had at least four pints, but surprisingly her skinny frame held the alcohol wonderfully. She was never drunk and even if she was, she held herself well because I never noticed a difference.

Our food hasn't arrived yet and Alice begins telling me how Paul was rude last night. "He kissed me and then went to his own bed claiming tiredness. Who does that?"

"Apparently, Paul does." My eyes crinkle with entertainment. Alice is always forward with her words and open about her life. It was one of the things that had drawn me to her. Because of those characteristics, I found her easy to talk to. She had trained with me most days at the research facility before I got sent out with this crew. It hadn't taken long for us to become friends. Now I couldn't envision my life without her.

Paul leans into Alice, his eyes heated as he says, "Tonight." Alice gives him a sultry smile at the promise. Their bodies speak volumes about their relationship and I have to look away.

Blushing from feeling indecent about witnessing their lust for each other, I look to the pier and mumble under my breath, "Get a room."

Paul's stare reminds me of the look Percy had given me the night of my twentieth birthday. An ache of sorrow finds me and burrows itself deep within my chest. I haven't seen Percy since that night, and I miss him.

The waiter arrives and sets down heaping plates of oysters. Licking my lips with hunger, I rub my hands together with drooling anticipation. Being in the cold was so worth it.

Alice looks at me and mouths a countdown from five to mark the start of our eating contest. Each plate to ourselves of over one hundred buttery oysters and who shall come out the victor?

Five.

Four.

Three. I inch closer to my plate. A hint of parsley and garlic wafts toward me, causing me to drool even further.

Two.

One.

I dive for my plate, but at the same time Paul yelps out a strangled cry. Jerking away, I look up in time to see him throwing his chair back before running at a dead sprint to the pier. The other two team members, Clio and Thalia, look after Paul with indifference. The terrified screams from the pier have Alice and me chasing after Paul, forgetting about our food and not giving our apathetic teammates a second glance. By the time we catch up, Paul has already stripped and is diving into the water.

"My son! My son is in the water!" a middle-aged woman wails as she and another woman clutch onto each other.

My heart goes into a panic—a *child* fell into the water. It's winter and the waters are freezing. An untrained adult would seize up from the cold and drown, a child would have an even greater chance of that happening.

Paul's head breaks through the water along with another man, both coming up for a huge gasp of air before they go back under. It's only been minutes and still too much time has already passed. The child has been under the water for far too long. Thinking that three is better than two, I run and dive into the water.

Honing in on what I can see and hear, I look around and see Paul and the man searching to my right, under the pier where the two women are standing. The choppy water seems to be fighting them whereas it's calm where I am. I don't see anything around where they are searching, so I turn my attention to my left. Quickly searching the open ocean and sea floor, I see the boy. The undercurrent must've swept him along because he's a good distance from the pier. As I swim toward him, I get a better look at him and my heart twinges; he's such a small boy he probably wouldn't even go above my knee. I grab onto him to lift him off of the floor, but his foot catches onto something. I look and see that it's a glass jug half swallowed by sand. In a panic, I tug wildly at his foot, unable to think of anything else to do at the moment. It takes only agonizing seconds until his foot slips free while his shoe that was holding him back floats up to the surface. For a split second, I wonder just how his foot even got caught in the first place, but I'm happy it did because otherwise he would've been lost completely to the sea from the current. Holding him above my head, I push my feet off of the seafloor and launch us to the surface.

I swim over to the pier as the medics arrive and take him from my outstretched hands. Paul and the man are back on the pier with me after noticing my successful rescue. Everyone gives the medics space, but we all lean in with anticipation as the medics perform CPR. After what seems like the most painful and longest minute of my life, water sputters out of the boy's blue tinged mouth. His eyes are sluggish to open and when they do, they close again after less than a second. A male medic taps the boy's pale face to get him to open his eyes. When he does, the medic sits the boy up while another medic throws a thermal blanket over him, rubbing his body furiously to try to get the cold out of the kid. The middle-aged woman rushes to him and kisses his face all over while she weeps tears of joy and garbles out repeatedly, "I love you."

While I watch the scene in front of me transpire, a medic comes over and hands me a blanket. I had been so enraptured by seeing through to the boy's recovery that I hadn't noticed my own body is wracked with shivers. The wind chills my soaked body all the way to my very core, leaving my jaw in such a fit of chattering that I can't even voice a thank you for the blanket. The medic is able to understand, though, and nods his head. He checks my vitals and makes sure I'm not going into hypothermic shock. After several minutes of checking Paul and me, he advises us to rest and spend the rest of the day inside. He hands us both several heating packs before turning to his paperwork and having us sign a waiver, declining an ambulance ride.

"You're a hero," Alice exclaims once the medic heads to his vehicle. I wrap the blanket tighter around myself, trying to block out the wind. The water felt warm to me, but as soon as I got out of the water, I started shivering. My soaked hair is also not helping with my current predicament. Before I have time to reply to Alice, the other woman who was with the boy steps between us and throws her body to the ground.

"Lady of the Sea!" she proclaims as her wrinkled hands grab onto my feet. I look down as she starts kissing my shoes. My sneakers are sodden—my goal of getting to the boy was strong enough that I had forgotten to take them off before diving into the water. I have no idea what this woman is talking about. I'm not even sure if I heard her French correctly.

"Please, madame." I give an awkward smile as I step back to remove my feet from her grasp. "Please get up."

I take in the woman as she gets up off of her knees. Her head just makes it to my shoulders. If it weren't for her hunchback, she would probably be eye level with me. Her face is lined with wrinkles and has a tough texture from living a life next to the sea. Her look of worship quickly turns to worry as she sees the expression on my face. She gives out a small cry and says, as she leans forward with her arms waving in front of her. "I am so sorry, my lady! I did not think to be more discreet. Please forgive me!"

Her erratic behavior has me at a loss, and I have no idea what this woman is talking about. I open my mouth, but then close it with a dumbfounded scowl. I look around me to see if anyone else is as confused as I am. The boy and his mother are entering the back of an ambulance to be taken to the nearest hospital, so they don't notice. Alice is as bewildered as I am and then there's Paul with his arms folded, sporting a detached look on his face. To top it off, he doesn't look remotely cold. Not a shiver runs down him as the wind pushes his blanket off of his shoulder.

Alright guppy, no need to flaunt your inhuman abilities.

I turn my focus back to the elderly woman. "I'm sorry, madame, but I am honestly quite confused as to what you are referring to." I place my hand on her shoulder and give a little squeeze, hoping that my face shows compassion. With a resigned look, the woman gives a soft smile and nods her head.

Patting my hand that is on her shoulder, she says, "It is alright, my lady. May the good gods guide you." She then turns around without waiting for my reply and walks over to the boy's father. Or who I presume is the father. With her arrival, he looks as if he wants to come talk to me, but the elderly woman holds him back. She says something to him, but I can't hear what it is. Then the man clasps his hands together in a prayer and mouths, "Thank you." I watch as they both turn away and walk to their vehicle to follow the ambulance.

"Mon Dieu," Paul whispers as he runs his hand through his damp, dirty blonde hair.

I bark out a strangled laugh and say, "Mon Dieu is correct. What was that?" Then, without warning, I am consumed by uncontrollable laughter as my adrenaline wears off. That had to be one of the weirdest things to ever happen to me and *holy shit,* a boy almost died.

Paul pats me on the back while Alice joins in with the laughter. By the time we make it back to the restaurant, all three of us are in tears from laughing so hard, partly from the shock of the boy having a near death experience and partly from the old lady worshiping me. We wipe our eyes as we sit down to finally enjoy our lunch with the other two team members. Both Thalia and Clio make no comment as they continue eating their lunch.

"Uhm, excuse me?" A woman taps me on the shoulder.

With an oyster midway to my mouth, I look up at her in confusion. "Yes?"

"I saw what happened through the window where I'm sitting ..." She points to a window that's on the other side of the restaurant. "What you guys did for that family was valiant."

I slowly nod my head, a little uncomfortable with the added attention. I just want to enjoy these oysters and kick Alice's ass. I eye her to make sure she hasn't started the competition while I'm distracted. She hasn't, but she looks annoyed by the interruption.

The woman carries on, "I also notice that two of you are wet."

"Yeah." I draw out the *ah*. What does this lady want?

"What I'm trying to get at is, well, my partner and I would very much love to trade tables with you and your group."

"Oh." And then what she says hits me. "Ooh!" I look to my crew and then back to her. "Are you sure? It's colder than Jack Frost's butthole out here."

The woman snorts and waves her hand, motioning for her partner to join her. "It's not a problem. Just following one good deed with another."

All five of us bleat out *thank yous* as we grab our plates and scurry inside. I was strongly debating grabbing a to-go bag and heading back to the boat to get out of the cold. The thermal blanket can only help so much against the beating wind. Thank God for small-town people being so kind.

After Alice annihilated me in the eating competition, Paul announces that the next day is to be a free day to do whatever we please. That evening I spend the night combing through the internet for things to do. These past few months that I've been in Europe I haven't explored at all, which is fine because it is what I had signed up for. The first two and a half months were endless training and then I was off with the crew to Arcachon Bay, so I'm excited to finally have a free day to be a tourist.

My internet exploration is a small success: there is a local bakery I want to try out and then a small shop by the name of Tresor de Neptune. Last night I couldn't find anything online about the place but I still wanted to check it out solely due to the fact that it is named after Neptune, the God of the ocean. The name made me think of Percy and all the Greek mythology he taught me. I figured the shop is some kind of tourist hub, and I might be able to find a little trinket to give to him the next time I see him. A small part of me is hoping that he will magically appear on the beach here like he did at home, but so far, my hopes have been in vain.

The main street through town is bustling with life while everyone is hurrying to their jobs. I guess in such a small town, most people don't have a need to drive a vehicle to work. A family of four walks past me and enters the bakery I want to visit. An adolescent boy is yelling just outside of the entrance, "Paper, paper! Get your daily paper!"

Passing by, I give the newspaper a glance and am not surprised by the headline: "PRIME MINISTER FRAUD." It wouldn't be the first time that a politician turns out to be corrupt. I wonder how the Prime Minister is fairing with all the heat right now, but I could really care less. My guess is he'll only get a few months in prison, if that, or if the evidence is weak, he might even get away with the charges. Such is the world we live in.

I hold in my frustrated sigh and instead smother my thoughts with the freshly baked goodies from the bakery that I will be enjoying for breakfast. Politics is not a topic I enjoy, nor do I ever want a part in them.

Just outside, I can already smell the yeast mixed with soft hints of cinnamon, nutmeg, and sugar. My mouth immediately waters and I have to swallow before I start drooling. The smell is enough to make me want a second breakfast and maybe even a third, like the little hungry hobbit that I am.

The family that walked in before me is currently placing their order. Their two little ones have their hands and faces pressed up against the glass, drooling just as badly as I am. One of the staff, a middle-aged man with a goatee, takes a towel and lightly swats at the two children.

"Aiya aiya, go sit down. How many times do I have to tell you to leave my beautiful glass *alone?*" He swats at them again to get his point across. The children stick out their tongues, then giggle as they retreat to a window table. He shakes his head while placing four viennoiseries on a plate.

Handing the plate over, he says, "Marco, could you take Ma to the doctors tomorrow? I thought I could slip away, but we've been so busy."

Marco grabs the plate from the baker and replies, "No problem. Lucille has the day off so she can watch the kids. What time does she need to be there?"

"Noon. Thanks, bro." The baker tosses the rag to Lucille and she walks over to wipe away her kids' fingerprints and slobber. I take their place as they go over to where their children are seated.

"What can I get for you?" the baker asks.

I look at him with a smile and say, "A chocolate eclair with a coffee, please."

After he hands me my order, I choose to sit outside. I want to take in the surrounding town and I figure that the fresh coffee will keep me warm enough on this winter morning. I'm just thankful that today isn't windy.

I wince as I sit in the metal chair. The cold has turned the chair into a block of ice. It seeps into my jeans and I swear I'll get frostbite. Wrapping my gloved hands around my steaming mug of coffee, I take a sip. The coffee scorches my mouth, which gives the effect that I was hoping for. Hot coffee burning down my throat and warming up my body is the much needed distraction from a very cold butt.

I sigh in comfort. Nothing beats a hot coffee on a cold day. I hurriedly wolf down my eclair before the cold gets to it. It's still warm and must have been made right before I arrived. I can't stop my eyes from shuttering closed in ecstasy as my tongue takes in the flavor. The vanilla pudding inside is light, accentuating the rich chocolate covering the top. The eclair is so good that I'm tempted to buy a handful more. But, being on a budget due to no longer relying on *daddy's money*, it's best if I don't spend today's amount solely on breakfast.

Many people pass by, all in a rush not only to get to work but to escape the cold as well. I lean back and observe the people around me while I finish my coffee. I've never found solace in a city. Oxford, where I went to school, was beautiful, but it had always been too much for me. I never could quite get comfortable. I was too used to the solitude of the beach where I grew up.

Looking around this small town has me relaxed, though. It's nowhere near the size of Oxford. It's a charming fishing town with its cobblestone sidewalks and different painted buildings of blue, peach, and yellow. Even though it's a town that faces hard rainy seasons, the buildings are not weatherworn like neighboring seafront towns. It seems that Andernos-les-Bains works hard maintaining their town for tourists.

The last sip of coffee has me grimacing. It's already cold, and cold coffee is a taste I don't care for. I spent too long people-watching. Tossing my trash away, I head north up the road in search of Neptune's Treasure.

I thought I would have to pay attention to the shops I passed so that I wouldn't miss the one I was looking for, but there is no missing nor mistaking that I have found the shop. Sitting off to the side, a little in front of the shop's entrance, stands a greenish blue statue of the god, Neptune. It looks to be made of copper, if its weathered, greenish tint is anything to go by. Analyzing the tarnished statue, I am struck by familiarity.

No. Freaking. Way.

The statue doesn't look like Percy, but at the same time, it does. They share the same straight jaw and unruly hair. Even the arch of their eyebrows and shape of their nose are the same. The likeness is ... unsettling.

I'm taken back to memories of Percy when we first met. I believed that he had come from the sea and, on top of our bizarre introduction, he later even showed me that he's able to manipulate water. I wonder if he really is a deity

... a god. In a way, it would make sense. My mind trails off at the possibility, but then I laugh at my silliness.

Nah, there's no way that he's some sort of god. He was just a kid like me when we met. Gods are ancient, and besides, he may share similarities with this statue, but this statue is a depiction of a forty-year-old chiseled man and Percy is only in his early twenties. The likeness is just an odd coincidence.

I shake my head as if that could banish my absurd train of thought. It was just too ... out there. As I open the door, there's the chime of a bell and I am welcomed by incense. The smell of lavender and peppermint wafts around me and I breathe it in. Stores that use incense tend to burn too much and the smell becomes so overwhelming that it gives me a headache, but this store burns their incense with a delicate yet powerful touch. I applaud whoever chose those smells together and the quantity they decided to use.

The ceiling is vaulted; not something I was expecting to see. The other stores that I have been inside all have low ceilings. I stop inside of the entrance just to marvel. The vaulted ceiling is not left blank with wasted space, but is instead decorated with what must be hundreds of ribbons. Each one is a different color and material. Some are faded and some shine with the brightness of being new.

"Would you like to make a wish, my lady?" I am startled for a moment at the familiar voice. I hadn't heard anyone approaching me. The only people that have ever been able to catch me by surprise have been my father and Percy.

Looking around, I find the voice of an older woman sitting behind the counter. I hadn't noticed her there when I first walked in. The shopkeeper waits patiently for my answer.

"Is that what these are?" I reply as I walk toward her. Upon closer inspection, I realize why her voice is familiar. The shopkeeper is the same woman from the pier. The same woman who was practically worshiping me. Once I realize this, it's too late to turn back without being rude. I want to bolt for the door to avoid any awkwardness, but again, that would be rude, so I refrain.

At my question she goes back to crushing the herbs in her mortar. "Ah yes, wishes for love, lots of love. Wishes for riches, more so than love, and a few—very few—selfless wishes." She stops crushing the herbs and looks at me.

It feels as if she's looking deep within my soul. I hadn't noticed before, but her eyes are murky, as if she is blind. I wonder why I hadn't noticed this during our first encounter. Things happened so fast that I guess it makes sense then that I didn't catch every detail around me. She's not kissing my feet today, so maybe she doesn't recognize me. That would be a relief.

Just when I thought today was my lucky day, she sets her mortar and pestle down and asks, "Would the Lady of the Sea like to make a wish?"

"Excuse me?" My voice is stern with a bite to it. I hadn't meant it to come out like that, but I really don't want what happened yesterday to transpire today.

She winces and leans back into her seat. Clasping her hands together on the counter, she says, "I am truly sorry if I have offended you. Based on yesterday's events, I figured that today you would like a little discretion. If I am mistaken, I can give you a proper welcome that is befitting of a queen such as yourself."

Her murky eyes bore into mine. She speaks with respect, but I can't help but sense that at the same time I am also being scolded. Making sure that my voice has a nicer tone to it, I reply, "No, you are correct. Please forgive me for my earlier tone. I just feel very uncomfortable with the title you keep giving me and your worshipfulness yesterday." I clutch my arms for comfort and say, "I'm just a normal person."

Her knowing gaze assesses me further until she gives a sad smile. "I see," she says solemnly.

She swivels her chair around to come face to face with the shelves of books that are behind her. She runs her hands over the book spines with her eyes closed until she finds what she's looking for. How did she do that? I thought this woman was blind, but maybe I'm mistaken. But her eyes are closed ...

"Ah yes, there you are." She grabs an aged book, then sets it down on the counter in front of me. She pats the book and says, "Here is where your questions will be answered."

"But I don't have any questions," I say in confusion.

"Oh, but you do. I see now what I had not seen before." She taps her chest where her heart is. "Not complete, you are." She hands me the book, then waves me away.

I take it, but am still confused. "But—"

"Be off with you." She waves her hand again, but this time in annoyance. "You do not have much time. Your soul is fading, lady."

"I …" I do not know what to say. Her words are cryptic yet knowing. I want to brush them off as some delusional hearsay, but I feel the truth in them. Clutching the book to my chest, I make a beeline out of the store. The reason for exploring is long forgotten and is only remembered when I'm back on the boat. I don't have the courage to go back to the store for a gift.

Chapter Three

FIVE MONTHS AGO

My fingers trace lightly over the letter placed upon my vanity that bears the signature of Doctor Louis Blanchet. *Centre de Recherché de La Baie de Biscaye* is written in blue ink along the header of the beige-colored paper. I received this letter one month ago, shortly after my graduation, and have been in correspondence with Doctor Blanchet through email since then. The letter is regarding my acceptance into the Bay of Biscay Research Facility, where I will be working as an intern. A dream that has come to fruition.

Staring at myself in the mirror, I notice a stray lock of hair. I pull it away from my almond-shaped, green eyes and place it behind my ear. Due to my mother's love of our Chinese heritage, for every event I am supposed to wear my hair in the Hanfu style—half down and the other half up in a flower bun. This year for my twentieth birthday I have worn my hair completely down. It could be seen as a sign of great disrespect to my parents, but I hope my father does not see it in that way.

A soft knock against my door alerts me to my father's arrival. Before I call out that I am decent, I place the letter in my vanity. I have not yet divulged to my father my acceptance, for I fear seeing the look of betrayal and disapproval upon his face. He has planned on me taking over the firm, but his dreams are not my dreams. It's a topic that has led to many arguments that have concluded in me not discussing my aspirations with him any longer. I have spent my entire childhood constantly studying to meet his standards and I'm tired. I've finally realized that I want to live *my* life, even if it's something that will turn my father against me. Although I hope he loves me enough to accept this.

The door slowly opens and in walks my father. He looks charming in his gray tux with a silky, red bow tie to match my dress. The smile that he gives me as he stands behind me shows nothing short of parental devotion. The breeze from his entrance wafts around me with a smell of familiarity and comfort. He smells of Hermes, my mother's favorite cologne from the Neiman Marcus line. I return his smile through the mirror, hoping that my nervousness is masked well.

He raises his hands from the back of the chair to my hair. They're gentle as they run through my thick raven colored strands. "Did you not find time to wear it up today?" His tone is not angry like I thought it would be, but thoughtful.

"This was intentional, Father, I hope you do not mind."

"It is nontraditional and people will talk, but if it's as you wish, then it is as you wish." I wish his motto, 'as you wish'—which he started saying after we had watched *The Princess Bride* together—was the same for my career path. He shrugs his shoulders as if all these years I could have worn it down whenever I chose.

He holds his hand out in a silent gesture for the brush and I hand it to him. I hadn't noticed how wound up I was until the brush is against my scalp, turning me into putty as the rest of me relaxes into the chair. Getting my hair brushed is one of the best things I have ever felt. I can't help but hum in satisfaction as each stroke scratches against my scalp. By the third stroke, my father has started to sing the same nursery rhyme my mother would when she'd brush my hair. After my mother's death, Father had taken it upon himself to start doing these small tasks with me that she once did. Even when I was fourteen and more than capable of doing it myself, he still insisted. I think he did it more for the memory of Mother, to remember her once again in these little moments.

Sometimes when I closed my eyes, I could trick myself that it was her dainty fingers moving over my hair, each taking turns with the brush instead of my father's bulky, callused ones. If I tried hard enough, I could hear her honeyed voice over my father's. In those moments, I would lose myself to the memory of her and be taken to a time when she was still here.

I open my eyes when my father's tune quiets and I hear the light thud of the brush being placed back on my vanity. Clearing his throat, he says, "The last of the guests have arrived, which means it's time for you to make an appearance." He places his hands on top of my shoulders and leans in to kiss the crown of my head before taking a step back, waiting for me to join him.

As I stand up to take my father's arm, I glance at myself one more time in the mirror. The red satin dress hugs my curves, the material gliding down my body sensually. The dress falls all the way to the floor, hiding my black Louboutin pumps. My silky, straight hair falls down to my hips, covering the bareness of my back. The dress' back is cut open, with its sides falling in loose ripples all the way to my sacrum. Rolling my shoulders back, I take a deep breath and prepare myself for what I am about to do. I try not to think too hard as my father leads me through the villa and out into the yard where the event is taking place.

It's a beautiful night with the full moon casting its glow down upon us. The wind caresses the sheer curtains that divide the outside world from the tables underneath the white canopy. Candles adorn the tables to give a low-light, romantic setting, while all eyes can be focused toward the stage where the auction will soon take place. The candles are in a glass bowl of water with frangipani flowers floating around each candle. The white flowers are local to the area and are one of my favorites. They bring sweet memories of the flower crowns I would make out of them, often adorning Percy with one.

Twisting the end of the flower to connect with the rest, I hold up the crown and admire my handiwork. Percy leans over my shoulder and says, "Perfect." The single word whispered from his lips sends a trail of goosebumps down my spine.

"Not yet." I turn to face him and place the crown atop his unruly hair. "Now it's perfect."

He laughs, and the sound unleashes butterflies in my stomach. I look away to hide my blush. "I believe that statement was directed toward me."

"Was not," I mumble.

"What?" He prods, poking me in the rib. "My perfectness couldn't hear you."

I turn further away from him, wanting to hide my embarrassment and to get away from his tickling. I hadn't meant for it to come out like that; it slipped. Roaring in laughter, Percy picks me up and spins me around. His arms feel that of safety as they're wrapped around me. I can't help but to hold on to him just as tightly as we go in circles on the beach.

"Percy, I'm going to be sick!" I squeal.

"Say it again," he taunts.

"Ugh, say what?" He can't be asking what I think he is.

"Percy is perfect."

"You're so dumb," I whine. At my refusal, he picks up speed. A new wave of nausea hits me tenfold, and I cave to his demand. "Percy is perfect! Percy is Perfect!"

"See? That wasn't so hard."

My world spins as I lay on my back staring up at the clear blue sky, trying to regain my bearings. "Asshole." I mutter.

"A perfect asshole," he corrects.

I smile at the memory as we make our way toward the stage and let go of my father's arm. He kisses me one last time on the head before I walk onto the stage. My hands grasp each side of the podium that's centered in the front as I look out at the sea of faces that flicker against the candles' soft glow. In the past, it was my father who would stand in my spot to announce the beginning of the auction. He would give a speech about our law firms strengthening relationships with France, Italy, China, and Britain's major companies. This year I am to give the opening speech and announce that I'm taking over my father's firm, now that I am twenty and finished with school. The internship was brutal, and I bloody hated it.

My lips curve into a welcoming smile as I lean toward the microphone. "Good evening, everyone. I thank you all for coming tonight. It is splendid to grow up over the years to see the same faces and new faces joining this charity auction to celebrate my birthday. This year I have chosen a charity that is very dear to me. My father chose to live near the beach because my mother adored the ocean and everything that dwells within it. I share that same adoration with my mother and am saddened by the amount of garbage that has found its way into the ocean. Our ocean is dying. The marine life that lives in it is dying. This is not because of natural selection, but because of human interference. Your generous offers tonight will help with the cleanup of our beloved ocean." I look over to my father. He has a proud look on his face, and a single tear that makes its way down his cheek. It's a tear for my mother. Our wounds for her will never heal, and the pain of losing her will never diminish the love that we have for her. We had both agreed that this auction would be an excellent opportunity to once again honor one of the things that she had loved so much.

This time, instead of looking out to the audience, I solely stare at my father while I give the rest of my speech. With a strong, unwavering voice, I carry on. "Because of my deep love for the ocean, I will not be taking over my father's firm. I will instead be joining a research team with Doctor Louis, who is located in France. I hope to spend my life there to help with the restoration of the ocean and the aquatic life that is being destroyed." The audience is completely silent as they take in my refusal of the firm. My father's body has stiffened, and he no longer holds that proud look. I do not let his demeanor deter me from what I am about to do.

I grab the scissors that I told one of the staff to leave at the podium. They had given me a questioning look at my request but had not asked why. As one, the audience gives out a gasp and whispers in hushed confusion as they notice what I am holding.

My eyes are deadlocked with my father's as I hold the scissors close to my neck. My voice steady, I say, "To leave behind a life of luxury, I am cutting my hair to symbolize my detachment to this life. I do this not to insult, but to show my new, fulfilling life." The audience's whispers are silenced as I begin cutting my hair to shoulder length. There's a buzzing in my ear that began the moment I started cutting. With the last strands of my hair being met with the scissors, the buzzing goes away and is immediately replaced by a jolt through my body. It feels as if something is snapping inside of me. Like I have lost something that was with me my whole life. The place that it had been within my chest now feels hollow. I ignore the feeling, thinking it is nothing but the nerves I just felt.

As I finish my speech, one of the staff comes over to sweep up my hair. His face is composed, showing nothing of bewilderment that the audience is conveying. While most are confused, some look at me with awe. I have just done what most deem in their culture as disrespectful. "Do not let my announcement hinder this great evening. Enjoy the food and enjoy this night."

I give a small bow of my head before I walk off the stage. The director takes over as he starts the first bid, not commenting on what just occurred. I walk over to my father, but he gives a curt shake of his head, warning me to not be near him. He needs time to think, so instead, I change course and decide to go to the shore, away from everyone. My presence is no longer necessary now that I have turned my back on the firm and essentially the lavish life my father had set up for me.

Leaving the sounds and lights of the event, I find my way to the driftwood where Percy and I always spend our summers. Taking a seat, I lean back and tilt my head to look at the stars. Thousands shine down, so many more than when I am in England. A warm breeze tickles my exposed back. It gives me goosebumps now that my long hair is no longer there to shield me and I feel the tiny hairs on my back and down my arms stand up.

My thoughts, like they always do recently, drift to Percy. I have not seen him since last summer before I left for my final year at Oxford. I have been home for over a month and not once have I seen him wandering the beach. I haven't seen him at all. I miss him. My feelings for him have shifted from mere friendship into something more. I only realized that after I had dated a freshman in a class that I assisted in. He was a year older than me and far too gangly. At first, I had found him attractive, but the longer I dated him, the more I compared him to Percy. And the more I compared, the more I had longed for Percy to be the one holding me. For his lips to be the one whispering words of endearment. For him to be the one kissing me instead of my boyfriend. And when it hit me that my feelings for Percy had grown, I couldn't be with the clumsy freshman anymore. It wasn't fair to him, and also I couldn't bear his touch anymore. Not when it was Percy who I wanted.

Percy's full lips take over my thoughts and all I can think of is them tickling every inch of my body. What it would feel like to be wrapped in his arms, not as friends but as lovers. My longing for him grows with the days that go by. Each one with no sign of him leaves an itch that I can't seem to get rid of. An ache buried deep within my chest that drives me mad. I throw my hands to my face and let out a loud groan. "Oh for fucks sake! What have you done to me, Percy?"

There's a deep chuckle next to me that has me jumping up in fright. I had not heard anyone approaching, and it's rare for anyone to sneak up on me. I have my fists up, ready to defend myself, but put them down when I see that it's just Percy. The flood of relief that washes over me is intense enough that I almost buckle to my knees. My waiting has come to an end.

The playfulness twinkling in his eyes compliments his signature smirk. It's always been the left side of his lips that turns up more than the right. I find myself wanting to take a nip at the lowered side just to get him to grin fully. His chestnut hair is styled out of his face, which hides his sun-kissed streaks in this lighting. The hairstyle gives him a more masculine look, emphasized by his freshly shaven, square jaw.

"And what is it that I have done to you, my dear Amethyst?" His voice is husky as his eyes take me in. My face flushes in response to his stare, and my breathing quickens as his eyes find mine. I'm a little shocked that I see want within them. I've only ever dreamed of the idea of Percy reciprocating my feelings. I never actually thought he would look upon me as anything more than a friend. To see the heat in his eyes leaves me breathless, and a million butterflies in the pit of my stomach push against me, wanting to break free. I don't say anything as I take the few steps separating us. Never breaking eye contact, I take his hand into mine and place a kiss against his knuckles. My lips brush against each knuckle, one after the other, at a slow, ritualistic pace.

"Amy," he whispers my name like a prayer as he slightly leans into me. The sound of his strained voice is all I need to hear to know that he desires me. I don't know how much, but it's enough to see that he views me as more than just a friend.

"Percy," I breathe back.

Twisting my hand in his to where my palm is facing upward, he trails delicate kisses from my inner wrist to my elbow. His stubble rubbing against my skin mixed with his soft lips sends a pool of heat to my core. I inhale a sharp intake of breath and Percy's eyes flick to mine. The sight of them smoldering under the moonlight makes my legs shake and I wonder if Percy can feel my pulse against his lips beating as fiercely as a Jumanji drum.

"Percy." This time when I say his name I'm begging. But begging for what? The inferno he's causing within me is building and I don't know how to release it.

"What, my little dove?" I can feel his smirk against my inner elbow. He lets go of my arm and brings his hand to the nape of my neck, where he gently grabs a fistful of hair. His nose grazes up my neck to the crook of my ear. "I'm waiting." His hot breath against my earlobe sends another wave of shivers down my spine and I squirm under his hold, not answering his question. How can I when I don't even know what I want? Sure, I want him to kiss me, but what I actually want is for him to unbuckle his pants and dive into my pussy. But I can't even ask that because I don't even know what *this* is.

Have we turned into friends with benefits? Bedmates? Or lovers? I don't mind the latter, but if I'm being honest, I'll be any of those titles just as long as we're exclusive. I ... I wouldn't be able to share him.

He chuckles before releasing his hold on me and takes a step back. I blink, then blink again to clear my muddled brain. Percy hasn't even kissed my lips and yet here I am, quivering like a hot mess over his lips on my arm. *My arm,* for fucks sake. The skin where he had kissed me still buzzes like a live wire, and I can only imagine how electrifying it'd be to have his lips against mine.

I sigh out in dismay while absentmindedly rubbing my thumb along my forearm. I thought too hard and missed my chance, and now I find myself feeling bereft without his touch. Frowning, I watch as Percy takes another step back. "What are you doing?"

He holds up a finger. "I'll be right back."

My frown deepens but I shrug my shoulders and instead of standing there like an abandoned puppy, I pull up my dress and walk to the water. A warm wave splashes against my bare feet and tickles around my ankles. The beach is my favorite at night. The only sounds being that of the waves and occasionally a bat screeching in the distance. I tilt my head back, staring up at the moon. I've always been drawn to the beach when the sun goes down, especially after my mother died. Nights when I felt a tug to come out here, it felt like the ocean was in tandem with the darkness wanting to cocoon me in a blanket of security and understanding.

"Ta-da!"

I turn and see Percy sitting on a blanket with an array of hors d'oeuvres from the party and a bottle of sparkling cider. He pats the space next to him and says, "Sit. I saw that you didn't eat after your speech."

My mouth drops open and I sputter, "Wh-what? You were there?"

Smirking, he points to the empty space and repeats, "Sit."

"Only if I get a treat," I purr.

Percy's hand stills midair reaching for the bottle. A beat passes before his shocked face morphs into a mischievous grin. Shaking his head, he finishes his reach toward the bottle. "Once you put something in your mouth, I'll start talking."

"Yes, Father." I groan before walking over and taking my place beside him.

Percy raises both his eyebrows and says nonchalantly, "Speaking of fathers ... I also talked with yours." My eyes narrow as I eye him; it explains the deep blue suit he's wearing. Which is the most formal thing I have ever seen him in.

He usually sports shorts with an occasional cotton shirt. It's the perfect beach boy look.

He doesn't speak and instead stares pointedly at the food. Right. I hurriedly shove a stuffed mushroom into my mouth. Through bits of food I ask, "Happy?"

"Very." He unscrews the bottle and pours himself and me a glass.

"So what's this nonsense about you talking with my father? I hadn't realized you two knew each other. Honestly, this whole time I thought I was imagining you." Percy flicks my nose. "Ouch. What was that for?" I pout.

"Do you actually believe you could imagine someone as perfect as me?"

I roll my eyes and playfully shove him. "Don't forget the asshole part. But hey, don't avoid the question."

"I didn't know a question was asked." His slender fingers flick away an invisible piece of flint on his shoulder.

Grabbing the cheese knife, I point it at him. "Don't make me use this."

Hands up in surrender, he says, "Just business."

"Business," I state while folding my arms, not totally convinced. Percy looks back at me, and the shade of his eyes has become too dark for me to decipher. Most of the time, his eyes are swirling shades of turquoise. Over the years, I've noticed that the swirls in his eyes change faintly depending upon his mood. The darker the color, the more upset he is. The current set of his jaw and the furrow of his eyebrows could only mean that the colors his eyes are displaying now are indicating anger. But angry at my father? Or angry with their conversation?

"Yes." Percy's tone goes cold, and just the sound of it makes the hair on my arms stand up as if static were in the air. "Mister Wu and I had business that we discussed prior to"—he leans forward and twirls a lock of my hair—"you making a statement," he finishes.

The air whooshes out of my lungs at his nearness. He smells of fresh water with a hint of citrus. My tongue darts out and suddenly my throat is dry. I want so badly to lean forward that single millimeter that's separating us to kiss him, but I don't bloody know where we stand.

Deciding to let what was said between him and my father drop, I switch the topic. "Did you hear the part where I'm leaving?"

Percy leans back and takes a drink. I watch as his Adam's apple bobs with each swallow. My head swims with thoughts of licking it. Would he taste just as good as he smells? "I did."

"And?"

"And what?" He stares out at the ocean and I know he's purposely avoiding eye contact.

Frustrated and a little hurt that he seems to not care, I say quietly, "I don't know when I'll be back. Could be a year, could be two." He remains silent, so I carry on, "Will you visit?"

His head whips to mine and his eyes quickly change from a deep blue to a swirling turquoise with specks of violet. "Do you want me to visit?"

"Yes, of course."

"Then I will."

I wring my hands, unsure if his words are true. "How? I don't even have your number."

He wraps his hands around mine and holds them firmly to stop my agitating wringing. Bringing them to his lips, he whispers against my knuckles, "I'll find you. I'll always find you." And with that, I melt. From this moment on, I know I'll always melt for him.

By the time I find my way back to the villa, the moon is low in the sky. The guests have all gone, leaving only the cracking of furniture that the staff are quickly disassembling. A multitude of them work to take down the four-pointed canopy. I'd say poor fellas since it's past midnight, but I've seen how much my father pays them. The clinking of glass and shuffle of quick movement trails behind me as I walk by, everyone unaware of my passing.

My footsteps are a hushed whisper against the sandstone flooring as I walk through the house in search of my father. He has insomnia and tends to be awake at this hour. He's not in his office or bedroom, so that leaves only one other place. I want to discuss my declaration from earlier. I push down the uneasiness brewing in the pit of my stomach. I hope that he's had plenty of time to cool off and will be willing to talk *and* listen.

I find him in the part of the villa that is dedicated to the remembrance of my mother. The room is at the end of the house that faces south. The southern wall of the area is similar to the room where I practice cello. Similar, in that it is the only other room that has one wall made up completely of windows. The rest of its aspects are completely different. This room has thick glass as a roof with dozens of Amazonian plants lining the windowed wall, while the northern wall has a saltwater aquarium. Most of my mother's favorite fish that are compatible to share a habitat are in this aquarium. The only light in the room is that from the moon reflecting off of the water and a few floor lights placed at the bottom of the walls. The lighting is just enough to see where you're going but still dark enough to create a tranquil environment.

In the center of the room stands a fountain, and in the middle is a serene statue of my mother. Father had carved it himself. He spent endless weeks getting every detail perfect and spent hours chiseling her features. During those weeks, I had not once seen him rest. Lost in my own mourning, I had not begged him to take a break, instead I withered away, succumbing to a pit of hopeless abandonment. It was Percy who had found me by our log curled into myself, and it was he who brought life back into my shattered soul. He had been a beacon, giving me the comfort that I so desperately needed.

When Father finished, I couldn't hate him for his neglect. He had devoted himself to her memory, and the memory he had of my mother was flawless. One can not help but admire the love he put into creating her likeness. Her very essence seemed to shine through the stone. After that first inspection of his work, I had wept for hours. She was beautiful.

My eyes fall upon my father, who is kneeling before the fountain. His face is tilted up, looking at the statue of Mother. His back is to me, but I already know what his face will look like. I have never once seen him mad at my mother; not once had he ever raised his voice in anger at her. He always looked at her with adoration, as if his whole universe revolved around her. It was a love for the ages. Timeless and now gone.

Kneeling next to him, I look up at the depiction of Mother. He carved her in the image of what she looked like before the treatments started. Thick flowing hair, eyes twinkling with joy, cheeks full instead of sunken. The statue's likeness of her is strong enough that I have an urge to reach out my hand to try to touch her once again, but I resist and leave my arm clutched to my side. My arms burn with the ache of wanting to hold her, to feel her smooth arms encircling me. She had smelled of honey and lavender, and if I think hard enough, I can faintly smell her. It's been three years since she passed and still her absence left a hollow space in my heart that I don't think can ever be filled.

Trying not to succumb to oblivion, I glance at Father. His face is marked with sadness but still a hint of adoration remains. He feels my stare and turns to face me completely. "Your mother would have been so proud of you today." His voice is strong, unwavering. Not hoarse from repressed tears, like I thought it would be. Tears that are always brought on by the memory of the greatest love of his life.

"But you're not," I state. He is silent and looks away. I look away too, not wanting to see the disappointment that must be there.

I'm concentrating on the pool of water at the statue's feet, trying to not let his disappointment get to me when he finally replies, "All these years I have tried so hard to keep you safe. To give you a perfect life that any human would want. You are wrong, Amethyst. I am proud of you, so very *proud.* How could I not be? For if you had so willingly taken what I had laid out for you, so willingly given up on your dreams, then you would not be the strong, independent daughter I had raised." He is looking at me now and his face softens and becomes fatherly as he sees my tears escaping their prison.

"But you were so mad." The sob that leaves me wracks my whole being. Geez, why must every little emotional thing bring me to tears? He starts to shake his head but before he can reply I say, "And don't you dare tell me that you weren't because you were. You were so tense and couldn't stand to be near me."

He lets out an exasperated sigh and says, "Yes, I was so very mad, but not at you. I was mad at myself."

I am taken aback and use that moment to wipe away my tears. I clear my throat to ask why, but before I can Father says, "And Amethyst, for the love of all the oceans please do not ask me why. I will not give you reasons for my emotions, but please do believe me that my anger was not directed toward you, and I am pleased with what you are doing and who you have become."

This makes me laugh and I lean into him. It feels like he has finally accepted the different turn my life is going to take. He holds me tight and kisses me on top of the head. The fatherly gesture chases away any regret I had and fills me with the ease that has always been an undercurrent between us. We stay like this, relaxed and enjoying each other's company until our legs go numb.

Chapter Four

PRESENT

The leather-bound book lies on my bed while I sit across from it, cross-legged and unable to open it. The book seems ancient enough that it's most likely a relic. I'm a little scared that with another touch it'll turn to dust, which leaves me honestly surprised the woman had given it to me, no charge. The leather is pliable with a title that is so worn out that I can't discern what it says.

Chewing on the inside of my lip, I stare blankly at the book. Treachery oozes from its closed pages and a strong part of me screams to throw it out, to never open it, to never read whatever its secrets are. The woman's warning resounds in my head, *"Your soul is fading."*

Fuck.

Honestly, I'd rather be reading Tolkien, but if what she said is true, that would be insane. It makes no sense. But if it were true, what could I possibly do to prevent something like that from happening? How would one even stop their soul from fading? I don't feel like anything is currently changing in me.

"Curiosity killed the cat," I ponder out loud. The book sits there, silent. Patient. "But satisfaction brought it back." I reach out my hand, finally making up my mind, but when my fingers skate across the leather edges, my heart rate picks up into a staccato beat. Higher and higher it transcends until I am light-headed. Sweat forms at my brow and my breathing turns into fast panting. I jerk my hand back, wiping my brow as I try to calm my breathing back to a steady rhythm.

In ... Out ... In ... Out ...

I scoot myself back away from the book, eyeing it like it had burned me. Why was I feeling this way? Knowledge is power, so why, why am I hesitating? Why is my damn body reacting like this book is my downfall?

So fixated on what I should do with the book, I don't notice Alice until she plops herself down on my narrow bunk bed. Her coily, onyx hair hovers over the book while she lies on her stomach, each hand holding her face up. She smells of elderberries.

"Are you sick?" I ask.

Turning one hand into a fist against her chin, she tilts her head, brows bunching quizzically. "No."

Huh. I lean toward her.

A feline grin curves her lips. "Are we going to kiss?"

Snorting but not at all abashed, I reply, "Funny." Taking a curl into my hand, I bring it up to my nose to smell. Elderberries.

"I'm into this." Alice purrs.

Rolling my eyes, I toss her hair into her face. "I smell elderberries and thought you had taken cough syrup, but it's just your shampoo."

"So no kiss?"

Resisting the urge to smile, I deadpan, "Ha ... ha."

She snickers. "You used to be so fun to tease. You would become the biggest tomato when I flirted with you."

"That was before I knew that you were never serious."

Taking notice of the book, she sighs as she picks it up. "I loved your tomato face, though." My gut wrenches as she turns through the pages. I hadn't planned on sharing it with anyone. Her eyes scan it, reading. I'm tempted to ask her what it says, but keep quiet.

Raising an eyebrow, she looks up at me over the book. "I never would have pegged you for reading smut."

I blanch. Sputtering, I say, "I ... I ... is that what it is?"

"Oh please, don't act like you haven't read it."

"I was debating whether or not to open it until you came in."

She looks at me over the opened spine. "Doubtful."

"Honestly." And then I voice, "What a load of shit. The shopkeeper said some nonsense about my soul fading and then handed me that book, telling me that my answers lay within."

Turning the page, Alice coughs. "Load of shit indeed, because this book is filled to the brim with kink galore and the worst images." She flinches. "A horse. Really? Interesting ..."

"What? Let me see." I move to take the book from her but she's quicker. There's a low thud as she closes the book and then moves it behind her back.

"I don't want my lovely Amy's eyes to be assaulted with such crude language. No, babe. I shall be taking this with me."

"But ..." My mouth is agape, unable to finish my protest as she stands up, book in hand. I was going to argue and ask for it back, but do I actually want to see something like that? A small part of me is intrigued, but no. Not in any of my days do I want to know what a horse is doing in a book like that. My ears redden at the annoyance I feel toward the shopkeeper. She had been so convincing that I almost fell for her cruel joke.

Alice shoves the book in her drawer of our shared dresser. Rummaging through it, she then tosses garments at me. Picking them up, I eye the black skirt with an matching long-sleeved cotton sweater. "Why?"

"To change into, of course." She bops me on the nose. "We're going out, silly."

"Oh, okay." A night out sounds refreshing. "But why a skirt and why your clothes?"

"We're going *out*. I want you looking *hot.*"

I stare at the clothing in my hand. "What's wrong with what I own?"

"No offense, babe, but your wardrobe cries grandma."

I frown. "No, it doesn't."

"When you don't show any skin, yes. Now change, we're leaving in ten." She walks out and then pops her head back in. "Oh, and put some color on. There's a tube in my drawer." And then she's gone, leaving me to my own devices.

"I'm working and it's *winter,*" I grumble, just a tad offended.

Standing at the bar, I pick at the hem of the borrowed sweater. My chest is larger than Alice's, making this piece of clothing a tighter fit than it should be. No matter how hard I tug it down, it immediately rides back up, exposing a ring of skin. I hadn't realized just how terrible the fit was until we were already here or I would've definitely ignored Alice's pleas and put on something that's actually my size. Sighing, I rest my elbows and forearms against the counter of the bar.

"Or not." I sneer in disgust, removing my arms and bringing them back to my sides. The countertop is sticky and not mere fresh stickiness from spilled beer. It's the kind of substance you get from a surface that hasn't been washed in ages. The contents of whatever it is has seeped into the wood and whoever finally got around to cleaning it up didn't do a thorough job about it. Leaving in their wake layer after layer of dried up beer and who knows what else. Could be barf, or from the looks of this place, blood. It's the kind of pub that seems to get too rowdy if you glance at someone wrong. The smell of cigarettes lingers in the air, and I try not to scrunch my nose in disdain. The pub is a town over and I'm not sure why Alice had picked this particular place. There seems to be nothing special about it, besides the naked wooden statue of a mermaid, if you call that special. The statue stood by the entrance, off to the side. She greets you with her bulbous breasts. A few drunken men have already leered and caressed her in the span of the five minutes I've been here. Pigs.

A male saunters over and stands next to me, casually pressing his back against the counter. By the size of him, he looks like he used to play rugby or hockey in his teenage years. Some sort of sport where you had to be big to hold your own when you got knocked into. His shoulders are wide and muscular. Huh, not bad. He's easy to look at, although a little rugged in the face. A white scar cuts straight down the left of his bottom lip and ends at his chin. If he has the right personality, it could be charming.

"Like what you see, darling?" He must have taken my curiosity over his scar as me admiring his lips.

"No, thank you," I say, friendly but not too friendly. I don't want him to think I am playing hard to get, but I also don't want to upset him. He is not, in fact, charming. I turn away from him to get my point across. I'm not interested.

He ignores my response and says, "You're not from around here."

I nod my head, not looking at him, but at the row of liquor on the shelf behind the bar. My fight-or-flight response kicks in. Something about this man is off. My body registers it and I try to not show just how unsettled he's making me. If he is a predator, he would get off on it.

Leaning in closer, he says, "You're too beautiful to be from here." My skin crawls. Ew. What is taking Alice and Paul so long? Looking at the clock, I tap my foot in impatience. Ten minutes. Bloody ten minutes alone in this pub.

I glance at him. "Thank you, though every woman has her own beauty."

He smiles. "Modest and beautiful, but I prefer them to be stupid and beautiful."

I stiffen. "Excuse you?" Yup, this man is bad news. Just my luck.

My eyes dart to the entrance, willing my friends to arrive. The tapping of my foot becomes more erratic. Alice wanted ice cream, I did not. Looking back, I should have gone with them. Then all of this could've been avoided.

Grabbing me by the arm, he says, "Don't make this harder than it needs to be. I tried to be nice, but you've made it so difficult."

I look down at his hands on me. My blood boils. "*Get* your *disgusting hand off of me,*" I say through clenched teeth. God, I'm seeing red. Why are there people out there that when they see a woman alone, can't help but take advantage? How many helpless women has he done this to? Scaring them into submission, forcing them against their will?

The man's only reply is to tighten his hold on me, using brute force to get what he desires from me. It is foolish of me and I should do something else, but I am royally pissed, so I do the only thing a royally pissed person can do. I spit in his face.

"You cunt!" he roars.

Here we go ...

I brace myself for the hit. Slightly bending my knees, I wait for his move. If he takes a swing, he will be off balance and I will have the chance to gain the upper hand. When someone is bigger than you, it's smarter to use their own weight against them. Not only is he bigger, but he is also already holding onto me. Two cons. Maybe the odds aren't in my favor, but I can already see how this would play out. He'd draw his arm back, hands clenched into a fist. He'd swing and at the last second I would duck. He might graze me—no, he most definitely would graze me. But the combination of me pulling him down with me and his body going in for the hit would be the momentum needed for him to lose his balance. I'd take my right arm, the one that was free from his meaty hand, and plant a solid punch right in his unmentionables. He would surely let go of me, then grab himself and bitch and moan like the pathetic man that he is. Probably calling me nasty obscenities in between his moaning. And then I would place my hands on his head, each against either ear while he was still bent over, and then I would finish him off by kneeing him squarely in the face, hopefully bloodying and breaking his nose.

It is an almost perfect plan but one that I don't get to see play out because right before he moves to deck me, a feminine hand clasps around his wrist.

"What are you doing?" It's Alice. I don't think I've ever been this glad to see her.

The man doesn't drop his arm, instead he pulls me tighter to him. My arm throbs. His fingerprints are definitely going to leave a bruise. I look around us, but all heads are turned away, as if purposefully ignoring what is transpiring in front of them. Cowards.

Alice hisses. She *hisses*. In that second, three things happen that I am vaguely aware of; Alice tightens her grip on him, the bones snap audibly, and he screams. With that, he finally lets me go. For good measure, and also because I know without a doubt that I am not the first woman he has done this to, I take my knee and make contact with his face. The sound of his nose breaking is nothing less than satisfying. I would do it again just to hear that sound all over again. The man is in so much pain that he is crying. It's actually a surprise that he hasn't passed out from shock. He runs out of the pub clutching his hand to his chest while his nose leaves drops of blood on the floor.

"I think I just fell in love." Alice beams at me, doe-eyed.

I roll my eyes. "Out of all the pubs, why did you choose this one? It's dingy and ..." I take a nearby napkin and slap it down on the counter. It rips as I peel it back. Raising my brows, I point at the napkin with my palms open. My eyes widen to convey my disdain.

Paul comes up behind her and she melts into him as his hands settle on her hips. For tonight she has donned ankle-length leggings with a spaghetti strap top. It's winter and how she is walking around without a jacket is beyond me. Incomprehensible. In my winter coat, it still felt like death until I was inside the pub. A pub that now had me wishing that I had stayed back with Thalia and Clio. My mood is soured by the scuz who just ran out.

Alice gives a throaty laugh, somewhat distracted by Paul. "This tavern serves the best crepes in the area."

My lip curls up. "I don't think I'd want to eat anything made in a place this filthy."

"You'll see," is her reply before hailing the bartender.

Taking our seats at a corner table, I set my coat down to sit on. I make a mental note to wash it before wearing it again. Does this province not have any sanitary regulations? I try not to imagine what all has touched the bench. It could be anything.

The waiter shimmies through the crowd of people to set down a bottle of Chartreuse, three empty glasses and a bucket of ice. Interesting. Being that I'm only twenty and have not had many chances to drink due to my strict and busy upbringing, Alice has taken it upon herself to expand my alcoholic experiences. I have not yet tried Chartreuse, but it looks ... strong.

It's an early morning tomorrow so I'll have to leave the drinking to a minimum. Alice and Paul may be able to hold their liquor well, but I can not. I am most definitely a lightweight and I sure as hell do not want to deal with a hangover.

Twirling one of the empty glasses, I ask, "Alice?"

"Hmm?" She drops four ice cubes into her own cup.

"How did you break his wrist?"

If I hadn't been paying attention to her, I would never have noticed her slight pause before she answers, "I didn't."

"I heard his bones breaking."

Taking the glass from me, she puts another set of four ice cubes in my cup and then Paul's. I wait, staring at her as she pours the liquor. She avoids my eyes as she slides the glass over to me. Paul raises his glass in the air, slightly distracting me from Alice. "To badass women putting misogynistic men in their places."

The distraction works. My lips twitch into a smile at recalling the man's hobbling form. "Cheers."

Before bringing the ridge of the glass to my lips, I swish it around, smelling it. The liqueur smells of herbs, reminding me of the Galliano I had tried not too long ago. It was the first alcohol that I was introduced to, also by Alice. It was my first night in France. I had only been in the research facility for a few hours and was settling in my dorm getting ready for the night. I was exhausted from the long flight. Even using my father's private jet with no layovers, it had taken seventeen hours to arrive here.

I was in the middle of unpacking and was craving nothing more than a cool bed when in walked this gorgeous runway model slash goddess. She introduced herself as Alice, told me that she is my dorm mate and then shoves the bottle of Galliano in my face, telling me to drink up. Probably due to the alcohol, I poured my heart out to her. Told her *everything* there possibly was to know about me.

The night ended with me passed out drunk on my bed with no sheets and my belongings strewn all over the place, not at all put away. The next morning, I remembered everything I said and was completely embarrassed. Alice had actually made fun of me in the most wholesome and friendly way someone could. Our friendship clicked, and I hadn't felt that close to someone so quickly since Percy. She must have felt the same because the rest was history, and our friendship seems to be unbreakable.

I take a sip, taking in the flavors on my palette. At first it's sweet, almost overwhelmingly sweet, and then the spiciness kicks in. Not so overpowering that it sets my tongue on fire, but that perfect undertone of spice that levels out the sweetness. I take another sip and then set the drink down, reminding myself to take it slow. I need something in my belly before I drink too much.

"How is it?" Alice asks.

I nod my head. "Not bad, actually. I quite like the kick it has. It's unexpected but very welcome."

"Right?" she muses. "It's one of my favorites."

Paul's arm is draped over Alice, his thumb makes circles on her exposed shoulder. I move my gaze to the different groups of people frequenting the pub. Sometimes it sucks to be the third wheel. If Percy were here, what would he be doing? I imagine him sitting next to me, his elbow on the table, holding his face up while his other hand played with my hair. And then he would tuck that strand behind my ear. The back of his hand would trail down my neck. I would lean into his touch, being pulled toward him. Percy is the very waves that crash and consume me. He is like the tide, and I am the moon. One always needing the other, always in a constant state of longing. Each essential for each other's survival; for I would surely be destroyed if Percy was not in my life. Just being away from him for this long is pure agony. He said he'd always find me, so why hasn't he yet? Maybe his feelings aren't as strong as mine. Maybe I am the only one in our duo that feels the pull for the other.

I watch as the waitress works her way through the crowd. I expect someone will smack her butt as she passes by, but I don't see anyone do that. Maybe I had encountered the one rude person in the whole pub or maybe they respect the waitress enough not to do anything. My bet is on the latter, judging by how a male just used a pool stick to smack the female next to him. The food better be worth it because this place disturbs me. It is too vulgar to women.

Pieces of paper stick out of the pocket of her apron. Her single braid is coming undone and her face is flushed as she sets down an assortment of cheese, cooked vegetables and meat, and a plate stacked high with crepes.

Oh, fucking hell and goblin dicks, this smells amazing.

At the same time Paul asks, "What?" Alice snorts out her drink. It sputters out of her nose.

My face reddens. I didn't realize that I said that out loud. I give an awkward cough, ignoring Paul and handing Alice a napkin to wipe herself.

"No, seriously, what?" Paul asks again.

"It smells good, okay?"

"Yeah, but who says that?"

"Yes, it's a weird thing to say. I got overly excited. Old news. Let's move on."

I can already see that Paul is indeed the furthest thing from moving on. His eyes sparkle with too much mischief that I know an onslaught of teasing will ensue the moment his mouth opens. So when it does, I hurriedly grab a crepe and bend myself over the table, careful not to lean against the food, and shoved the crepe into his open mouth. He just about chokes on it. I lean back, smug in my victory. Alice explodes into laughter, almost choking too on her hysterical giggles as unrestrained tears bunch at the corners of her eyes.

"Goblin dick, that was delightful," she says as she wipes her eyes.

My shoulders shake in amusement. "Fucking goblin dick." I should have never said that. Now it'll be Alice's new favorite term. One I'm sure she'll make good use of.

The savory crepes are one of the best things I have ever tasted. Alice was right about it being worth it. If I am ever in town again, I will seriously consider stopping by this pub just to be able to enjoy these crepes. The way the meat is marinated and the vegetables seared and seasoned are delicious and addictive. They pair perfectly with the Chartreuse and I find myself already five glasses deep by the end of the night, my belly full with good food and my head light from the drink.

Chapter Five

Time slips away while I look down into the water and admire the darker shades of blue that my body swims above. I have never felt cold being in the ocean. I always thought that was because the waters of the gulf that I grew up on leaned toward the warmer side but when I'm in the water here in the bay, even without a wetsuit on, I feel the same warmth as when I'm in the gulf. I usually get picked to do the tasks in the ocean because of my weird immunity to the cold water. But my immunity only applies when I am in the water. As soon as I hit the surface, I am taken over by shudders and the need to find shelter and warmth from the icy air. Paul also doesn't seem to mind being in the water, so sometimes he takes over for me. But today I had scrambled to be in the water just to rid myself of this bleeding headache. I woke up this morning with a splitting hangover. I didn't want to over drink last night and yet here I am, dying. The back of my neck is exposed and as the water laps over it and then recedes, the throbbing of my head is soon replaced by a chill so searing that it doesn't take long to rid me of my hangover. The cold today is a blessing in disguise. My eyes flutter closed briefly as I enjoy the feeling of no longer being sick.

With my hands gripping the manta tow, the boat glides me through the water at a leisurely pace. As I get lost in the quiet open of the water, my mind stills. The bay's waters are too dark for me to see further than a couple meters deep, so instead of focusing, I close my eyes and listen to the water's embrace lapping over me. With each tug and pull of the wave against my prone body, I hear the bay whisper, *mine, mine, mine.* I let the sound lull me into full relaxation.

When the boat slows down and gradually comes to a stop, I lift my head to see Clio signaling that the coverage that I was doing with the manta tow is finished. I take off my goggles and hook them to my belt, then hook the manta line to my belt as well. Once I secure myself, I give the thumbs up to Clio to tell her that I am ready. I float on my back and enjoy the water splashing over me as Clio starts the line to tug me and the manta tow back to the boat. The cold air burns my lungs like a bright, hot iron with each intake of breath. I ignore it and take in the beautiful sky. There's not a cloud in sight.

Closing in on the boat, I unhook the manta line and swim the rest of the way to the ladder in casual, lazy strokes, not at all looking forward to the burst of wind once I'm out of the water. After being in the water so long, my body feels heavy as I pull myself up into the boat. My legs and arms feel like lead, not at all wanting to do what I tell them to.

Teeth chattering, I hastily make my way to the main cabin. Being inside is not much warmer, but it beats the open air pounding against me. Not waiting another second, I strip the wetsuit in exchange for dry clothes and a heavy coat. I take off my swimmer's cap, thankful that I remembered to wear it today to keep my hair nice and dry. I pull my hair into a bun. It has grown quite a few inches since the big chop. I miss the original shortness, but having it this length comes in handy for tying it out of the way.

Making my way back to the stern, I notice dark clouds thundering across the horizon. All four members of my team are standing in a line, staring at the foreboding clouds. Lightning rolls behind them, making the darkness light up every few seconds. I wonder how I could have missed those clouds just moments ago. I'm sure I would have heard the thunder. It's so loud there's no way I could've not noticed. There's a mass of darkness under the incoming clouds and from this distance, it looks like a massive flock of birds. I tilt my head as I stare, trying to comprehend what I'm seeing.

"I guess it's a good thing we finished coverage today, would've sucked to get caught ... in that ..." my voice trails off as all four of them turn around. Clio's mouth is open in horror while the others are sporting looks of distress.

I stop short and ask, "What's wrong?"

Ignoring me, Thalia commands, "We must get her to safety. Now. We don't have much time until he arrives. Alice, take us to the island and step on it. Paul, use the wind to our advantage and Clio, you're with me." At her word, Alice rushes to steer the boat. We are thrust back and I have to grab a hold of the nearest seat to prevent me from falling as Alice puts her foot down on the gas.

"What is going on?" I protest as Thalia drags me back down to the main cabin. Clio is behind us and shuts the door. She starts frantically digging through the drawers of our shared sleeping quarters. She throws essentials into a bag while Thalia lets go of me and begins to practically burn a hole in the ground with her nervous pacing back and forth.

"What in the name of everything that is holy is going on?" I say again, on the verge of screaming at everyone's weird behavior and the lack of information. One moment I was in bliss and then the next everyone around me turned into a soldier in battle mode. Not having any idea what's going on puts my nerves on edge and is scaring the shit out of me.

Ignoring me, they both stop what they are doing and stare at each other. They act as if they're having a mental conversation; then Clio shrugs her shoulders and goes back to packing, but this time at a calmer pace. Thalia lets out a sigh and goes to sit next to me. She's silent for a moment as she watches Clio's back.

Still looking at Clio, she says, "Clio and I are sisters." My eyebrows knit together in confusion—they look like polar opposites. Both of them being ethereally beautiful but nevertheless opposite. Clio is as white as you can get, sporting red hair and freckles, while Thalia is olive-skinned with deep chestnut hair. Taking a closer look at them, though, I now notice that they share the same sharp nose and cat-like eyes.

Thalia nods at my confusion and continues. "Same father, but different mother. Our father has a taste for the finer things in life." I hear a bit of disgust in her voice and I wonder what part of what she said it is directed toward.

Feeling that this topic is just a diversion from my question, I ask, "That's great and all, but what does that have to do with this?" I wave my hands around to indicate *this* being everyone's odd behavior.

Thalia gives my question an ominous chuckle. "Everything, Amethyst. Our father has everything to do with this because our father is Zeus. And we all have been stationed here to protect and monitor your soul."

Now it's my turn to laugh, somewhat hysterically. "You mean to tell me that the almighty Zeus, a god, is out there rolling in the clouds on some chariot coming for us?" My voice is rising in pitch, but I'm trying to keep my cool. This is the real world, not some made up fairy land. And this business with my soul again? Alice must've mentioned to them what the shopkeeper had said to me. None of this made any sense.

"Like hell am I falling for this, Thalia. You think of this as just some messed up entertainment? I refuse to fall for it." I shake my head in indignation as my confusion is quickly turning into rage. Thalia and Clio have always been cold and business-like. They have never shown any kindness toward the rest of us, just strict professionalism. This was some warped joke. But for Alice and Paul to also be in on it ...

My arms are folded to keep me from shaking, but before I can tell her to piss off, she says sternly, "This is not a game. I would never lie to someone I respect. Those you know of as gods are real. It's time for you to open your eyes. How can you think this is not real when you know Poseidon?" I stare at her blankly, not processing what she's saying. "Poseidon ..." she says again and then, "*Percy.*" His name on her lips is like a slap across my face. I flinch away, still unable to wrap my mind around what she's saying.

So many questions run through my mind, but I ask the most important one. "How do you know him?" Percy is Poseidon? It doesn't make sense, and yet it does. It's starting to make perfect sense, even though I don't want it to.

Thalia no longer looks stern, but pleased with the change in my tone. In a patient tone, she says, "Think, Amethyst. I know you are knowledgeable of mythology."

I rack my brain through all the stories Percy has told me. My mouth opens in wonder at the realization. "You two are part of the nine muses. But where are your other sisters?"

Thalia gives a sad smile as she says, "They have chosen a different life."

"Thalia. Clio. We need you out here, harpies are rolling in." Alice's voice booms over the intercom. Harpies? What in the bloody hell ... My heart kicks up a notch at the flood of information and the fact that some harmful being that is putting everyone in panic mode is almost at the boat. If Zeus is out there, how do I fight off a god? How would any of us survive an attack from a powerful being who seems to be able to control the weather?

Clio takes off toward the door with Thalia and me right behind her. I follow, mainly because I still have no idea what is going on and since they do, I'm betting the safest option for me is by their side. Thalia's explanation is poor and leaves me with no answers and more questions that pile up with each word she says. Before Clio opens the door, Thalia says, "I know you're in shock. We should've explained who we were earlier, but our orders were to keep silent. We honestly thought he wouldn't find us. Someone must've tipped him off ..." She trails off, lost in thought in how Zeus could've found our location.

I look back to her. "Then explain now."

Thalia just shakes her head. "I have already said more than I should. I'll be punished for this, but you need to know. We can't tell you more. Not because we are under oath, but because you have a test and because of this test you have to know as little as possible." I open my mouth to ask what bloody test she could be talking about, but before I can there's a sudden crash, and we are thrown to the floor. I feel a sharp pain on the side of my head and then my world goes black.

Chapter Six

FOUR YEARS AGO

I stare hard at the words that Percy has given me to learn. My brow creases as I try to make sense of the sentence. After the struggle it took to translate, I recognize it as the first line to one of the many works from Plato. "*Human behavior flows from three main sources: desire, emotion and knowledge.*"

The first day that I met Percy, I placed his weird speech as an accent and asked him where it came from. He replied that it's an old language that is no longer spoken except for where he comes from. I then proceeded to ask where that is and he just stared out at the sea, sadness hooding his eyes. Sometimes I believe that Percy is derived from the sea itself.

Having finished the translation of the old language, I set it down on the beach towel and make my way over to the water. Percy is waiting for me in the water up to his neck. His body moves to and fro with the tug and pull of each calm wave. It's a warm summer day that makes a swim feel perfect.

I gaze at his chiseled jaw and make my way up to his oceanic eyes that have always captivated me. With just my toes in the water, I'm a couple meters away from him. I stand there and take in his features. He's my elder, but I am not sure by how much; he's always vague when it comes to his age. He never gives me a clear answer when I ask. There was another charity auction this year to celebrate my sixteenth birthday like there is every year. When I made a small complaint at never receiving any gifts, Mother scolded me and said it's good to be giving, and to use any excuse for it.

Mother ... the thought of her pulls me into a pit of depression. She was diagnosed last fall with cancer. She hasn't been doing well. *Not well* is an overstatement. I see her get weaker and weaker every day and it seems that with each day, she deteriorates even further toward death. Her skin is pasty and her once full cheeks are now hollow. Her eyes have sunken in and remain closed more often than not, as she struggles through the pain. Morphine would help, but she has chosen to only take it at night because she would rather be here with her family, present and not lost in her high. Though sometimes I do wish she would take it more often, it breaks my heart to see her in so much pain. Father has moved her hospital bed into the house so that she is closer to us. She finds comfort in hearing me play the cello, so I play a piece for her in the mornings when she's the most aware, hoping and praying that this small comfort that I give her will help ease her pain. I make sure to keep the music light and to not flow into the darker tones that I feel toward losing her.

Percy swims tentatively toward me. When he gets to shallower water, he stands and begins walking. Reaching me, he takes my hand into his. "What's wrong?" he questions. "Was the translation too hard?"

I shake my head no and reply, "I was just thinking about my mother." My voice cracks at the word *mother* and I cover my face because now I can't stop the tears from flowing. I have cried years worth of tears in less than a month and yet they still come. The tears spill all the same, like a never-ending well of despair and frustration. The ache in my chest that was dull a moment ago, turns into a sharp stabbing that wishes to consume me. And I let it. I let all of the hurt take over as I sob even harder. I will soon no longer have a mother. The sound of her voice when she sings lullabies has already been replaced by her now-raspy tones. How long after she's gone will it take before I forget what she looks like too?

Percy wraps his arms around me, cocooning me into his chest. His frame is warm and solid and as my cheek is squished against him, a blanket of security soaks into my soul. Rubbing my back in gentle strokes with his thumb, he whispers, "Shush,It will be okay." Those are the only words of comfort I get because even he knows that she won't pull through from this. What human has ever survived stage four metastatic cancer?

On the shore, we sit in silent comfort with a box of chocolates lying between us. We meet here a couple times a week during the summers, when I am not at Oxford for school. Percy has taken it upon himself to teach me the old language. Sometimes he'll even tell me a tale from Greek mythology. Tales of the once-noble Zeus who grew twisted and drunk on power. Or of Hades, who had a heart made up of ice until the goddess Persephone melted it. Although the amount I see him has lessened with the spread of my mother's sickness. This is the first time I've spent with him in two weeks and it's been a nice reprieve from the somber atmosphere within the walls of my home.

I wish I could see him every day, but besides my mother's waning health, I don't have time. The expectations of being in Oxford at my age, at times, are suffocating, but I carry on, wanting to only appease my father. He's hoping that I'll finish my Masters in a couple of years so that I can join his law firm when I turn twenty. I am not too keen on that idea. I would much rather spend my days studying the ocean. I continually fight a war within myself between wanting to please my father and needing a break from endless studying.

I'm growing tired.

I had a huge argument with him about my major. In the end, he let me major in marine biology just as long as I minored in law. He wants me to take over the firm some day. I get it, it's a family business. I just wish that he would see that law is not my dream. The ocean is my dream; it's where I find peace and solace.

"Sometimes I feel as if the ocean is calling to me. That if it could, it would bring me deep within its waters and never let me return to the surface." I admit the feeling out loud while fumbling with the hem of my bathing suit.

He stills and I feel his eyes on me, but I don't look toward him. Eyes down, I reach for another chocolate.

"You belong to the ocean," he whispers.

With the chocolate halfway to my mouth, I stop and turn to him. "What?"

He shakes his head and playfully smiles. "It's nothing. Nevermind." Something about what he said feels right, but at the same time it's so asinine. But maybe I didn't hear him correctly. I shrug my shoulders and bite down on the chocolate.

"I think I'm going to go for a swim. Care to join?" I ask as I stand up.

He shakes his head. "I'm good. The sun feels fantastic right now." To further his statement, he tilts his head back and closes his eyes, grinning up at the sun. "Ahh," he sighs.

I shrug my shoulders. "Alright."

Floating on my back, I enjoy the warmth of the sun soaking into my body when something bumps into me. Percy? But it felt slimy against my thigh ... I am not too far out, so I straighten myself and my feet touch the seafloor with my head still above the water. I look around trying to see what had touched me. All I can think about is a shark testing to see if it wants me for an afternoon snack. I've never encountered a shark before, but there is always a first for everything. Whatever it was, it bumps into me again, but this time into my back. I start with fright and then turn around to see who my attacker may be. I'm praying that it's not a shark because I honestly wouldn't know what to do.

"Oh, you precious thing," I coo with delight. My attacker isn't a hungry shark but instead a curious baby manta ray. The ray glides its pectoral fin across my skin in a hello as it swims around me. I reach out to touch it and my fingertips trace ever so gently down its back. I am so wrapped up in the baby ray that I don't realize the dozen other rays that have joined us until I am being bumped from all sides. Twisting in a circle, I look around me in wonder. Repeating what the baby ray is doing, they all swim around me, each in turn gliding their pectoral fins over my skin. Their dance reminds me of a welcoming ceremony. I swear I can faintly hear their whispers, *We welcome you. We accept you. You are ours. Ours.*

As the rays dance around me, my eyes scan the beach to look for Percy. I want to share this unforgettable experience with him. I thought he would be sitting on the sand where I left him eating the chocolates that he is so obsessed with, but instead I see him walking along the beach with a noddy perched on his shoulder. Just before I call out to catch his attention, I see his lips moving. I can't hear what he's saying, but I see the bird nod its head as if it can understand Percy's every word.

Intrigued by what is happening, I swim closer to Percy, trying to be stealthy about it so that he won't notice me. As I draw nearer, I hear Percy say to the bird, "I have waited so long for the—" The bird gives out a piercing squawk, cutting off whatever Percy was about to say. Within a second, Percy turns and faces me. Rage is written all over his face and his eyes blaze an icy blue. Feeling ashamed of maybe hearing something that I shouldn't have, I yell out sorry and dive under the water.

The moment I shared with the rays is broken as my dive scares them off. Mad at myself, I try to swim out to the reef to get away but am overcome with tiredness before I come anywhere close to the reef. I float on my back, hoping that Percy didn't follow me, and take a moment to catch my breath. I feel humiliated for taking off, acting scared of Percy when I have no reason to be scared of him. It was childish of me to run away.

With my last steady exhale, I look around for him. Thankfully, he is not in the water although now a part of me wishes that he was. I don't see him at all. He's not in the water or along the shore. Was he so mad at me that he took off? The thought leaves me devastated, so I swim back to the shore in search of him.

My heart is pounding when I make it back to the shore. I run out of the water and land on my hands and knees, panting for air. I am in the middle of thinking about how dumb it was of me to try to swim out to the reef when a set of sandy toes comes into my vision. I slowly tilt my head up to find Percy with his arms crossed. At first I think that he's mad, but the longer I look at him, the more he looks uncomfortable. Nervous, even. We say nothing but stare at each other. So many emotions play across his face but the ones that keep reoccurring are worry and fear. I don't realize how long we have been doing this until my neck starts cramping. Grimacing, I rub the back of my neck and flip over onto my back. I don't even care anymore about the embarrassment of swimming away from him. Damn it all into the deepest pits of oblivion.

He's still standing over me when he says, "What all did you hear?" There's defeat in his voice and the forlorn sound shatters me.

The words rush out of me as I stand up and wrap my arms around him. "It's okay. I'll still be your friend even if you talk to birds and it's a little strange. I'll still be your friend and I didn't hear anything. I promise." I take a huge breath in after the flight of words and lean back to see his expression, but he holds onto me so I can't look at him.

He laughs a dark laugh and says, "You don't find that unhinged?"

"I, well ..." I trail off. He's got a point. But I sometimes talk to myself, so what's the difference? Never finishing my train of thought, Percy holds me tight and doesn't say anything for a long while.

He never brings up the birds again, and I never do tell him about the manta rays. There are so many questions surrounding Percy. If I ask my questions, I don't think Percy would lie to me; rather I think that I am not ready for the answers. Some things are left better unsaid, and maybe the mystery surrounding Percy is one of them.

Chapter Seven

PRESENT

The weight against me feels as if I'm at the bottom of the ocean. The pressure is like a weighted blanket cocooning me into a forceful sleep. There's something ringing next to my ears and I try to bat it away so I can drift back off, but I can't lift my arm. I'm stuck, drowning in this darkness.

The ringing gets louder.

As I open my heavy eyelids, the ringing turns into battle cries. I hear screaming and a cry so inhuman that I wonder what could make such an awful sound. There's scraping and stomping on the deck and I lift myself up to look around me, but someone pushes me back down. I wince at the disturbance to my equilibrium and press my fingers against the back of my head. There's a sensitive lump and I hiss in a breath of pain.

"Be still," a voice commands. "You hit your head pretty hard and there was a lot of blood. Normal for head wounds, but you may have gotten a concussion." The hand that pushed me down is now patting my head with a towel.

"Clio?" My voice feels heavy like the rest of me. "Where's Thalia? What's that noise? What happened?" Clio shines a light in my eyes. She looks from one eye to the other, then clicks it off. The light is bright and if she hadn't been holding my eyelids open, I would've shut them at the intrusion.

"They caught up to us. Damn harpies are fast, but even faster when Zeus is aiding them with the wind. Your speech seems fine. How are you feeling? Dizzy at all? Nauseous?" Her questions are quick and as she asks them she scans over my body.

"I feel a little groggy, but no, not dizzy or nauseous." I stand up and this time Clio doesn't stop me. I wobble on my feet and grab onto the bunk bed railing to stabilize myself. When my world stops spinning and the weighted feeling leaves me, Clio removes a gun and a jian from the backpack she was packing earlier. My eyes widen as I realize that she has my jian, a family sword that my father had given to me. I've only practiced with it a few times. *A few times* meaning only twice. If I'm expected to use it I don't know how good I'll be.

"How?" My mind is reeling. How could she have fit that in the bag and how does she even have it in the first place? Clio only gives me a smirk and hands me the jian.

I shake my head as I take it from her and say, "Why am I still surprised? By chance, you wouldn't happen to have Percy in there as well?"

Clio rolls her eyes and says, "Don't be ridiculous. Now come on, you're in good enough shape to fight. Poseidon said that you're good with a sword?" She says it as a question but doesn't wait for an answer before she continues speaking. "Keep an eye on their claws and be mindful of their beaks."

Their ... what?

The screams that woke me up had become background noise, but now with the reminder that we're under attack the sounds of battle become crisp. I take off my jacket—it'd only hinder my movements. I unsheathe my sword and follow Clio out the door. Fighting can't be that much different from fencing, can it?

As we make our way to the deck, there are creatures everywhere. Spindly arms draped in feathers and ... *God,* a human face with a beak strapped to it. They are walking nightmares and I have to hold back a scream. To see something that looks human but is so morbidly twisted into a bird sends shivers down my spine, and not in a good way. The shivers almost send me into a state of panic, but then one of the creatures lunges for me and my fear turns into adrenaline. Lost in the now, all thinking comes to a halt and is replaced by years of training. Like I do with my cello bow, I imagine that the jian is another extension of my arm, and thanks to the extra training with my father, I let the sword become a part of me. I breathe in and then breathe out as I cut the jian down through the air. I find contact and slice off a wing, and then I'm plunging my sword into the beast's chest. It drops to the deck and is replaced by another bird-like human.

Arm up, breathe in.

Release, breathe out.

I slash it from shoulder to hip, and its guts spill out, littering the deck. I ignore the putrid smell of fresh guts and blood and instead focus on my breathing as another one readily takes its place. It moves out of reach of my lunge, its clawed hands reaching for my throat, but Clio is there and shoots it in the chest. It gives out a piercing screech from its warped human face and staggers back from the blow. It falls to the ground and its screams become garbled as it bleeds out, its purple blood pooling around its head.

Everywhere I look, I'm surrounded by feathers and claws. I have no time to take in my surroundings or check how the others are faring. I barely register Clio as she shoots another one down. There are too many of them and all I can do to survive is not lose focus. Time seems to be an illusion; we have been out here for mere minutes and yet it feels like hours. My arm is losing strength and with each bird that lunges for me I find it harder to hold my own. There's a gash in my inner thigh from a few dead foes ago. Luckily, the wound is not too deep. The adrenaline coursing through my veins is so thick that I'm able to ignore the pain that otherwise would have brought me to my knees.

Just when I think that I won't be able to raise my sword anymore, the boat sways. I lose my balance and stumble across the blood smattered deck. One of the creatures that I had been battling with uses this opportunity to try to rip me to shreds. I don't even have enough time to block the attack. One moment I'm staring into its human eyes, claws long and lethal reaching for me, and the next moment it's engulfed in water. I almost cry out in relief—I was *this* close to running out of luck. To being ripped apart by its sharp beak.

As it's ripped away from me, I get up to fight the next one, but as I look around, I see that water is engulfing the entire deck. The water touches everything except for the crew and myself. An endless wave gushes around the creatures on the deck and the ones that are left in the sky. Some claw at their throats gasping for air while others wobble their limbs around in panic, trying to escape their fate. The unnatural water formation drags its unwilling guests down into the body of water. I lean over the edge of the boat and watch as they disappear, arms outstretched, swallowed by the deep ocean.

With the battle over, my hands start to shake and queasiness takes over. I can't hold it in any longer and barf over into the ocean. I continue to heave a few more times until bile starts coming up. I take in deep breaths, trying to calm myself. I wipe my mouth, but end up smearing blood all over it. Looking down at myself, I realize for the first time that I am drenched in blood. Not one part of me is free from the red of my own or the purple of the human-like birds. Harpies? Is that what Clio called them? I don't even know. I'm having a hard time processing what just happened.

No matter how much I try to focus on my breathing, I can't stop shaking. I must be having a panic attack. My whole world as I know it is collapsing in on itself and instead of turning to fear, I turn to anger. I whip around to yell at everyone and instead come face to face with Percy.

Now the unnatural water makes sense. Percy is here, and he's a *god*. Oh fuck, I think I'm going to have a panic attack. I wrap my arms around my torso and hold myself tightly. Percy just manipulated *water*. A laugh barks out of my strained lips. "This can't be real," I mumble to myself. What just happened is playing through my mind at a dizzying speed and I can't quite get them to stop.

"Breathe, Dove." Percy says as he takes a tentative step toward me. He's not wearing a shirt and for some reason, my mind focuses on every beadlet of water that's dripping down his tan chest and over his abs. And I especially notice a drop that accumulates and drips from his pebbled nipple. It reminds me that when someone goes through a traumatic event their mind tries to distract itself with something mundane. But let's be real, Percy's toned body is far from mundane. He raises his hand outward, reaching for me like one would do with a scared animal that's about to bite. I snap back to reality.

"Breathe?" I taunt back at him. "You're a fucking god and have been lying to me all these years!" No wonder he never found me once I came to France. I was a mere human who had a zero chance of being with a god.

Rage takes over and wipes away the whiplash from monster gore to Percy half naked. Everything around me is blurred out leaving only a tunnel vision of him. The one person whose neck I want to wring. I have never been so angry in my life. I embrace the anger over the fear of not knowing what is going on or that I may mean nothing to him. The sane part of me seems to be letting the wild me take control because it knows that even if I gave it my all, my attempts would be futile. Percy is a god for fuck's sake and could easily stop my advances. I can't help but think that I have been played for a fool. A lone human in the middle of some sort of battle between gods. I almost died with not a clue as to why. And all for what?

Percy sees me coming. When he assesses my demeanor, the way I hold my jian and the bloodthirsty look on my face, he stiffens and his face goes blank. Devoid of any emotion as if he's cold as stone and that my anger isn't justified. I want him to be angry back or at least show me that he's sorry. But this unresponsive coldness is something that I don't want to deal with. It makes me even angrier.

I find myself in front of him, seething. Panting so hard I could cry. My anger then turns to mortification because I don't want to hurt him. I am so mad at myself for stooping that low. Before I can calm down, his mask of indifference turns from me and as if I don't exist, he walks past me. For the first time, I look for the others. None are paying attention to me, instead all of them are huddled around each other.

"No," I whisper, my voice cracking.

Paul is laying on the deck, his head cradled in Alice's lap. So pale and yet so red. I hadn't felt myself moving but somehow I am on my knees huddled with the rest of the group. There's so much blood surrounding him. One of the wretched beasts had gotten him. The attack must've happened right as Percy showed up. He's still alive with only seconds left. There's a gash in his lower stomach with his guts hanging out, barely contained as Alice tries to hold them in. An intestine slips out of her hand and she sobs out in anguish, trying to quickly put it back.

"Poseidon." Paul's voice comes out barely above a whisper. His eyes fluttering open and closed in quick succession.

Percy is next to him and takes his hand. "I am right here, my son."

Knowing that his god is with him during his last moments, Paul gives a faint smile and then goes limp. His eyes that once held so much humor now look at me, dead and soulless. I can't look away, even when Alice's cries turn into heart-wrenching screams. It'll be a sound that will haunt me for eternity.

Clio, Thalia and Percy leave the circle to form their own and are speaking in hushed tones. I'm too numb to care about what they're saying. I get up and go down to the main cabin. With a body that doesn't feel like my own, I strip out of my bloodied clothes and step into the small shower stall. The water isn't warm, but it is bearable. Although I'd rather it be scalding to burn off what just happened. I feel hollow as I scrub every inch of me to rid myself of the stain of death. No matter how hard I scrub my fingernails I can't seem to remove the blood from underneath them. I want to scream but don't. What's the point when Paul is dead? I give up trying to remove the blood. Let it be a reminder of this terrible new reality. At this point, I'm too numb to care. I am merely a husk wishing to be blown into the abyss.

Once I am finished cleaning I dress the wound on my leg and clothe myself in something warm but easy to move in. Who knows when the next attack will be? The world that I knew is more than I thought. Am I even safe? How often does one get attacked when involved with a god? I can only speculate the reason for today's events. A feud? Bitterness? Or simply just jealousy? My readings mentioned quite frequently that the gods were prone to bouts of jealousy, that they were easily angered. In my ignorance did I somehow piss off a god?

I've known Percy for practically my whole life, and to now come to terms with him being more than just magical but an almighty being? It was becoming hard to grasp. I had to wonder if he was at all anything like Zeus. Was he just as capable of killing so callously? At the slightest annoyance would he wipe a person from existence? It was a train of thought that I want to ignore but it keeps eating at me. But I have to tell myself that he is different, he has to be. If not, then …

The fabric of my leggings rubs against my bandaged leg, causing me to flinch in pain. I am beyond lucky that the harpie wasn't close enough when it lashed out. If the wound was any deeper, I would be laying next to Paul, with the same blank look and lifeless form.

Feeling loss settle on me like a weight, I huddle in my bed curled under a blanket, and shroud myself into a deep pit of grief. I repeat in my head that what happened to Paul is all my fault. It has to be. Nothing makes sense right now but the one thing that does is that if Zeus wasn't looking for me, Paul would still be alive.

I thought it would be Percy who would come down to see how I was doing but to my disappointment it was Clio. She sits at the end of the bed and places her palm upon my curled form. With a comforting tone she says, "The funeral is about to begin."

This information shouldn't surprise me but it does. I sit up and ask, "Funeral?" My voice is emotionless. The last time I felt this broken was when my mother passed. I just went into battle without knowing why, just that I needed to survive, and right after I watched someone who had become a friend die. Just like that, he was gone. I haven't even cried yet. I'm just laying here hating myself and hating this predicament. It's all my fault.

"Yes," Clio says as she looks at me with concern. "Paul was a potamoi, and even though we are too far from his home for a proper funeral, this part of the world will do just fine."

I wrack my brain over the familiar word until I remember a small lesson about them. Potamoi are the male versions of nymphs. Their domain is usually rivers, and they are known to be protectors of the young. This explains why he was watching the little boy on the pier and why he jumped into the water without a second thought.

My chest tightens with an emotion that I want to push deep down and not feel at all. He didn't deserve this. I look away, trying not to cry. Trying to harden my heart to the loss. It was easier said than done.

"I know how you're feeling." I can't bear to hear the empathy her voice exudes. It sickens me, it's something that I do not deserve.

I whip my head back to face her and spit out, "How could you possibly know?"

She doesn't flinch from my tone and says, "I have lived a long time. I have seen many loved ones pass from this world." She pauses, taking in a shaky breath. "Zeus is a very cruel man. He is possessive of his treasures and he views his daughters as such. He says he does what he does out of love."

"Let me tell you my story," she continues. I lie there unresponsive and her eyes become distant as she recounts a memory. "I was lonely. I wanted to share laughter with a friend. You see, Zeus loved us so much that he didn't want to share. He did warn us." She sneers. "But I took this warning lightly. I had not yet seen who my papa truly was. He showered us with so much that I did not think of the extent of what he'd do when we disobeyed his commands.

"Seeking friendship with someone who wasn't stuck up like my sisters, I frequented the bathhouse at my nearest shrine." She gives a sad laugh. "You see, I was told that a bathhouse was where all the women would go to have fun without men telling them what to do. I thought it was perfect, because Zeus controlled every aspect of my life. Back then women were very oppressed, so the bathhouse was an escape for them, and it became an escape for me. I had made many friends, every single woman that would go to that bathhouse, in fact. It was a few short months later when Zeus had found out what I had done. I was so unbelievably happy and on that same day so utterly ..." She doesn't finish what she's saying, instead her face is torn, as she's stuck in the past.

"Clio?" I grasp her porcelain hand to give her courage, now riveted by her story.

She shakes herself. Pushing a fiery-red strand behind her hair, she gives me a smile that doesn't reach her eyes. "When Zeus found out that I had friends he acted delighted. He invited them all to my home for a party. My friends ranged from just twelve-year-pubescents to fifty-year-old women. I was elated that he was accepting my friends. That he was happy for me. But when he had them all in one room, he had his men hold me down ... *he made me watch* ... I kicked and screamed for him to stop."

She's silent and this time I don't encourage her to go on. I stay quiet, giving her the time that she needs. After a deep, rattled intake and release of breath she says, "He killed all thirty-two of them. I watched as an entire village of women who were beloved by their community were ripped apart by a man who I had loved dearly, who I had called Papa.

"He wasn't nice about it; he'd tear an arm off of one and have the others watch, petrified, while she would bleed out, and then he would go on to the next. He took his time. He took his *sweet* time. Hours had passed by before he was finished with his massacre. He had called it a *lesson*.

"The room stunk with piss and fecal matter. It was a living nightmare to hear the cries and morbid screams of those being tortured, counting down the minutes until it was your turn. My screaming had stopped long ago, my eyes unseeing and body limp as I was lost in my own little world of hell. When he was done, he came over to me and placed his bloodied hands against each cheek and said, "I love you so much, my dear daughter. This is how it is to be, you see? No one can love you as much as I." And then he kissed my forehead and walked away whistling a merry tune, like all that I held dear was a passing fancy to be wiped out."

She goes silent again and I wait for more, but that was it. I am speechless. What is there to say to someone who went through something like that? I should feel fear, Zeus had tried to kill me as well. He succeeded in killing Paul. Yet all I feel is anger. Anger at the injustice, at the proclamation of love when that so clearly was not love. No, that was an obsession. One fueled by control and that took countless lives. I could ask what was the point in all that, but when it comes down cruelty, there is no point. Evil does not need a reason.

"How could you live on after that?" I finally ask, gripping her hands.

She studies my face before replying. "Purpose ... I could not let them die in vain. I owed that to their memory and to their families. It did take me a long time to find that purpose, though. I spent decades being his little treasure, blaming everything on myself. His manipulation made me believe that what he had done was what was best for me ... that anything bad that ever happened was my fault. Every day that ate away at me. I would wake up, look in the mirror and repeat how it was my fault, that I was the reason for their deaths."

She stills, struggling to get the words out. I rub the back of her hands. "It's okay, you don't have to finish."

"No, I need to." She takes a deep breath, steadying herself and then she says, "It eventually got to the point that when I looked in the mirror, I saw them. They appeared bloodied and would hiss at me that they hated me. That I did this to them. I couldn't take it. It was too much, and I needed to escape. You see, I can't die." She laughs, but it's broken. "Something that I'll explain to you later, but for now all I'll say is that for certain reasons I am unable to die, but that doesn't mean that I can't feel pain."

Her attention turns to her hands in mine and she releases my grip on her to pick at her cuticles. "At the end of each day, I would lay in the tub and cut myself. Most of the time I would slit my throat, bleed out and then wake up, perfectly healed. The beauty of being immortal." I have way too many questions, but now is not the time to ask them, so I keep as still as a statue, listening. The only thing you really can do for someone who is hurting and telling their story.

"On the days that were more unbearable than others, I'd get a little rough with the knife. I wanted to *feel* something besides this grief and self-hatred. I wanted my friends back, and it was all my fault. So on those days I'd go to town on myself like a butcher. I was so far gone that most of that time in my life was a haze. I look back and it's foggy. I see snippets of what happened, but most of the time ... It's like I was in such a dark place that my mind blocked out that part of my life. Only a few memories remain. And the worst part was that I soon began to forget what my friends looked like."

A tired sigh leaves her, one filled with years of misery. "It wasn't until I had the help of a very special nymph that I opened my eyes. Once she did that, I was able to break Zeus' chains. My sister and I fled and have been running ever since."

"I am so sorry!" I throw myself at her, holding her tight against me. I have never known such cruelty. My heart bleeds for her pain, all the loss she's had to endure. The self-hatred that ate away at her. I wish I could take it all away. No one should experience something like that.

"It wasn't your fault," I choke out.

"It's not your fault either." I stiffen, it totally is. Paul's death was undeniably my fault. "It's not," she repeats, steel in her voice. "Zeus was coming for us, not you."

I don't know if it's because of her story or the unyielding resolution in her voice, but the tears finally come. They flow out of me, wracking me with uncontrollable sobs.

She strokes my hair and whispers, "Shh it's okay, it's okay. I am free now and am much happier. We must learn to move on. If our mourning is never-ending, how will we ever find happiness? No, it is not what they would have wanted. They will always be in my heart, but I vowed to never shed another tear for what I have lost. Now stop your crying and let's go; we have a good friend to honor." I calm down and break my grasp from her. Wiping my nose, I nod my head.

"Good," she says, and gives my leg a firm pat before making her way to the door. She only looks back to make sure that I am following before going up the stairs.

In the middle of the Atlantic Ocean, Percy stands above the calm water. At his feet floats Paul, completely naked. The rest of us sit in the rescue boats that are required to be on the research boat. Thalia and I share one, while Clio and Alice share another.

With the aid of Percy's manipulation of water, we were able to make it out here in less than an hour. Thalia explained to me that this ritual is usually done at the river or the body of water that the Potamoi dwelled in during adolescence. While we were getting the rescue boats into the water she was saying that when a Potamoi's time expires, they turn into foam and are one again with the water, as the circle of life requires of them.

I watch with great intent. Looking at Paul's cold, blue-tinged form, I am stricken with sadness. I grit my teeth, trying to not let the wave of anguish consume me. My life has made a dramatic turn and I must be strong. I have a feeling that this won't be the last death that I will see.

Percy walks in a circle around Paul's floating form, his feet making small ripples in the water. Each step he takes, he splashes water over Paul. As he does this, Thalia, Clio, and Alice start singing an eerie hymn.

"Who shall bring you
Into the death-sleep sling you.
When you walk on the Path of Death
And the tracks you tread
Are cold, so cold.
When you stand by the Gate of Death
And you have to tear free,
I shall follow you.
With my song,
You shall be free from your bond."

When the last of the song finishes, Percy goes to his knees and places his hand over Paul's face. Light shines forth from Percy's hand. The light becomes so bright that I have to look away. As the light dims, I draw my eyes back to Percy and Paul. Paul's body is now replaced by sea foam in the shape of him. Quick as lightning, Percy plunges his hand into what was once Paul's chest. I hear a gasp of shock from the other boat as Percy's hand retreats from Paul's sea foam chest. His hand is holding onto what looks like a cloud. He lets go of it and the wisp of fog turns into a solid form of water that's in the image of Paul. Paul's watery form stands confused and quiet as he waits for Percy to speak.

"Today you saved my greatest love." Percy's voice booms over the silent waters. "You gave your life to protect her. For that, I am giving you a gift. Instead of dying and joining the never-ending cycle of life, you have died and been reborn. I announce you as The Protector of the Atlantic Ocean. Here you shall dwell. Here you shall protect and cherish every living creature within your domain. With those before me as witness, it shall be done." I was expecting a clap of thunder or a large wave to end the ceremony, but instead Percy just places his hands to his sides and stands there, feet floating on the water.

Paul bows his head and says, "Thank you, my king." He then gives each one of us a nod before diving into the ocean. Suddenly, all around us, blue whales start splashing and blowing air out of their blowholes. Water sprays us while I hold tightly onto the boat. The whales are so close that they cause a giant wave to come our way. We have to rock with the waves to ensure that we don't flip. I feel as if I'm on an amusement park ride.

"What's going on?" I shout out, confused and a little worried. This was not normal whale behavior.

For the first time today since Percy arrived, he finally speaks to me. "They are celebrating their new ruler. The species of this domain have not had a Protector for centuries." Even though he speaks only a few sentences, his voice caresses my heart. I've missed hearing his deep tones that end on supertonic and mediant notes.

"What are they doing here?" I ask. I hadn't even noticed that they were here until they started dancing around.

"They are the witnesses," Percy states. I furrow my eyebrows in further confusion. I thought he was referring to us when he spoke of witnesses earlier.

When the splashing finally dies down, Percy walks over to me and reaches his hand out. His fingertips gently glide from my temples down my jaw to my chin. His thumb rubs my bottom lip in possessive strokes. My skin flares up where he touches and I lean in, wanting to kiss him. Damn it all. I'm so confused. One minute I'm upset over not knowing where we stand and the next I'm fawning over him. Forgetting where I'm at, I topple forward.

Percy catches me, saving me from falling into the ocean. He gives a satisfied smirk as he holds me in his arms. I look around me and see the others laughing. Everyone is laughing except Alice. Before I can make sense of her menacing glare, she turns away.

"Get a room!" Clio calls out.

"I think we shall," Percy replies. The drawl in his tone makes my stomach dip and curl. My face blushes in a mixture of embarrassment and desire. I internally slap myself. I shouldn't be feeling this way toward him, but he has such a pull over me that my body can't help but react.

Water rushes from beneath us, carrying us over to the research boat. I clutch onto Percy as we shoot out of the water and onto the deck. It still freaks me out a little bit that he can control water and I try to fight down the hysteria bubbling back up. Clio and Thalia start whistling and hollering lewd things at us, which distract my new brewings of distress. I quickly hide my beet-red face in Percy's chest. Gosh, they couldn't be any more crude, it's embarrassing. It's not like we were going to do anything. We haven't even kissed yet, or discussed what we are to each other. And he's a god. What does that mean for us? I'll eventually age and die while he'll be gallivanting around, doing whatever it is gods do. Instead of setting me down, he carries me to the cabin where the sleeping quarters are. He tosses me onto the nearest bed and I slightly bounce against it.

"Percy, we need to talk and this isn't my bed," I protest as he crawls on top of me.

He ignores me and crushes his lips against mine. His assault catches me by surprise, but as his lips ask for entry, I melt and open myself to him. He grabs onto my hip and kneads it as his other hand cradles my face. Delirious from his touch, I hungrily run my hands through his grown-out hair. Grabbing a hold of a bunch at the nape of his neck, I tug his head back to remove his lips from mine. "We need to talk," I repeat, staring at his exposed neck. His Adam's apple bobs, and I lick my lips, resisting the urge to taste him there.

"I need my woman," he growls, pinning my hands in a deadlock grip above my head, which pushes my chest against his. *His woman.* I guess that answers my insecurities about who I am to him. I squirm under him, his body flush against mine. I feel his bulge straining against his shorts as it presses against my core. I grind against him, wanting to feel more, but he only tuts before securing my arms and going back to kissing me. This time slower, but still an undercurrent of hunger remains. I've dreamed of his lips since my birthday and yet all that dreaming is not comparable to this. They're soft and warm and holy shit, he tastes exactly like he smells. His tongue trails slowly across my bottom lip. Before he removes his tongue, I quickly bite down on it and give it a light tug.

When I release him, he chuckles. "Always so feisty."

"Honestly, after today, I think you deserved to be bitten harder."

Leaning his forehead against mine, he lets out a heavy sigh and then lies on his side. He moves me to where my back is against his chest. I feel his need to have me close, so I allow him this small gift, even though I think he doesn't deserve it. I feel his heartbeat coming to a steady pace against my back. The beat sings to me, *I'm here, I'm here, I'm here* and my heart replies, *never again, never again, never again.* Because never again do I ever want to be separated from him. He is mine and I won't allow this new cruel world to ever take him from me. Whatever grudge Zeus has against him, we will weather it together. That's what I've realized after tonight. Percy by no means is anything like Zeus. Percy is kind, something that I learned Zeus is not. Whatever immortality has done to Zeus, it hasn't changed Percy. And honestly, whatever things Percy kept from me, I don't think I'll ever be able to let him go. Whatever trials we face, as long as he's by my side, I'll be able to set aside my fears and traverse this new life with him.

Not letting go of my anger completely, I ask, "Why did you never tell me who you are?"

Percy squeezes me, which brings me closer to him. He breathes so deeply against my hair that I feel his nose pressed into the top of my scalp. "Honestly, I wanted you to like me for me." The back of his fingers skim down my arm. "But that's also why I talked about Greek mythology with you. I was hoping and at the same time not hoping that you would put two and two together." He shrugs his shoulders.

I snort. "Well, I didn't."

"Which was surprising." He buries his head in my hair once again and takes a deep breath.

I twist in his arms to face him. "Are you okay?" I ask between giving him kisses on his chest. His chest hair tickles my nose and I take a moment to breathe him in as well. He smells of home, clean ocean water with underlying tones of citrus. It's pleasant. I want to give him a little bite, but refrain. Something seems to be bothering him so I wait patiently for his answer.

He lets out a shuddering breath. "You were covered in blood. I thought I was too late. I thought I was going to lose you. But you were ... moving. You were still swinging that sword. Your face was weary and I could see your arms shaking and growing tired. And then I was enraged. All I could think of was how *dare* anything try to harm you." Percy's jaw clenches so hard I can hear his teeth grind. I move my head up and kiss his jaw. He relaxes when my lips make contact.

"I thought you were mad at me," I admit.

Percy holds me tighter before saying, "Oh, I was. A good friend was dying, and you decided that was a great time to throw a tantrum."

I try pulling away from him, but Percy firmly holds me in place. I close my eyes and take in deep breaths to calm myself down. I'm tired of letting my anger control me, and even though his comment makes me angry, he is right. It's out of embarrassment that I am angry. I hate myself for letting my emotions get the best of me, especially because I was so mad that I was oblivious to Paul bleeding out. It was not one of my finest moments.

Counting down from ten, I think about what Percy had said. When I get to four I ask, "Good friend? You knew Paul?"

"Yes." Percy stiffens, which lets me know that there is more to it that he's refraining from divulging.

I sigh and through clenched teeth, say, "Spit it out, *Poseidon*."

He flinches at the way I say his full name and then, with a defeated sigh, says, "I guess there's no point in keeping this from you. You have already witnessed so much and know the truth about me ... Remember that bird you caught me talking to?"

I pull back. "You mean when we were teenagers, and you always had a noddy on your shoulder and it never left your side?"

"Yes, that's the one. Well, it wasn't just any bird ... it was Paul."

"Ha ... ha." My voice is dripping with sarcasm.

"No, I'm serious." Percy goes on, "Paul was an advisor who became a friend, and then I granted him the power to shift into a bird so he could advise me on land unnoticed."

"Wow." I'm kind of shocked that the bird turned out to actually not be a bird. "And what about the other birds? You always had an army of them flocking you."

Percy snorts. "They were just Paul's admirers. I guess for a male bird the others found him very attractive. I thought it was funny while he thought it was bothersome, quite amusing to witness though. Have you ever seen how a female noddy asks for a mate?" Even though the birds were almost always around when I was with Percy, I never saw them do much interacting besides acting like little mini guards.

I cuddle into Percy and say contentedly, "No, but I'm glad that you're not some lunatic who talks to birds."

In mock horror, Percy lies on his back with his hand raised to his chest and says, "Lunatic! Is that how you perceived me?"

"Oh, quite the contrary, dear," I say with an American accent. We both laugh at my botched imitation.

"No, but really," I say. "I am glad. It's amazing what you did for Paul." It also lessened my guilt. Something that I was not keen to share.

"He deserved it," Percy says in all seriousness.

It's crazy to think that this whole time I had known Paul for years and yet at the same time I hadn't known him at all. All those years he was just a bird to me, while these past few months I got to know the real Paul. I wonder how he felt during our interactions. He watched me grow up. Knew every secret I told Percy. He knew my heart and soul.

How did he feel when I could finally talk to him? Was he exhilarated to finally converse with me, or was he sad that he couldn't explain who he was? He knew me on such a deep level, and yet I hardly knew him at all. Some nights when I couldn't sleep because I missed home, he would come out and talk with me. We would talk until sunrise, sitting at the edge of the facility's pier. And yet I was the one who always did the talking. Paul never talked about himself. It's now understandable why, but I wish I had known who he was. That he'd been able to open up to me, as well. So that I could have been the same friend he had been for me.

I must doze off, because something startles me awake. There's thumping coming from above. My heart hammers in my chest and I fumble for my jian in the corner. I worry we are being attacked again, but quickly realize that it must be the rest of the crew arriving from the funeral turned ceremony because Percy is completely relaxed.

"How long have I been asleep?" I mumble, while snuggling back into Percy. My eyelids feel so heavy that it's hard to keep them open. Wanting to drift back to sleep, I don't fight the urge and close my eyes.

"Only a few moments," he replies as I feel him slip out of bed.

I open my eyes to see him searching the room. "What are you looking for?"

Opening the drawers around him, he says, "Paul's clothes. I can't be half naked all of the time."

My bottom lip pouts out. I would very much enjoy myself if that were the case. With regret, I point him to Paul's corner of the room. I can't help but admire his backside as he leans down to grab something to wear. His whole body is well-defined with lean muscle. I can't help but think what an utter snack he is as his lats ripple when he leans down.

Hot damn. Snack indeed.

After throwing on a long john sweater, Percy walks back to me and smirks as he wipes the drool from the corner of my lip. "Like what you see?"

I roll my eyes. "I'm just tired, that's why I was drooling." Even though that totally wasn't the reason. "Come back to bed." I reach out my hand to grab him but drop it when he shakes his head no.

"We have to get going. Soon Zeus will get word that the harpies have failed and he will send another wave, if he hasn't already." Percy runs his hand through his hair in distress. "It's faster to get to the Underworld if we use a portal, but you are unable to travel that way, and there is no way that I'm allowing you out of my sight again." My heart hums in agreement, *never again*.

"Oh," is all that I can get out. I'm still a little taken aback by what I have jumped into. *The Underworld?* Yet another thing that is being thrown at me without my consent. It takes everything in me to not show just how unsettled this new development makes me. Why exactly are we going there?

Percy's face softens. He leans in under the bunk bed to caress my cheek. "I won't let anything harm you," he declares. That's not what I'm worried about, though. I'm more concerned about his well-being. Are we going into a realm of another fickle god?

"Get some rest," he says, kissing my forehead before turning to the door.

"Where are you going?" I ask, my voice rising an octave. I don't want to be alone right now.

Percy gives me a haughty smirk before saying, "Somebody has got to steer the boat, and since Zeus knows our location, we have to use the other door. Wouldn't want another ambush."

Right ... "But one of the others can steer," I state. I don't want him to leave; we just found each other again.

"Yes, but can they get us to Bermuda in less than a day?" He raises his eyebrows, waiting expectantly for my reply.

"No, but ..." I'm a little confused and then it dawns on me that I'm looking at *Poseidon*. He was able to use the ability he has with water to get us out to the middle of the Atlantic in such a short time. My mind is such a drowsy blur that I had momentarily forgotten about his skill with water.

"Ugh," I groan. "Of course." I shoo him away with my hand and say, "Go do your thing." He gives me a wink before bounding up the stairs. I get out of Clio's bed and into my own. Tugging the blankets over me, I flip to my side. Feeling more comfortable in my own bed, I drift off into a deep slumber.

Chapter Eight

The fierce pounding of my heart wakes me from my dream. My blood beats heavily in my ears, which cancels out any other noise there may be. It's just me and my short breaths of panic as I lay there, running through the emotions of the dream. I can't recall what it was—the memory of it is already fading fast. There was a woman with breathtaking blue skin and a searing pain, followed by forgiveness. The forgiveness of what, though, has jumped to the edge of my memory, out of grasp and unattainable.

I flip my wrist over for the time on my watch: 3:01 AM SUNDAY DECEMBER 5, 2008. My eyes bulge out of their sockets. Sunday! Geez, did someone slip me some drugs? I was asleep for over twenty-four hours. Throwing my blankets off, I jump out of bed. The movement causes my stiff muscles to tighten up. I buckle from the unexpected pain lancing down my body and hit the floor with an unpleasant thud.

"Fuck." This was already a delightful start to my day. I painstakingly stand back up, using the edge of the bed as leverage. It feels like I got hit by a wrecking ball. No, scratch that. It feels like I got thrown around like a ragdoll, shit on, and then hit by a wrecking ball. I roll my shoulders back, trying to relieve the tension. I wince some more as the movement once again causes pain to shoot over my shoulders and down my back. I immediately regret my decision to move as a muscle in my lower back cramps up.

Someone stirs in the bed next to mine. It's too dark to see who it is, but their little mumble tells me that I'm making too much noise. Breathing through the cramp so that I won't wake them, I tiptoe out of the room and quietly close the door behind me. Just doing these miniscule movements is agonizing. My muscles must have gone weak from going months without sparring with my father. I roll my eyes; who am I kidding? Even if I had still been sparring weekly, no, *daily*, I still wouldn't have been prepared for the battle against the harpies. They were fast and the number of them was overwhelming. It took every skill I had and then some to be able to keep up with them. Sparring with my father was nowhere near as exhausting as what I had endured Friday afternoon.

A shiver runs down me, coating my skin in goosebumps. The shiver is not from the pain that consumed me with every little movement, but in response to the mental image the harpies elicited. Their gruesome beaks disfiguring human faces. Their arms stretched out, coated in feathers, ending in hands with long thick nails that are razor sharp. They were like the bird version of Edward Scissorhands. They even shared the same pale complexion.

I limp to the kitchen in hopes of satisfying my grumbling belly. I find lasagna in all its holiness shining at me like a beacon in the fridge. I'm too hungry to warm it up, and devour it cold within seconds. I even lick the plate like the uncivilized animal that I am. God, nothing tastes more delicious than when you're starving. I could eat dirt at this point and still think it was a fine damn meal. I fill up my water bottle and guzzle that down. I feel like a dried-up fish left on land to fry away in the sun. There is nothing but orgasmic relief as the water gushes down my throat. Filling it up a second time, I drink it slower, savoring the flavor of the water.

Satisfied with my hunt, I put on my jacket someone left hanging over a chair. I try not to think about how I never got a chance to wash it after using it as a barrier between me and the bench at the tavern. There are gloves in the pockets. I put them on along with a beanie, knowing how cold it will be outside.

Securing myself against the cold, I mentally prepare for the trudge up the ten steep steps. I could really go for a massage right now alongside a nice steaming hot bath, but obviously that is not on the agenda for today. Instead of thinking of the pain that each step will bring I distract myself with daydreams of Percy's masculine hands kneading into my shoulders, working out the knots that have accumulated between them. I mumble out a satisfied, "num, num" at the image of Percy releasing my aching muscles. I swear I would sell my soul this very moment just to get a massage from him.

When I open the door, I am slammed with a strong warm breeze. My feet slightly lift back but the wind isn't strong enough to move me any more than that. Still inside, I close the door.

Bollocks.

I forgot that Bermuda is along the equator where it is much warmer than France right now. I stare begrudgingly down the steps. I really don't want to walk down those steps and then back up again just to put my extra layers away. I internally debate stripping here and tossing my extra layers to the bottom of the stairs, but that feels childish. And even though it's something I would more than love to do right now, I would hate it if someone else left their clothes right in the middle of the walk area. Letting out an irritated exhale, I head back down the stairs. Today is definitely not my day. Everything hurts to the point where I'm trying really hard not to cry, but my eyes still tear up.

By the time I make it back up the stairs and out on the deck, I am panting, exhausted, and feeling like I could collapse at any moment. Percy is immediately by my side, hovering above me like a distraught mother hen. If I wasn't already at my breaking point, I would think it was cute and also ask him what the hell he's doing awake at this time.

"What's wrong?" His voice is panicked. I've never heard him this anxious before. I start laughing at his reaction and instantly regret it. I hold the side of my ribs while wincing. My face is distorted in a grimace of pain and a small cry escapes my lips.

"I'm just really sore from Friday. Literally feels like someone ran me over." I finally make eye contact with him. The lines of his face are strained with worry. I notice that the swirls in his eyes have turned a deep blue. I long ago determined that this color occurred when he was stressed or worried.

"It's really nothing to worry about, Percy," I state. But my words immediately become lies as the urge to puke overtakes me. I don't even have time to move before the puke is expelled out of me, splashing onto the deck and covering our feet as well. It smells of the lasagna I just ate with pink chunks to confirm it. Ew. I lean back up to wipe my face but before I can apologize I am convulsed with shakes so strong that I lose control of my body. Percy catches me before I fall to the ground.

"What ...?" I faintly say as Percy lays me on the ground away from the puke. I want to ask what is happening, but the words seem to be trapped, the convulsing worsening. My tongue feels stuck in my throat and the fact that I currently have no control over my body terrifies me.

Suddenly I am covered head to toe with water. It feels as if it's absorbing into my body and heating it from within. The convulsing stops and I lay there, too weak to move. I barely register Percy as he picks me up and briskly walks to the edge of the boat.

In a rushed voice, he says, "Your soul is almost gone. Dammit! Hades warned me, but I thought I had more time." Before I can ask what he means or comprehend what is going on, he plunges us into the water. A bubble of air surrounds my head so that I am able to breathe. Nothing surrounds Percy's, so I guess he can breathe underwater. Huh, intriguing. I want to look around us and see where he is taking me, but my body is tired. I let my fatigue win and go limp in Percy's arms, where I drift off once more.

Chapter Nine

I wake to the smell of sulfur. I sniff a few more times before opening my eyes. The sulfur is not overpowering but still tinges the air, though not enough to cause harm. Sitting up in the bed that I find myself in, I take in my surroundings. Every square inch of this room is covered in rock that is smoothed out to form a flat surface. The rock is obsidian black, with glistening swirls. The room looks like it was carved out of a mountain and crammed full with out-of-place Victorian era furniture. There is no electricity, just candles giving light to the room. In the center, there's a crystal chandelier with an assortment of candles of varying heights providing the majority of light.

I press the side of my watch to see how long I was asleep for this time, but the screen doesn't light up. I tap the side again before realizing that the screen is cracked. How ... odd. The last thing I remember is Percy holding me in his arms and diving into complete darkness. Just how far down did he take me for my watch to break? I vaguely remember him mentioning the Underworld as being our next stop. If that's where I am, then this Victorian furniture is really throwing me a curveball. Victorian furniture meets Underworld? Those two just didn't seem to mix. But I was digging the gaudy vibe; it had a homey appeal to it even if it didn't scream Underworld.

I lift the down blanket and give a sharp intake of breath. I am as naked as the day I was born. I don't remember undressing myself, which means someone else must have. It leaves me feeling violated. I just hope that whoever did it, hopefully Percy, did not get too handsy with my sleeping form. Even if it was Percy, though, it still feels wrong to be touched romantically when you're not aware. Which also begs the question, where is he?

Before I have any more time to ponder on where I am and where Percy is, there's a knock on the door. Not waiting for my answer, the person—or should I say the wisp—enters the room. I'm not quite sure what I am seeing. It appears to be a person, but her form isn't solid and yet her footsteps make light noises against the ground. Her smock is tattered like she has been mauled by a bear. Dark gray splotches mark her clothes, giving the illusion of wet blood, as if her form remains stuck in her dying moments. Her face is expressionless as she sets a piece of clothing at the edge of the bed and takes a step back. I glare at her as I clutch the bedding to my chest to cover myself. The audacity she has to waltz in without a word of permission. Judging by the clothes placed before me, she knew I was indecent. What if I was out of bed? Then she most definitely would've seen all of me. I don't like the idea of almost being that exposed. I already feel helpless being in unfamiliar territory, I don't need to add public nudity to the mix.

"Where is Percy?" I question, trying to keep my voice calm, but no matter my efforts, I can still hear it quiver slightly, not from anger but at the idea of communicating with a ghost. She doesn't seem harmful, but one can not be too sure.

She remains unmoving, hands clasped behind her back. Without a word, she stares at me then slightly moves her head to look at the clothing then back to me.

"Am I to change into that?" I ask. The hollow woman nods her head once.

"So you understand me. Don't you speak? Is it Poseidon who sent these garments?" I switch over to his real name, thinking maybe others don't know him by Percy. The words flow out of my mouth fast and I clench my shaking palms to try to control my anxiety. I wish I had a weapon merely to feel more in control. I doubt I could harm this woman before me. How would one go about killing something that is already dead?

Neither nodding her head yes or no, she continues staring at me as if I haven't spoken. I want to scream, but instead I oblige. I grab the piece of clothing and stare at her expectantly. She stares back, her gaze unwavering and still emotionless. Her lack of expression is disquieting. I have an urge to stick my tongue out at her to see if that would get any emotion out from her blank face. Even a slight twitch would suffice, but I rein in the impulse. No need to start making enemies on my first day down here.

"Can I have some privacy?" It's unnerving to have her unwavering eyes pinned to me. There's no color to them. The grayish white of her form also saturates her eyes even further, making her look like a fish that has been dead for too long. She slightly turns her head to the side and gives another nod. I look to the right of me and see a door—-it must be a bathroom.

I stare back at her, eyebrows raised as I wait for her to leave. She doesn't. Instead, she remains where she is, fish eyes still vacantly upon me. Internally screaming, I wrap myself in the comforter to shield myself from her prying eyes, and walk to the closed door. I look over my shoulder with my hand on the round doorknob. She finally moves, but it's only to tilt her head to track my movements. This ghost is fucking creepy.

Closing the door behind me, I let out a long, exasperated breath. This ghost shit is becoming too much for my sanity. I can barely process what got me in this predicament, and now I have to deal with a mute pervert. I throw the comforter off of me a little forcefully. My patience is wearing thin. I want answers, starting with why I woke up alone. It seemed a bit cruel to have me deal with this solo.

After my fit of frustration, I inspect the bathroom around me. Two mirrors line the wall to the left with wooden cabinetry below. In the opposite corner is a stream of water that cascades down from an opening in the ceiling, where it pools in a bed of river rocks. The water accumulates, forming a little pond of clear water. The excess water overflows and splashes onto the bottom tier of the makeshift pond, where it drains into another hole to disappear somewhere else. There are no sinks, so I assume that this must be what constitutes one, as it's too small to bathe in.

Coming to my knees, I cup the water and splash it over my face. To my disappointment, the water is tepid. I was hoping to dash something cool on me to distract my racing thoughts. Face dripping, I place my hands over my bent knees and deeply breathe in and out, trying to calm myself.

It works.

Barely.

The events that have occurred over these past few days keep taking over my every thought. It's a lot to handle in such a short amount of time, but I'm trying. If not for my own sake, then for Percy's. The anxiety I feel over this new world being thrust upon me is crippling, but I can't let it consume me, not when I have bigger things to worry about. Prime example is my soul. The shopkeeper said it was not complete, and then Percy mentioned it as well. How could one not have a complete soul? Did it mean that I was dying? But then ... My life ending is nothing short of terrifying. I don't want to die; I finally feel like I am truly living. They say happiness is always followed by misery. Is this how it is going to end? I will do everything in my power to stop whatever is happening. We are in the Underworld, and I know Hades is the keeper of souls. He should have answers. Maybe that's why Percy brought me here in the first place.

I rub my thumb and index finger against my forehead, trying to relieve myself of this dull headache. Answers, I need answers, and I will get them no matter what. Grabbing a nearby cloth, I dry my face. Pulling myself up, it dawns on me that I am no longer in pain. My muscles no longer cry out in agony at the littlest movement. Everything had gone numb after Percy had covered me in water. I wonder if that had anything to do with easing my pain. I'll have to ask him when I see him. Whenever that may be. I am becoming greatly frustrated at being left here alone, and the idea of punching him is becoming more tempting with each passing moment.

Picking up the piece of clothing, I rub it between my fingers. The fabric is a deep purple silk. It easily slides down my body as I put it on. Looking at myself in the mirror, I laugh at the dress that was given to me, which turns out to actually be a toga. Of course, a Greek god would have me wear this in place of modern clothes. The human population must be nowhere near, but this just confirms it. No one goes traipsing around in this attire. Though whatever that woman is tells me just as much. No human would come back sane after encountering a ghost.

I search for underwear but I come up short. I guess it's going to be a commando day. I'd ask the ghost for a pair, but knowing her she'd just stare at me, all melancholy and lifeless. The less her eyes stay on me, the better. There is just something about how her stare follows me, bored yet very curious. I'm about to leave the bathroom when I see a pair of sandals at the bottom of the door that I know for certain weren't there a moment ago. I pause only for a moment before putting them on. It is still hard for me to come to terms with magic. The door never opened, so those shoes had literally materialized out of thin air. It is something that I am going to have to get used to.

I take one last glance at myself in the mirror and admire how the toga looks. The folds and waves of material give it a loose look, yet it's sophisticated and appealing. I can't help but to be pleased with how I look. I can't wait to see how Percy's eyes shine when he sees me in this. I can already imagine the heat in them.

With a smirk of my own that I'm sure would put Percy's to shame, I walk out of the bathroom, striding with confidence. The phantom of a woman is still standing where I left her last. She still frightens me, but I grasp that fear and push it way down. I will not allow my ignorance to control me. I stop short of her and give her a deep, curt bow.

"I am greatly sorry for my rudeness earlier. It was unnecessary and uncalled for. Please accept my apology." I end my bow and look into her hollow face. I swear I see the edge of her lips curve up into a slight smile, but before I can be certain, she slightly tilts her head and turns around. She walks out of the room, only once looking back to indicate that she would like me to follow her. Do I even have a choice?

The cavernous halls are dimly lit with flickering pale blue flames that are placed roughly every four meters. It's hard to see, and I frequently stumble over my own feet. The woman takes me through twists and turns until even if I wanted to head back to the room, I would be completely and hopelessly lost.

Trying to look at my feet so as to not trip over myself as much, I didn't notice that the woman had stopped walking. In my peripheral vision I see a glimpse of white, but before my mind can process that it's the ghost-like figure, I walk right through her. Complete ice washes over me, like I just went for a polar dive. From the shock of it all, I once again trip over my feet, but this time am unable to catch myself. I stumble headfirst into a rock stairwell. I twist my body at the last second, but to no avail—I still hit my head.

"Bloody ... *hell*," I groan.

To help relieve the pain, I rub the side of my throbbing head and shoulder. Sitting on the bottom step, I look up to see the woman holding one of the blue lit torches. Her face remains expressionless as she waits silently for me. Figuring that if she could talk she would ask if I am okay, I reply to her unspoken question. "Yes, I'm alright. Let's carry on." Although I do feel extremely stupid answering a question that wasn't asked.

She hands me the torch and then walks past me up the spiral staircase. I take it that ghosts have night vision? I should be surprised, but I'm really not. How else would they go about haunting? I get up and follow her. This time without any stumbling, thanks to the torch.

"Thank you!" I call out gratefully. I can only imagine the nightmare of an adventure it would've been to climb these steps without the added help of the torch. I undoubtedly would've tumbled down to my death and my corpse would've made a lovely addition to the ghosts that already live here.

After what seems like ten minutes of the stairwell not coming to an end, I start counting the steps. I grow bored after three hundred and give up. It feels as if we have been climbing these stairs for hours. My legs can't bear to take another step and my lungs are burning. I never liked the elliptical at home, but it was Mother's favorite. I want to ask for a break, but decide not to because I doubt this ghost would wait for me. Just when my shaky legs feel like they're going to give out, we arrive at the top. The woman grabs the torch from me, placing it on the wall, then opens the door. Suddenly, blinding light washes over the stairwell. I have to stop walking and close my eyes to better adjust them to the dramatic change of light.

I open my eyes slowly. What stands before me is complete, utter beauty. Pillars of white marble line a walkway made up of gems like rubies and diamonds. Is that amethyst that I see? And peridot? I am in awe of the workmanship and have a hard time reining in my amazement. The floor is awash with a rainbow of different gems, some I don't even know the names of. The gems are polished flat for a smooth surface to walk on. As I step onto the path, I have an even deeper appreciation for it. It is not only a beautiful rainbow of colors, but the gems are carved flat into flowers themselves. As I walk further, the flower gems turn into mythical creatures. So much detail is put into these gems that, judging by how long the path is to the next building, it must have taken decades to finish. The woman takes her time walking while I trail behind her, and I am thankful. It gives me more time to admire the scenery around me and to take the break I was wishing for.

Outside of the pillars on each side of the walkway is a garden of flowers. Most of them I have never seen in my life. It's a chaotic flurry of flowers, trees, and plants, but the way the gardener placed everything also gives it order. It's as if the plants are living in harmony with each other.

As we near the building, I hear the laughter of children. A group of them outside of the building are making flower crowns and chasing each other around. Their skin is a charming jade color that pairs well with their earthy brown hair. The children see us approaching and when they notice me, their frolicking stops. They run off to hide behind a nearby tree.

"Do not be frightened," I call out and then regret it. That's exactly what every stalker says before they take a kid.

One of the braver children briefly sticks their head out, their elfin ears back like a scared cat. The child gives me one quick glance and then hides back behind the tree. The ghost woman is waiting patiently for me, so I give up my attempts and follow her the rest of the way into the building that she's led us to.

The building is an open coliseum. There are no walls dividing, just more white marble pillars holding up the outer walls. There is no ceiling, just complete openness to the bright sky. But the sky is strange. It's not the normal blue, but an extreme white that it hurts to look at. The kind of hurt you get when you try staring at the sun.

The building is swarming with more people that look like my escort, all of whom are buzzing with conversation. None of them seem to be talking to each other, but to the man positioned on the other side of the building across from me. He sits languidly upon his throne of more white marble. A black crown with five spikes adorns his head and contrasts with the white toga he's wearing.

White, white, and more white. Did this man have no taste?

The woman brings me to the man, motions for me to stay and then leaves me to fend for myself. I stand by his side, not sure what to do or say. My arms hang limply at my sides while he ignores me as if I don't exist. His head tilts every so often in different directions, as if he is listening to everyone talking at once. The voices are low, hissing whispers, so I can not discern what they're saying.

Using this as an opportunity, I inspect this man who I can only presume is Hades. His hair is made up of dreads with gold strands braided into each one. I follow the length of one of his dreads that brushes against an ebony nipple peeking out of his toga. He flexes his pecs. Intrigued as to why he did that, I look at his face. His lips curve slightly upward, deviously. I quickly look away. He caught me staring and wanted me to know. I don't know what is worse, being caught, or that he seemed to enjoy the attention.

I scan the crowd of people for something to occupy my mind. The ghosts here seem to be the same as the one that escorted me, but something seems different about this group. I don't know a better word to describe the difference other than *alive*. The ghosts before me seem more fresh than my escort. I cringe at my terminology. It seems such a morbid way to describe the dead, but it's true. Their eyes have a spark to them and their bodies appear less hollow.

Not too much time passes before all talking comes to a stop. "I have heard your case and judgment has been made." The man before me snaps his fingers and everyone disappears at once. With everyone gone, the room looks immensely bigger. There must have been at least a thousand of them, if not more. He stands up and stretches before turning to me with a broad grin, his teeth straight and pearly white. His eyes are completely onyx, with no whites or color showing.

I try not to show how disturbing it is but seem to fail as he says, "Oh. I am sorry, Amethyst." He then lifts off his crown. As soon as the crown is removed, the onyx color swirls inward to pupil size and are then surrounded by light brown irises with specks of the same gold woven in his hair.

The man proceeds to explain. "You see, one of the five abilities this crown has is to allow me to listen to every passed soul simultaneously. My eyes turning black is a benign side effect of the use of the crown." He smiles at me again with a nonchalant shrug.

With that clarification, it all makes sense, and my suspicion of him being Hades is confirmed. He's darker than I thought he would be. I imagined he would be extremely pale due to living in the Underworld, but his skin is a stark contrast to that. His skin is as dark as the night. At the inner side of his elbow where the skin is the thinnest, there's a faint glow. It almost looks like the sun herself is trying to shine through his skin. It gives off a light sheen and I notice it in other parts of his body, like under his eyes, and the inside of his wrists. The effect makes his skin look unbelievably smooth. It's enchanting. To put it simply, he is the most breathtaking man I've ever laid my eyes upon.

Percy had briefly told me a story about Hades and Persephone. About how the Underworld was a harsh domain until Persephone came into the picture and brought life to the realm. I wonder how much of the story I was told I can trust. It could all have been a lie, or simply all true. I don't remember much though, because this particular story was not my favorite. If I had known I'd be meeting the gods depicted in Greek mythology, I would have paid better attention.

"Where is Poseidon?" I ask, cutting right to what I want to know. He already knows who I am, and it's obvious who he is, so there's no need for introductions. I feel on edge, almost itchy being here without Percy. Something seems off, but I can't put my finger on what.

"Ah yes, my dear brother. I have him busy with other matters at the moment." Hades gives me an appraising look. "I knew that shade of purple would look marvelous on you." I am flustered by his comment. I thought it was Percy who had set up this whole thing, but I guess I was wrong. It irks me that he had picked out my attire.

"Does Poseidon *being busy*"—I put my hands up in air quotes—"and you wanting to see me have anything to do with my soul?" I can't help but to think that ties into all of this. Hades, is after all, the Keeper of Souls. It seems to me too much of a coincidence.

Frowning, Hades says, "*That fool has said too much.*" It takes me a moment to understand his words, but I recognise it as the forgotten language Percy had taught me.

Replying in the same language, I say, "*Clearly he has said too little, because I still do not understand what is going on with me. So tell me.*" Each word that passes through my mouth leaves me angrier until my next words are nothing but venom. "Tell me *how making me aware of something about my life makes him a* fool." I leave it not as a question but as a statement, because I really don't care for Hades' answer. I am Percy's partner, and it would only make him a fool for keeping things from me. Trust is not built on secrets and trust is what's at the core of fruitful relationships.

Shock crosses Hades' face, followed by a disapproving shake of his head. "I should have known he would teach you the First language."

If looks could kill, Hades would be lying on the ground right now. I'm starting to dislike him more by the second. He's hiding Percy from me, and for what purpose? And on top of that, he wants Percy to keep me in the dark. Nothing good can come from lies and deceit.

Hades chuckles, and it seems wholly inappropriate for the moment. "Poseidon also told me that you have a quick temper." There's a twinkle of playfulness in his eyes, but I ignore it.

I fling my hands up in the air, my patience gone. "So? You think you can hide Percy from me and leave me in the dark?" I turn around and stride back to where I had entered. I've given up on having Hades help me. I'll find my answers somewhere else.

Hades calls out, "Sweet Amethyst, I am not hiding Poseidon. He is simply hiding from you."

I stop at that statement. I turn around and march right back up to him. With my finger pointing up at his face, I say menacingly, "And why would someone who cares about me hide from me?"

"Precisely for that reason." Hades lowers my hand from his face and sighs. "You are honestly a very trying woman, Amethyst." Still holding my hand, he says, "Walk with me."

I remove my hand from his grasp and without following, I ask, "And why should I?"

"If you want your answers, then you shall take a walk with me." Hades states it as an invitation, but the note in his voice makes it a command.

"I don't trust you."

"It would be prudent of you not to, but I don't ask for your trust, merely your cooperation. Time, as always, will eventually tell." He tilts his head, eyeing me. "Have you ever wondered why your body started to give out at an alarming rate when prior you were doing just fine?"

"Because my time was running out." I roll my eyes. Does he think he's going to tell me something I don't know?

"Yes, but not quite." He smiles slightly as my body stills at his words. "You could've stayed human but if somebody hadn't gone and cut their hair with such *love* then the magic keeping your broken soul alive never would've been destroyed."

I try not to move as I process what he's saying. Is that simple act really what started this all? But I still don't understand how turning my back on a path set out for me would be powerful enough to break magic.

"Now, shall we?" he asks and holds out his arm, not giving me a chance to question him any further on it. His eyebrow is raised as he waits for my acceptance.

I weigh my options, which I would say are limited, but in reality, are none. Ignoring his arm, I wave my hand out for him to lead the way. He throws his own hands up in exasperation while shrugging his shoulders. "Do try to keep up."

I resist the urge to spit a curse at him, but I don't hold back rolling my eyes. I take back him being breathtaking. He is vexing beyond belief. We walk on in silence, neither one of us glancing at the other. He takes me along a different route than when I arrived. The elven-eared creatures are less afraid with Hades next to me, but are still leery of my presence. I want to keep my silence out of sheer pettiness, but my curiosity gets the better of me.

"What are those creatures following us?" I glance behind me. The one-meter-tall beings let out a squeal at my glance toward them and dart back into the foliage. As they run , I hear the jingling of bells.

"Those *creatures*," Hades says in a voice that tells me he doesn't appreciate that terminology for them, "are nymphs from my domain as well as Persephone's. Although only a few of hers dwell here."

I wonder why that is, but decide not to ask that question because we have come to the end of our walk. In front of us, at the end of the trail, is a metal door engraved into the flat surface of the obsidian that seems to be the norm around here. It gives off such an ominous feeling that my body shivers and goosebumps trail down my arms. No flowers or plants grow in the vicinity of the door. Everything surrounding it is dead. The soil is so parched you can see thick cracks in it, and two burnt trees are on either side of the door. They've long been lifeless, yet they seem to remain for a purpose, almost like a warning. I realize now that the nymphs had not squeaked in fear from my glance, but at the realization of where they would be if they followed any longer, for I can not bear to be here either. My body screams for me to retreat. That this place is not *right*.

I wait anxiously, wringing my hands. We stand feet away from the door, at the edge of the pathway that ends where the cracked earth begins. I have no intention of placing my feet on the forsaken dirt. An eerie feeling tells me that whoever steps off this path will meet a tragic end.

"You will find your answers behind this door," Hades states in a solemn tone.

"Must my answers be there? Can't you just explain to me what's going on?"

Hades lets out a sad sigh. "I am sorry, Amethyst, but I can not. To find your answers, you must enter this door. Alone."

My mouth drops open, and my eyes widen in terrified shock. "You ... you c-can't possibly expect me to ... to go there alone?" I had meant for my words to be firm and unrelenting, but all that comes out of me is a hoarse croak that was barely above a whisper. I shake my head frantically. My whole being is telling me to stay far away from this place. My mind is screaming at me to run. This can not be happening. I refuse to do this alone. No, I refuse to do this at all. It's a death sentence.

Hades places a steadying hand on my shoulder. "Amethyst!" His voice is solid and commanding. "You must. This is the only way. I would not ask it of you if there was any other way."

"Why am I so scared?" I look up at him with bleary eyes. My unrealistic fear has brought me to tears.

"It is merely the magic that surrounds this place. There is nothing to be afraid of if you belong there."

"But I don't belong there." I wipe my eyes as I try to calm myself. It's just more damn magic playing mind games.

"Trust me." His eyes lighten a bit as he says this.

"But that's the thing—I don't trust you."

"Then trust Poseidon."

"Poseidon." I whisper his name and hold on to it. If the only way I'll receive answers is behind this door, then I must. I want to live. What happened on the boat was not from exhaustion but from my body dying.

I give Hades one last glance before bravely stepping off the walkway to face my fear. Nothing happens. I take a few steps more and still nothing happens. Exhaling a long breath, I confidently erase the distance between me and the door. As soon as I walk between the trees, they start shaking. I'm about ready to bolt back to Hades, but then the trees stop their movement.

"Alright." I nod my head to cope with the creepiness. "That wasn't weird." Hades snickers. The only attention I give him is my middle finger before I take the last few steps to the door without anything else occurring. Grasping onto the iron latch, I pull to unlock it. There's a clunk, followed by a breeze of cold air as the door opens, resting ajar.

Well, let's get this party started.

I push the door farther open and walk into darkness.

Chapter Ten

As I walk further into the narrow tunnel, the feeling of foreboding disappears. Whatever spell this place had cast on me is no longer there the further I walk from the entrance.

How curious. I mentally mark it down on my already long list of questions I have accumulated about this new frightening, yet intriguing, world. There is so much that I don't know, but I find myself wanting to learn more, even when it seems like with each hour, my sanity is disappearing. How can one be sane when so much wonder surrounds them? And yes, wonder, because even the terrible things that have happened were beautiful in their own way. The harpies were disgusting, but the way they moved was pure elegance.

The Underworld is nothing I could've imagined. It's an oasis that's coated layer upon layer of paradise. I haven't even seen all the Underworld has to offer and I'm already in complete awe. Everything will seem mundane after having my worldview split open and the greatness of all this splayed at my feet. Who would've thought that my worldview would change, not from flying out of my father's carefully built nest, but instead by having my wings almost clipped. Although I'm loving that my eyes have been opened to the different layers of our world, a small part of me still wishes I had never left my father's nest at all.

Coming to the edge of the light where it meets the darkness, I furrow my brows as I ponder at how I will find the end of the path without a lantern to guide me. If I place my hand on the wall, I will be able to use that as a guide, but the only problem is that if there's a second tunnel leading in another direction, I won't know.

Bloody hell, this place could turn into a maze.

My anxiety rises at the revelation that I could become eternally lost in this damn place. Hades could have at least given me a map. A lantern would've been fantastic, might I add.

You know what? Screw this. My fight or flight kicks in while staring into this pit of darkness, and I choose to run. I am growing increasingly tired of games; all I want to do is rest. I have been so, so tired. It's like no amount of rest can ease this weighted feeling , and I've done my share of sleeping lately. But no, this is a different tired. This type seeps into my very bones, solidifying itself where it weighs me down the most. It leaves me struggling to put one foot in front of the other. I am tired of the mind games and the struggle for answers. No one has been completely honest with me and it's left me feeling like lead. It shouldn't be hard, and yet the people surrounding me find it so. I turn around to head back to the door, but just as I turn my feet, the door slams close.

"No!" I run straight for the door and collide with it, my hands searching frantically for a handle that isn't there. This can not be happening. A cleithrophobia nightmare coming to fruition, that's what this is. I slam my shoulder against the door over and over, trying to get it to budge. I am met with only the cold bite of the metal that soothes my throbbing shoulder. With all the slamming and kicking I do, the door never moves in the slightest. I feel around the frame for anything and still find nothing. Not giving up just yet, I bang my fists against the metal door. "Hades! You bastard, let me out of here!"

Do I care whether I offend the man who walks with the dead by calling him a bastard? No, I do not. Locking me in here makes him a bastard and I will gladly, after curtsying to *his majesty,* of course, call him a bastard to his face. Because that is exactly what someone is when they lock you inside a cave with no way to see and no map. Who does that? Bastards, that's who.

"Bastard!" I scream it out again, just for good measure. Maybe he'll get mad at the name-calling and open this door back up.

Only silence greets me from the other side of the door. I am so beyond frustrated that I want to scream at the top of my lungs until I go hoarse. But I don't, because as I lean my head back, I realize I can see.

Light.

In all of its glory, light is twinkling in the darkness. I turn back toward the long tunnel. My mouth opens at the beauty surrounding me. Speckled across the walls and ceiling are twinkling lights. They fade in and out, but there are so many that there is always enough light to see the tunnel clearly. The glimmering reminds me of the clear, starry night spent with Percy on my last birthday. The water was so calm that evening that even the ocean looked like it had its own set of stars.

I walk up to the wall to inspect the lights to see exactly what they are. I assume that they will be some sort of unknown rock, but to my delightful surprise, the lights are glowing worms. I've only read about these worms but have never had the opportunity to enjoy their presence. For a moment, I forget why I am here. The worms have charmed me with their luminescent glow. I swear I could just pull up a seat and watch them for hours. I felt like a moth to a flame, or better yet, an unsuspecting fish caught up in an angler fish's snare. But the need I have for answers, and most of all, preservation of my life, leaves me with little time to marvel at my surroundings.

I don't journey far before the narrow tunnel opens up into a cavernous room. There is no need for the map that I am so desperately wishing for. The tunnel never branches off, and brings me directly into a cavern where a body of water the size of a lake dominates the open space. In the center of the lake is a small, sandy island.

I pinch the bridge of my nose. You have got to be kidding me. Above the island is a floating *trident.* I assume it's the one and only. I have a feeling that this is what I'm here for, and somehow connected to whatever plan Hades has for me. Why is it so much work just to get answers to what's going on with me? Images of tomb raiders setting off booby traps skitter across my mind. I swear if anything jumps out for me when I touch the trident, I will take it and shove it up Hades' arse.

Rolling my shoulders back, I let out a frustrated sigh. I seem to be frustrated a lot today, it's a wonder I don't have a headache. As I walk near the edge of the water, it parts, making a dry path leading straight to the island. Which is actually nice, because I was not looking forward to a swim. As I step onto the path, I reach out to the wall of water, curious. I hear a faint screeching coming from the water's depths.

"Curiosity killed the cat!" I yelp as I run for the island. The water starts pouring back over the path as soon as the screeching starts. Just as my feet hit the island, a skeletal fish glides over the surface, right where I had just been. The screaming grows quieter as the water calms back to total stillness.

Holy fucking hell, I am going to *kill* Hades.

I feel like my heart is about to beat right out of my chest. What the hell was that thing? Scurrying back, I get myself as far away as I can from the shore. I assume that it can't go on land, but I'm not taking my chances if that thing decides to jump out at me. Who knows when its last meal was. I shake myself, as if doing that would help clear my head.

Thump, thump ... Thump, thump ... Thump, thump.

I turn toward the sound of the beating. A blue glow emanates from the trident, pulsing like it's a living, breathing thing. I take a step toward it, and with every step closer, the beat quickens. It sounds just like my heart was a moment ago, beating as fast as a conga drum readying for a sacrifice.

A trance overtakes me, coaxing me to reach my hand out and touch the trident. The beating has become so loud that I just want it to stop; and then it does. The noise ends just as abruptly as it began. My fingers are just a hair away from touching it. The glow is pulsating leisurely. I breathe in deeply; it's the moment of supposed truth. I flex my hand, a mere twitch, and the distance between me and the trident disappears.

At a dizzying speed, my world starts spinning in circles. I want to scream but can't, air refuses to enter my lungs. I try touching my throat, but my body won't listen to me either. I keep spinning and spinning until suddenly I stop.

My body finally listens to me, but it doesn't matter because I fall to the floor, knees shaking. I can hardly hold myself up as my guts spill out of me.

I wish I had a glass of water to clean out my rancid mouth. With that thought, a glass of water appears in front of me. What? I look around. I'm no longer in the cave, but instead an endless universe of white. It's just me, a glass of water, a puddle of foul-smelling puke and a lady. Her features do not stand out, and yet they are defined. I focus on her strong nose and the rest of her blurs. The same thing happens when I look at her eyes that swirl like a galaxy is hidden in them. She blurs again as I focus on her thin lips.

I stand up immediately, already on the defensive. The lady laughs. "Do not be afraid, I shall not harm you." Her entire being floats, and her clothes sway as if she's drifting in the ocean. Her hair is a pale blonde and her dress is multicolored, like a kaleidoscope. Everything about her screams *not human*. The bile taste in my mouth has become too much. With my eyes still on her, I lean down and rinse out my mouth. Ahh, much better. I think of a cloth, and just like the glass, a folded cloth appears before me. I use it to dry my mouth and hands.

"How is this possible?" I'm dumbfounded by where we are and how my desires keep becoming reality. Is this reality, though? This endless white seems to say otherwise.

Her voice reminds me of the calm sea and starry nights as she says, "This is merely a space for me to communicate. A world that only exists in my mind, if you could say I have one, of course."

I look at her in confusion. "What do you mean?"

The lady only smiles. "You will soon find out."

Before I have time to react, she appears directly in front of me. Her hand has morphed into scissor-like claws, and she stabs me in the heart. "Show that you're worthy," she says gently, and then my world once again goes black.

Chapter Eleven

T he world around me is unfamiliar, yet like it would be in a dream, it's as if I already know this place. Percy sits across from me at a dining table made of yellow coral. He calls me Amphitrite, and I am taken aback. Amphitrite? My tongue moves, but it's not the words I want to speak that come out.

"The refugees housed in the East Sea received supplies this morning," the despondent voice says from my lips, but it's not my voice.

"That's good. And what of our remaining storage?" Percy asks.

I sit back, stunned, as I come to terms with whatever is unfolding before me. Clearly, whoever's eyes I am seeing through are not my own. I try to listen to the conversation, but Amphitrite has stopped paying attention to Percy. I am left with only what she sees and hears, which isn't much given her disregard for what Percy is saying. She barely pays him any mind as she finishes her fish salad, and without a word of goodbye, she gets up and leaves the room. I strain to turn her head so that I can get one last glimpse at Percy, but lose the mental fight. I clearly have no control over this body.

On the walk to what I assume are her chambers, Amphitrite stops at every mirror just to admire herself for a brief moment before she continues her walk. I internally roll my eyes at her conceit, but now as she sits in front of her vanity, I can truly examine her. She's breathtaking. There's no better word to describe her. She is the most ethereal being I have ever seen. I can't even compare anyone else to her. Her skin is a pale blue that has a light shimmer to it when she moves. Her lips are voluminous and pouty, contrasting with a petite nose. What I find the most attractive about her is not her feminine curves or her opal-colored hair, but her eyes. They swirl just like Percy's, but unlike Percy's stormy ocean blues, they are deep and light tones of green. The kind of green you find in calm Mediterranean waters.

Knowledge of Percy's and Amphitrite's circumstances floods my dream mind. I don't get the full details, but it's enough to know their relationship is more complicated than one would assume. Something brought about a hatred on Amphitrite's side of things. Whatever the reasoning for the lack of love is, I do not know. The knowledge I have access to seems to only be what she's actively thinking. I am simply a passenger in her mind.

"Oh, oceans! You scared me, dear sister." Even Amphitrite's voice is beautiful. She could whisper words of hate and it would still bring you to your knees, panting for more. My gaze follows Amphitrite's as she turns to look at her sister standing in the shadows.

"Well, don't just stand there. Come in." I can sense Amphitrite's lips curving into a smile that I can only imagine as decadently sweet. I feel her adoration for her younger sister. As children, they were inseparable, until Amphitrite's arranged marriage with Percy. When she became queen, her free time was limited, and when the war started, that was doubly true. Being queen made her people her first priority.

Her sister stands in the open double doorway that leads out to Amphitrite's secret garden. Only immediate family can access it and gain entrance into her quarters. No one could ever enter through her water portal located in the garden unless they were a blood relation. Even with this precaution built in, after the war began, the portal was shut off. She would have been more concerned about how her sister had gained entry had she not been so happy to see her. It had been too long since their last visit. The last time she'd seen her family it had just been her Papa. It was not a family visit, but a meeting among the war generals on their next move. No one knew that before the battle that marked the beginning of the war, Amphitrite was unknowingly a spy for the enemy. It was her knowledge that led to their many losses. The amount of blood on Amphtrite's hands was sickening. She hated herself for her naivety. If only she had seen through the enemy's true nature, maybe then there wouldn't have been as many casualties. She wants to tell Percy who was actually behind this war, that it isn't who they believe, but if she does that, she will damn herself. And that is something she is not ready for.

Amphitrite turns back to the mirror and combs her locks with the bones of a swordfish. It glistens in the candlelight, glowing like the moon. "So, what brings you here this evening? We just had dinner. Poseidon would have loved for you to dine with us. Oh, it's been too long, sister."

Amphitrite's sister stands behind her with a dark look of malice enveloping her face. "Doto?" Amphitrite puts down her brush, but before she can turn to ask her sister what's wrong, Doto plunges a knife into Amphitrite's back.

No words escape Amphitrite's mouth, only blood as it trickles down the side of her lip. She coughs from the wound to her lung and her blood splatters across the mirror in tiny specks of blue. Doto stabs her again, this time catching her spine. Falling out of her chair, Amphitrite tries to run for the door, but her legs give out. The blade is still embedded in her spine, already causing damage to her mobility. Her legs have gone numb, and as she lies on her back staring up at her sister's form towering over her, she no longer registers the burning feeling of the blade tearing through her back.

Why? She wants to ask, but words fail her. There's too much blood. Her mouth tastes of iron, but that thought is fleeting. *Why?* She thinks again.

Her face must display confusion because Doto says, "I am the one that loves him! You don't deserve him! I should be queen, not you!"

Amphitrite's body feels cold as it begins to shut down. She stares at her sister, her favorite sister. The only movement she can manage is to reach out her hand to Doto. Her thoughts blaze through the chill that is now consuming her.

I forgive you.

A welcoming breeze brushes against her face, followed by the scent of fresh citrus water. "Amphitrite!" The love in Percy's voice fills Amphitrite with sorrow. Why had she spent so long hating him? She once loved him, but certain knowledge that she had gained from the enemy had warped her opinion of him. Now it is too late. She needs to tell him who is behind the attacks, but the blood is too thick. The words that she tries to speak only come out in garbled bubbles of blood.

"Guards!" his voice roars. He cradles me against his chest and the warmth of him feels like an inferno against my cold body. The last thing I hear is, "Dove, stay with me."

Chapter Twelve

E yes fluttering open, I am brought back to the world of white nothingness.
My heart is racing like it would when you wake from a nightmare. My
hand is outstretched. Twisting my wrist, I close my hand into a fist and then
bring it to my chest. Something feels familiar about the dream, as if I have
dreamt it before. It is almost like déjà vu with my hand reaching out. The
gesture is all too familiar, I swear it's something that I have recently done.

I look up at the floating woman. "What was that?"

"A memory." The way her kaleidoscope dress floats around her reminds me
of The Lady of the Lake in the movie *Merlin*.

"How old?" Percy was there, and I was his wife. A wife I never knew he had.
Before being faced with that memory I wish I had known about it from Percy
first. It hit a raw nerve to know this bit of history about him. It's something
that should have been said between us instead of me hearing it essentially from
a stranger.

"Eons," is her reply.

Eons. The word echoes through my mind. The relationship they had together from what I gathered was anything but affectionate, but still, it must
have broken his heart to have his wife die. I wonder if he loves her, even eons
later. Amphitrite's death seemed so unjust. How could she forgive her sister

so quickly? In her dying moments, she had experienced forgiveness. If she had lived, would she have punished her sister instead of offering forgiveness?

"You have lived through this memory and now you have had time to think about it. It is time." Without any explanation or warning, I start spinning away from the woman and out of the world of vast whiteness.

Thankfully, this time the journey does not leave me nauseated. I'm left standing where I was on the island with my hand grasped around the trident. It's still glowing, but no longer pulsing with a rhythmic beat. I think of the woman's mysterious words. *"It is time."* It is time for what? Why does everyone have to be so cryptic? It is aggravating me beyond belief.

Splashing behind me catches my attention. I turn around, trident ready in hand. As I feared, it is the fish, but thankfully it's still in the water. Its eyes stare into mine, never breaking contact. For some odd reason, this fish reminds me of something. The association is just out of reach. Like I'm trying to grab something solid in the fog but keep coming up empty-handed.

I sit down cross-legged with the trident across my lap. My hands rest on the trident just in case the fish has extra appendages that allow it to walk on land; which, I should point out, would be a living nightmare. The only sign of any movement is the ripples of water around it, showing that it's using its fins to stay afloat. The more I stare at it, the more human-like its face looks, especially its eyes; they show more intelligence than your average fish.

Human. Oh my God, that's it.

"But you weren't human, were you? You were a nymph."

The fish slowly blinks, as if to answer my question. I let out a sigh and rub my temples. I now realize what the woman meant when she said it was time. It's time to make a decision, and I need to make it soon. I can feel my body draining and I now realize my fading soul is the cause of my exhaustion lately. It's only a matter of time before I pass out again. I look at the fish and then at the trident in my lap. I can only imagine how long the fish has been in here if she is who I believe her to be. Eons, blimey, that is awful. It's a fate worse than death to be trapped by yourself for all of these years. With nothing and no one to keep you company but the darkness? I would go mad.

Forgiveness. That is what I felt as Amphitrite was dying. So forgiveness is what I shall give—she has served her sentence long enough. A part of me doesn't want to give her freedom, but my mother's voice plays in my head. "*Whenever you are mad, do not hold on to that hatred. In the end, you are harming yourself more than who did you wrong. Always allow your heart to be free and open so you do not poison yourself from within.*" It was something she said to me on her deathbed. She and her sister had a falling out before she got sick and never reconciled.

I nod my head resolutely. Trident in hand, I walk to the bank, waiting for the fish. If the fish is who I think she is, then she will gladly come to me. As she swims closer, I'm able to get a better look at her. Her skin is taut against her bones, giving her a waxy look. Starved but unable to die. She stares at me, waiting. I lift the trident and efficiently stab her with it. She doesn't shriek like I expect her to, but instead lets out a sigh, her body sinking into itself.

Smoke rises from the deflated form and Doto's wisp-like figure stands before me. "Thank you, sister." Her voice is scratchy from eons of silence.

Before I can say anything, her form gets sucked into the trident like a vacuum. As soon as she's gone, the trident starts glowing. Heat radiates off of it, burning so hot that I drop it. Light shines from where I was stabbed earlier by the woman in the vast realm of white. It hurts. Oh gods, it hurts so bad. I fall to my knees, clutching at my chest to try to appease this pain. It feels like molten lava is being poured down my throat. I want to scream, but nothing escapes my open mouth. Tears stream down my face in an endless wave as the agony rips me apart. This pain is like nothing I've ever experienced before, and it's becoming unbearable. At this moment, it really does feel like my soul is fading. No, not fading. It feels like it's being *shredded.*

I reach for the trident. It's causing this pain, maybe there's something I can do to make it stop. My mind is in a frenzy. I can't even think properly because the pain is too much.

Where the trident once was, the lady in the kaleidoscope dress is standing. Next to her is Amphitrite. Both of them look down on me with angelic smiles. They look ... pleased? Based on the trident's response, my decision had been wrong; but looking at them, it is clearly what they had wanted. I was played for a fool and now I will suffer for it.

Why? I plead with my eyes. They give no answer. Instead, Amphitrite kneels down in front of me. Lovingly, she wipes away my tears. I jerk back, but she holds me in place and then gives my lips a gentle kiss. I want to shove her away, but the pain has left me too weak. As Amphitrite deepens the kiss, the pain subsides just a fraction. It is such a relief that when her tongue grazes mine, coaxing me to return the favor, I cave and give her my all. I'd do anything to make the searing pain stop. Our kiss becomes heated as I drink her in, whimpering into her wet mouth as the pain lessens. My tongue searches for more. The release of pain is beyond pleasure, and I want more of her until I can no longer feel. I never want to feel this tearing apart ever again.

When the last of the pain leaves me, I let out a gasp, finally coming up for air. I could cry tears of joy from the release the kiss has given me. I feel refreshed, renewed. I feel ... whole. It's the oddest thing to feel suddenly whole when I hadn't felt fractured before. Does this mean that whatever just happened fixed my soul?

The cavern is empty as I look around. Both Amphitrite and the lady are no longer here. All that I'm left with is the trident and a dead fish at my feet. Looking out, the water parts for me, anticipating my departure. I walk back the way I arrived with the trident in hand, not looking back.

Chapter Thirteen

As I exit the cave, I expect to see Hades, but to my relief, I find Percy. *I wish the trident was smaller; it'd make it so much easier to tote around.*

With that specific thought, the trident shrinks. Staring down in shock, I open my hand to find it nestled in my palm.

Did ... did this thing just read my mind?

I look up to Percy for clarification—didn't this once belong to him? He shrugs his shoulders in a, *yeah it does that sometimes,* kind of way. I'm not sure what exactly to do with the trident. Do I give it back or is this a finders keepers type of thing?

"Amy?" The concern in Percy's voice brings me back to the present. Saying fuck it to my questions, I run the rest of the way to him and he catches me in his arms. The hug is stiff and hesitant and then he's holding me so tight I wouldn't be able to free myself if I wanted to. But I don't. There's security in Percy's arms, and after what I just went through, I really need this. I breathe him in. The feel of him is almost comparable to the kiss with Amphitrite. I will never in all of my days get enough of Percy's scent. He will always be my favorite smell. The smell of the ocean. Fresh. A hint of salt with citrus. Home.

I don't realize how tired I am until I'm in his arms. I haven't eaten in what's probably been days. I'm physically and mentally drained from the cavern and what transpired before then. It's been a long week, and it's finally catching up to me.

"Percy?" My voice is a croak. Lack of food and drink does that to you. He pushes me back to get a better look at me. His eyebrows are raised in question, face etched with concern as he massages soothing circles with his thumb on the top of my left shoulder.

"I'm so hungry," I state.

Percy's eyes swirl a deep blue of concern. "Ah, hell." He runs his hand through his sun-kissed hair. It's gotten so long, I like it. It's oddly even longer than the last time I saw him. Did his hair grow that fast? It's grown about a good seventy-five millimeters and is now shoulder-length and curling slightly. I envision tugging it to expose the tender part of his neck. The pit of my stomach warms at the thought, followed by a starved growl. I'm shaken out of my reverie to playful chuckles from Percy. I look at him and he shakes his head before I can question what he was laughing about. I open my mouth to demand he explain, but he lifts me into his arms.

Before I can ask him what he's doing he says, "I'm taking you to food, and you look like you're too weak to stand a moment longer."

"Why am I always being cut off?" I grumble against his chest. Percy is silent, so he's either ignoring me or didn't hear. He's right, though. My legs were beginning to get shaky. Probably from low blood sugar, which is a sure indicator that I need food right away.

I rest my head against him and close my eyes. I still have so many questions. Hades said they would be answered behind that door but they weren't. I'm still as confused as ever. Even more so now with the trident nestled in my palm. After a meal and a nice bath. Yes, that sounds lovely. I have been craving a good bath. One with Percy ...

Percy takes me down a flight of stairs and down a short hall, to the bedroom I had woken up in. It's a completely different path than the one the ghost had taken me on, and this one is actually lit by pale blue torches. I must have been on the ghost's bad side, because the way she led me was dark and treacherously long.

"Is there another way to get to the room?" I ask.

"There is but its purpose is for the servants, why?" He sets me down on the bed and pulls a rope that dangles next to the headboard. There's a light knock and the ghost that had escorted me earlier enters the room. I ignore Percy's prodding and focus on the filigree stitched onto the comforter. I'd rather not give this ghost any of my attention now.

"We will dine in the bathroom," Percy says as he walks to the door that I had gone through earlier to change. He turns back and as an afterthought he says, "Oh and a bottle of Ambrosia." The ghost gives us both a nod before leaving the room.

"Bathroom?" My voice raises an octave in bewilderment.

Percy shrugs. "I figured it'd be more relaxing." He hesitates before warily asking me, "Do ... Do you remember anything?"

I frown. "What would I be forgetting?"

He lets out a shaky sigh. Walking back to me he says, "Maybe we should eat here first." His hands run through his hair again. A nervous habit. He sits next to me, his hands now rubbing against his thighs. I've only ever seen him this nervous once, and that was years ago. When he was talking to the bird, to Paul ... My thoughts trail off. What was it he had said? He had waited. Waited so long for what? And then I think about Amphitrite's memory. Percy had called her *Dove*.

The revelation has me gasping in shock and I quickly cover my face as I start heaving out in sobs. This can't be true. It can't. I feel the worst thing anyone could possibly feel, betrayal. I look at Percy between my vision that is now blurred from tears. His face has become impassive. He's once again put on a mask to hide his emotions from me. That hurts even more. It feels like my heart is breaking into a million pieces, even more so with him shutting me out.

"Is it true?" I spit the words out in an unattractive manner. "Did Amphitrite's soul combine with my own?" Percy only nods his head, his eyes guarded as he watches me carefully.

"Why?" I half scream. I'm standing in front of him now. "Are you that selfish?"

Percy stares back at me, voiceless. His eyes search mine. They're swirling with so many shades I can't determine what he's thinking at this moment. But I don't care. He betrayed me, and that's all that matters.

I sink to my knees. Giving up, I whisper, "Did you ever love *me*?" I can't even look at him anymore. I'm scared of what I'll see. When I look at him will I only see the love that he has for her? Or will there be disgust because I'm not her? He has to see that I'm not. I never was. And this combination of our souls, her taking over mine and replacing me, is the worst act of betrayal there ever was.

Before Percy speaks, he kneels down in front of me. He gently wipes my tears away before sliding his hand down my jaw. He cups it and raises my face to look up at him. "I have always loved *you*."

I jerk my head away. Now he tells me he loves me *after* my body is sharing a soul with his dead wife. "I'm not her." The words hurt so bad. I was just a pawn. A vessel for her soul.

He reaches to hold me but I push him away. "Don't." The tears sting my eyes but my sadness has turned into anger. I really don't want to hear his excuses. "You're a pervert. You came to me as a child and spent my whole life trying to make me fall for you. How old are you, anyways? Should I call you grandpa? Did you have fun tricking me? Say something you fucking bastard!"

"It was a glamour," he says so quietly that I almost didn't catch it.

I have forgotten that I am still holding onto the trident, only remembering when it starts pulsing the second my sorrow turns to anger. For a hot second, I envision stabbing Percy with it. My anger *craves* blood. I imagine the trident sliding so easily through his gut. With that thought, the trident grows back to full size. The shock of it makes me shudder. What was I just thinking? How could I?

The trident slips out of my hands with a clatter against the stone floor. I close my eyes, breathing in and out slowly. No, I don't want that. That's not me. My anger subsides, the pulsing along with it. All I'm left with is sadness and utter defeat. It was never me. Only ever her. I'm so hurt and betrayed. I can't bear to be here any longer. Frightened by what I might do if the anger comes back, I rush out of the room, leaving the trident and Percy behind. I don't know where I'm going but anywhere is better than here. Away from the trident. Away from Percy.

Chapter Fourteen

I keep running until I'm out of breath. My shoulders heave in racking sobs that are broken up by my gasps for air that doesn't enter my lungs fast enough. I'm glad Percy didn't chase after me; if he had, I would've kept running. Lack of air or not, I don't want to see him. I don't know if I can handle anything he would say to justify what he's done. Just the thought of him is more than I can stand. It leaves a pain so deep within me I want to rip my chest apart to rid myself of this anguish. It's like someone cracked me open to expose my heart and left me there to bleed out. The burning in my lungs helps greatly to distract me from the stabbing pain of betrayal that is deeply lodged within me. Every choking intake of air is more pleasant than the alternate ache that I ran from. Gods, anything is better than the truth that slapped me across the face.

It was never me.

This whole time it was never me. I was just a damn vessel to be shared with his past lover. I sneer in such disdain at the irony. *I'll always find you.* When Percy said those words, I had thought he meant the first time we met at the beach, that our meeting was destiny, *not* him referring to always finding Amphitrite. Does he expect me to roll over as Amphitrite's subconscious takes over *my* body? How does all of this work out? But who knows, I may have easily agreed to it. No one wants to die. But then again, no one wants to share their body with their boyfriend's ex-lover.

And then I scream like a bloody banshee coming in for the kill. How dare he do this to me? I would've welcomed death with open arms over sharing my body with another soul.

As my rageful scream turns back into broken sobs, I wish for nothing more than to lose myself. To no longer have to think of what will become of me.

With the last dregs of repressed air leaving and making way for steady breathing, I straighten my hunched body to observe my surroundings. I had run fast and far in hopes of not being found, which led to me getting lost. It was foolish, but one does lose all care when their heart is broken.

The strange sunlight has left, making way for what I suppose is night. I say that because this is the Underworld, where the sun and stars do not exist. Instead, what makes up stars are a million glittering worms that light up the area like a full moon would. The way the light shines down on the surrounding flowers is breathtaking. The veins in some of the leaves shimmer in an array of deep blues and purples that were not present during the day hours. Amongst the flowers is a thick sea of vegetation. Trees of varying heights shoot up all around me, and an assortment of leafy bushes litter the ground, intertwined with the flowers. It has the look of a tropical forest, but minus the muggy air that instantly coats you in perspiration.

The aroma coming off of the flowers is strong. Their smell of honey and strawberries leaves me lightheaded in delirium as I savor their aroma. The scent is rich and with each inhale I can taste it on my tongue. A yearning groan of hunger flies out of my mouth as my stomach grumbles and tightens, leaving me wondering if the flowers are edible. I sure hope so because I am beyond starving. I can already feel my body starting the process of eating itself from going so long without food. The act of starving yourself is a most torturous process and eclipses any rational thought. When you get past a certain point of hunger, you will do anything to ease that gnawing ache curling between your intestines and crawling up your throat. Even wanting to take a bite out of an unknown plant sounds rational to a person so deprived of food. And I currently am said person.

I reach out to pluck a white-petaled flower to get a taste when a piercing shriek stops me. I whip around at the noise. My heart flutters against my chest like a bird trying to escape its cage. If my stomach wasn't empty, I would have barfed from the combination of adrenaline and the queasiness that hunger brings along.

"What the bloody hell was that for?" I fume incredulously at the servant-ghost, who is standing there holding a tray of food. Glorious, glorious food. I take a step toward her, ravenous need propelling me. I have no doubt that I look like someone who has gone rabid. I wouldn't put it past myself to be foaming at the mouth right now.

With a straight face, she points to the flowers then to her mouth. She shakes her head no and mouths the word *bad*.

I stop short. "Poisonous?" *Fuck ...*

She nods her head. Just then my stomach lets out another thunderous growl. She lifts up the tray higher, bringing it toward me. Taking the tray from her, I don't say thank you. I remain silent while I watch her for a moment, tapping my foot. The part of me that is still sane wants her to leave so I can shovel whatever is on this tray into my face. The smells wafting up to me are making me salivate like a dog, and I currently don't care to wipe the drool pooling out of my slacked mouth.

She looks me up and down briefly with no emotion, and then turns and walks away. I can see through her, and yet she can hold objects. It's a mystery that has me shaking my head. Tray in tow, I walk on in search of somewhere to sit. And then I will shove every last piece of food into my mouth.

The sound of rushing water has me looking around in search of a stream. I see no sign of water, but there is a narrow path that leads through the forest in the direction of the noise. In hopes that there will be a bank for me to sit on while I wolf down this food, I follow the path. The sounds of cicadas and frogs disappear, drowned out by the roar of the nearby water. Pushing aside a fern blocking my way, I am greeted by a flowing river skating down the edge of a cliff, creating a waterfall. The water flows steadily down into darkness.

Searching for a place to sit, I spy a circular, moss haven off to the side. Little, white flowers are sprinkled around the grove, giving off fairy-like light. The jingle of bells chimes as my legs brush against the petite flowers. Their petals are closed in, giving them the shape of a bell. Their ringing reminds me of something Miss Justine once told me: "*Every time a bell goes off, an angel earns its wings.*" The thought warms my chest in content nostalgia. It was a line from Miss Justine's favorite Christmas movie. Even though I never saw it, her words still echo in my head every time I hear a bell.

Sitting in the middle of the grove, I place the tray on my lap. It's too dark to see the contents of the wooden bowl, but the twisting in my stomach doesn't care what it is. I grab the matching wooden spoon and devour the food like the ravenous beast I have become.

Soup. *Oh, fucking goblin dicks,* I internally moan with each slurp and swallow.

The soup is heavenly. It could be because I am past the point of hunger but it is the best soup I have ever tasted. The meat is soft and the potatoes are filled with so much flavor it should be illegal. Within seconds the soup is gone and the ache in the pit of my stomach has dimmed but still remains. Moving onto the sliced bread, I take each bite slowly. This time I actually savor every bite. It tastes of sourdough with rosemary undertones and is generously lathered in garlic butter. Every bite makes my mouth water with the need for more. Note to self, stop skipping meals. You're not you when you're hungry, Amy.

Finished with my feast, I lie back into the pillow-soft moss and close my eyes. I empty my mind of Percy and roll my shoulders back to try to relax. The water is loud enough that it acts as white noise. I welcome it. I breathe in and out with intention and in turn my body becomes dead weight that allows my mind to drift into nothingness. For the first time in what feels like a lifetime, I can just be. My mind finally getting the rest it desperately craves, I lie there unmoving, as I imagine floating on clouds.

A strand of hair tickles my nose. It wakes me up from the sleep that I had slipped into. I scrunch my nose to relieve the itch. My eyes still closed, I try to settle back into nothingness. The wind moves my hair again, followed by another tickle. I open my eyes, frustration coursing through me at the disturbance. I just want to forget my worries but this damn wind won't let up. Something whizzes past me, skimming across my nose. The image of wings and spindly limbs is fleeting as it flies away, too fast for my eyes to follow.

Flailing my hands in panic, I jump up looking around for the bug. Bugs always tend to get stuck in my hair and then are mad at me for that. Once a beetle got stuck and then bit me when I released it. That experience ended any neutrality I had toward bugs, now they can bugger off.

Heh, bug. Bugger. I chuckle at my own joke. But in all seriousness, bugs flying around my head are not my favorite.

Whatever it was is no longer flying around me. Squinting, I scan the grove trying to find what it was, but the area seems to be empty of any life, despite feeling like eyes are upon me. I brush off the feeling; nothing is out here. Picking up the tray, I follow the trail back to the gem walkway. The feeling of eyes stays upon me until I'm out of the grove. I don't think about how uneasy it makes me, and instead try to find my way around. I'm still too upset to go back to Percy. I think what hurts the most is that he didn't trust me enough to tell me anything. I was left in the dark. No *"hey, your soul is incomplete and for you to live my ex-lover has to combine with your soul."* And the worst part is that he didn't even ask my permission.

My aimless wandering away from Percy has left me completely lost. I can't see too far ahead, so I trudge along in hopes of finding someone to speak to. I'm sure I'll run into someone eventually. With nothing to do, I take my time with my search and admire the different plants along the path. Remembering the ghost's warning I keep my distance from the plants. The science-loving part of me itches for gloves and goggles so I can better examine the flowers. I wonder if they're all toxic or just a select few. The nymphs run through them, so maybe they're just poisonous to eat? I am astonished by the beauty that surrounds me.

Who could've imagined the extent of all of this growing in the Underworld? The gardener behind it is brilliant, and I'd love to pick their brain.

The darkness is starting to lighten and with it laughter and music float over to me. My walk has led me to a clearing where nymphs of varying shades of brown, black, and green dance around a bonfire. I stand at the edge of the clearing, entranced by the freedom of their movements. A green nymph jumps into the air and a shower of pink blossoms rains down from her hands. A few of the nearby nymphs catch the blossoms and put them in their hair. As soon as the green nymph's feet touch the ground she continues her dancing of endless twirls.

"Amy!" My head whips toward the familiar voice.

"Alice!" I exclaim back at her. We tackle each other in a tight embrace. Through everything I had forgotten about my crew. Not once had they crossed my mind. Guilt creeps into my conscience, but I ignore it. She's here. That's all that matters. With my best friend holding me so close, I want to cry. To break down and tell her everything about Percy and his betrayal, but I hold it back. She also knew what was going on, she is just as guilty, but it's something that I don't want to bring up. Not right now at least, when all I currently want to do is forget.

I push Alice back from the hug. My hands remain on her shoulders as I yell through the noise. "What is this? How did you get here? Are the others here as well?"

Alice giggles at my torrent of questions. Her unrestrained laughter sounds like bubbles and champagne. It is a laugh filled with mischief. Her face is flushed and perspiration beads around her forehead. Leaning into me with a full-blown smile she says, "Come. You HAVE to try the ambrosia. Babe, it's out of this world!" Her breath smells of honey from whatever she had to drink. It's a pleasant smell, so when she leans in to speak I don't back away. I instead breathe her in and enjoy the feeling of affection and true friendship that she elicits.

Alice's voice is all cheer and her onyx curls bounce as she tugs me along and brings me to the others. Sitting on fern-covered chaise lounges are Clio and

Thalia. Hades sits on a separate chaise with a woman wrapped in his arms. Their bodies are entangled, enjoying each other with soft kisses and words of what I can only assume are endearment as Hades' eyes become clouded with lust and the woman blushes, wriggling her body closer.

Clio and Thalia look at me with heavy-lidded, drunk eyes.

"You're alive!" Thalia slurs.

Clio rolls her eyes at Thalia, elbowing her in the ribs. "Of course she is. I had no doubt that she'd succeed." She stands up and gives me the tightest, most genuine hug she has ever given me. She breathes me in and says, "It's so good to finally have you back after all these years."

I stiffen just the slightest. *I'm not her. I'm not her. I'm not her.*

Clio doesn't notice my change in body language. She squeezes me once more before letting go with a content sigh. So much reverence lingers in her eyes. The intensity of it is stifling, and it makes me want to put space between us. What could Amphitrite be to her for her to act this way? Then it dawns on me. Clio sees the understanding and nods her head, her face alight with gratitude. "Yes, you're the friend who opened my eyes. *You* saved me."

I want to scream at her that I'm not Amphitrite. That it wasn't my guidance that led her away from Zeus, but I hold it back. There is no point in telling her the truth, and how could I crush her happiness? She believes her long-lost friend is finally here, back from the dead. Little does she know that Amphitrite hasn't yet tried to take over her new body.

I'm trying to remain calm, to not think about my body being a vessel for someone else's soul, but the thoughts won't stop intruding. Not when Clio is in front of me so blatantly enraptured by my presence. Just as the urge to bolt is beginning to overtake me, Alice comes between us and hands me a goblet of wine that smells richly of honey.

Alice is clearly a godsend, one that I could kiss right now. I am that thankful. She somehow always sees when I'm about to have a mental breakdown and is there to get me out of it before it consumes me.

I chug the contents of the goblet in hopes that it'll help me forget about the worries plaguing me. *Please* be alcohol. Too much has happened in so little time, I need a breather. Something to help me forget for a while.

Every millimeter that slides across my tongue brings my tastebuds to life. My mouth pops with what I can only describe as fireworks. It's euphoric. I let out a laugh. Then another. My mind begins to float and all that I can think about is how amazing this stuff is.

Alice senses just how badly I need a break because as soon as my goblet is empty she replaces it with another that is filled to the brim with this liquid that is beyond orgasmic. I've never tasted anything so ... so addicting. I gulp down this one too, leaving not a drop behind. I even lick my lips in hopes of catching any stray drops. The drink brings me to a high where I'm no longer aware of my troubles. No longer thinking about my soul. No longer thinking how I'm not *her*.

My pulse begins to beat to the drums, willing me to move. Letting the rhythm guide me, I find myself by the fire. It's as if something ancient overtakes me as my limbs move to a dance that I myself never learned. The nymphs surround me and our bodies become one as we flow to the music. I throw my head back and laugh and laugh and laugh. Whatever has befallen me prods against what I can only describe as the barrier of my mind. It feels like shadows are pressing against my barrier, looking for a way in. I envision a door and mentally open it to the shadows.

Welcome, I greet cheerily, as if the shadows have a consciousness. Not a second goes by before the ancient shadows consume every inch of my mind and then I'm gone. They have taken away any thought that I have, leaving me only with ecstasy and the need to dance, dance, dance.

The temperature is warm enough where you can sleep out in the open without needing a blanket and that is exactly what everyone is doing. The music has been silenced and the only noise left is the crackling and popping of the dying fire. All of the nymphs are content and sprawled out on the grassy floor. I wonder if it's magic that keeps it warm or if it's just how it naturally came to be.

Clio is dozing in one of the moss lounges. Even with her amber hair covering her face I can still see that it is slack in bliss. Her lips part and little snores escape as she lies there, her arm hanging over the side. Hades and the woman left before the music stopped, shortly followed by Alice. Where she was off to, I don't know. She didn't say, but I assume she went to her own chamber. I should've asked where to find her bed, because I certainly did not want to go back to Percy.

Thalia and I carefully walk through the mass of bodies to find a more secluded place to relax. Outside the ring of flickering ember light is where we find a spot devoid of any sleeping bodies. We lay on the grass at an angle from each other where our heads slightly touch at the crown. The high has worn off, along with the shadows. When the shadows took over I was someone else. I have never felt that loose, that content and happy with my life. It was like the world had stopped. The universe froze in time and there was nothing but joy filling every crevice of my mind. It was a perfect bubble of zero worries. Remnants of that feeling still cling to me, humming against my skin, craving more. If I'm not careful, that divine drink will surely become an addiction.

The remnants shatter when Thalia speaks. "I take it you got your memories back."

"No. I did not." There's a bite to my words. They are curt, dripping with disdain.

"Then why aren't you with Poseidon? It's either that or you took his explanation badly."

"I didn't listen to him either. I'm not her. That's all that matters. I'm not her," I choke out.

I'm not her …

Thalia stays silent. Moments pass and I think she's going to leave the topic alone but then she says, "You are her, though."

The words sting. I'm about ready to tell her no when she continues, "You were born with half a soul. That half is the sister to the other half that combined with you. You are Amphitrite reborn."

"I ..." My mind whirls. It can't be true. So many thoughts spin around but I speak the one circling me the most. "He kept me in the dark. I knew nothing, *nothing* about this. And then to have this thrust upon me?!" My hands fly up, shaking with anger and hurt. They fall back to my chest with a thud befitting how I feel. Which is defeated and hollow, like I have just lost a war and come home to find my family slaughtered, and now nothing matters.

"He couldn't tell you, none of us could."

"What do you mean?"

"Poseidon knows more than I do, even Hades does. I just know the gist of it so you should really ask them for better detail." She flicks her wrists in dismissal. "Anyway, when we were sent to protect you we were told not to give you any hints to your past life. If you knew too much, then the other half of you might not accept the half that was in you. I don't know how Hades was able to preserve your soul. Souls of nymphs don't get reborn. Their soul instead flows back into the earth, giving her energy. Preserving a nymph's soul has never been done. It's impossible, but Hades is full of secrets and he knew a way. Just telling us a tiny bit about you was taking a huge risk. Not only because if we were to tell you any of this it could jeopardize your chances of success, but also there are plenty of immortals out there who would do anything to get their hands on that knowledge. If a nymph's soul meant for the circle of life could be salvaged, why not an immortal's? That information is powerful, even dangerous, so we don't even know how it happened or what went down in that cave. All we know is that Amphitrite's soul was somehow preserved and for her, for *you,* to be reborn, half of you had to be born into a mortal body while the other half waited."

I lay there in silence, stewing on the information. I think I know how it was done, but I don't share my thoughts for obvious reasons. If Percy didn't trust Thalia with that information then I shouldn't either.

I'm still mad at Percy but I do need to hear him out. If he expects me to be Amphitrite I don't think I can stay with him. Maybe as friends but not ...

Even knowing that our souls aren't separate and living in this one body but are instead just two halves that found each other again, I am still not *her*. I do not have her memories. I have lived my own life and I'm a completely different person who has had separate experiences from *her*.

My chest tightens once again. I want us to work so badly. If Percy can't see that I'm not her, if that's the only reason he loves me, then I'll walk away. I will not be valued only as a shadow of someone he used to love.

Chapter Fifteen

I push around the braised vegetables and runny eggs with my fork. The vegetables are sprinkled with melted cheese and the smell of it makes me queasy. I spent my first hour of the morning dry heaving. Eyes bleary, Thalia and Clio walked me over to a mini-colosseum-shaped building to get something in my stomach. Into all of our stomachs. Both of them look just as bad as I feel, with their eyes swollen and hair strewn about so much that it looks like birds made a nest out of them during their sleep.

I experienced a different side to Thalia and Clio last night. I had grown used to their standoffishness so last night when they were warm toward me, I welcomed it. It was a side of them that I can get used to. I now understand why they chose to keep their distance in the past. It was the safest thing to do. Knowing that, I can let go of my first impression of them. Which honestly wasn't that great to begin with. So, lucky them.

Alice and Paul on the other hand, chose differently. They became my friends and made my experience at the facility feel like home. I don't know why Alice broke her silence but for Paul I think I can understand. He watched me grow up and maybe when he finally had the chance to talk to me, he couldn't hold back. Maybe he had this urge to have me care for him just as fiercely as he had for me. At least that is what I think, because if I watched silently as someone grew and knew everything about them, I would undoubtedly love them.

I sit in the middle of the long, maple table next to Alice. Hades and the woman wrapped around him last night are seated across from me. Earlier she introduced herself as Persephone. I assume she is a nymph, given her pointed ears poking out of her chestnut locks, the tips of them a lush green. Everything about her is brown. Her skin is a russet tone with eyes the deepest browns of the earth. She's practically half the size of Hades, who when standing, towers over her. Her heart-shaped face reminds me of a spring flower's first bloom after the last of winter's frost. Vibrant and strong, yet delicate and soft.

"Ugh." I groan, pressing my forehead against the table. I move my plate to the side so that I don't have to breathe in what I currently feel like barfing out. "Can we please just eat in the dark?" The light shining down from the non-existent roof is making my headache worse. I just want to envelope myself in total darkness. Or even have someone knock me out. Anything to make this split in my head disappear. Thalia and Clio groan in agreement while Alice, Hades, and Persephone laugh with pure enjoyment at our misery.

"That must have been your first time drinking ambrosia." Persephone smiles. "Most of us have gained a tolerance to its effects. Did no one warn you to not drink so much?" Her voice sounds like dew, if that is even possible. Everything about her really is spring incarnate. She even *smells* like spring. The sweet fragrance of crocuses with an undercurrent of melting snow wafts over to me as she speaks.

I don't lift my head up as I grumble, "What the fuck, Alice." She had handed me two sloshing cups full and I'm pretty sure another one but my memory is foggy. I practically begged for another but a little warning in advance at what the aftermath would be like would've been nice. Now it makes sense why she was never drunk, even though she literally had some sort of alcohol in her hand every time I saw her. Ambrosia had built up her tolerance.

I could feel her shrug next to me as she says nonchalantly, "I forgot that's a thing." I roll my eyes, the movement causing more pain. I pinch her calf.

"Ow!" she exclaims.

Turning my head to stare at her I open one eye and say, "Revenge. Oh, so sweet."

She goes to flick my nose but I turn my head the other way. I feel her lean into me and her lips are against my ear. "The best thing is revenge," she says it in a sing-song voice, and for some reason it gives me goosebumps. I shake off the chill. Alice just laughs as she goes back to eating, stabbing the savory potatoes like they are her foe.

I can't stomach any more food, so I opt for peppermint tea. With a raise of my hand, a ghost comes over and hands me a mug. A teapot and loose leaves of varying herbs are already stationed at the table. Each peppermint leaf that I drop into my wooden mug floats above the steaming water. The aroma of it is soothing and helps settle my queasy stomach.

"What exactly were we celebrating last night?" I ask, sipping my scorching tea.

"Winter solstice."

I startle at the reply. I don't turn around to look at him. Instead, I bury my face in my cup while he comes around to find a seat. Percy sits across from me, next to Hades. I watch his every move over the rim of my cup. His hands are big and his slender fingers expertly apply butter and jam to a scone. I stare at his lips as he takes a bite. He slowly grazes the top of his lip with his tongue and then his succulent lips smirk. I look up to his eyes. Sky blue swirls around his pupil, playfulness dances behind them. I immediately hide my own eyes back behind my cup. I blush, embarrassed to be caught. I don't want to add whatever this is sparking between us to my already-overwhelming confusion. At this point, still being head over heels for him after what he did feels like an act of betrayal to myself.

"We missed you at the festivities, brother," Hades comments, raising his fork.

"My apologies. I had a lot on my mind."

"Ah, yes." Hades stares at me with a grin. It reminds me of a wolf. "It seems Amphitrite has passed the test."

"I am not *her!*" I don't know what comes over me. I boil with rage at my identity being stolen. The wooden cup splinters and then shatters in my hand,

and with that my rage turns to shock. I just shattered a mug with my own hand. It must have been poorly made, because how is that even possible?

Everyone at the table remains silent as a servant comes over to clean up the mess. He works around me as I stay unmoving, staring at my hand. There's blood but no wound. Hades coughs and I hear the others resume their eating. I keep staring at my hand. What just ... happened?

"It would seem that your body is finished transforming." At that I look up to Hades.

"What do you mean?"

"Did you think an immortal soul could be contained by a mortal body? You would wither away, your soul destroying what was." Hades hand makes a fluttering movement, as if envisioning my body turning into wisps and drifting away into the wind.

I ponder his words. "What makes me immortal? I don't feel any different."

"Aside from the strength you just displayed? You will never age. Never get sick. Extreme healing capabilities. Of course we all have our own special attributes." Hades rubs his chin in contemplation. "I wonder what yours will be. I can only assume it'll have something to do with water, given you are the Queen of the Sea. Or maybe ... " He trails off.

"I'm to be a *queen*?" I can't hide the shock from my voice as it raises several octaves. I look to Percy, violet specks of yearning swirl in his blue eyes.

Hades booms, "You are not to *be* a queen. You are *already* a queen. The oath to your realm is soul-binding. Your death as Amphitrite does not unbind an oath. Especially one signed with your soul. As long as your soul is in existence you will always be queen."

I keep eye contact with Percy during Hades' explanation. I'm yet again blindsided. I'm a queen all of a sudden? Thalia's words tug at my memory, "*If you knew too much, then the other half of you might not accept the half that was in you.*" I owe it to Percy to hear him out. I am the one who walked out on him and I also deserve an explanation. Maybe if I had listened to him instead of running away this new knowledge wouldn't be such a shock.

"Walk with me?" I ask. My teeth tug on my bottom lip as I wait for his answer.

He must sense my urgency because he doesn't say anything, only nods his head once slowly before rising. Or maybe he feels just as anxious as I do to forgive and move on. We leave, not saying farewell to anyone. Too much lingers on my mind to care for pleasantries. I hear Alice calling dibs on my barely touched breakfast and Hades' huff of irritation from being ignored. As we leave, the sounds of the surrounding forest block out any noise from our friends.

Percy guides me to another walkway of intricate colors. He notices me staring at the path and says, "The main walkways all tell a story. If you look closely, the gems become shapes."

I look up at him, squinting my eyes in question then I look back down at the path. I had noticed the shapes, but I didn't know they told a story. The ache in my chest has dimmed due to my conversation with Thalia, but it still throbs with betrayal. On top of technically being reincarnated I am to be a queen of a realm I've never been to. I doubt my trips to the beach count. It's comical to think that I, someone who loathes politics, am now having a crown jammed onto my head. It's hard to fathom, and I'm not even sure if it's something that I want. But do I even have a choice? It sounds like I don't. Not even death broke this oath that Amphitrite made. And now in this new life the oath is bound to me. What will that mean for Percy and I if we can't work out whatever this is between us?

I focus on the path to give myself more time to think. My thoughts become such a jumbled mess of anxiety from thinking about my future that I decide not to think about it at all. Instead, I ignore my raging thoughts and take a closer look at the path now that I know the gems tell a tale. I notice an eye, an ear and then long, flowing hair that transforms into a field. I must be a fool for not realizing there is a message behind the images. Once told, it becomes blatantly clear as I stare at the path. It is a work of art, intricately arranged into colors of vibrant yellow to darker browns. My curiosity gets the best of me so I ask, "What is this path's story?"

"I believe it is how Persephone and Hades met." His hand brushes against mine. A tingling wave of shock burns up my arm that sends jolting vibrations to my chest. I jerk my hand back and look up to him to see if he felt it too. The only indication that he did is the downward turn at the corner of his lips and the slight furrow of his eyebrows. The rest of him is unfazed and even the reaction that he shows is fleeting.

"Hmm." Curious now, I bring the back of my hand to graze against his. The shock is there but has dimmed. It's not as intense as that initial sting. I leave my hand against him to see how long the vibrations will last.

Percy releases a frustrated sigh. He clenches his hand that was touching mine and looks at it so fiercely that one might think his hand would cave and give him answers from the intense scrutiny. In the end we continue our walk in silence, neither one of us testing out the reaction any further. I wonder why our bodies are reacting this way when they didn't when we were last in each other's arms. Is this a side effect of being immortal? I kind of want to ask Percy, in hopes that this tingling won't be a long-term thing.

My thoughts have come full circle and they leave me at a loss. So much has happened that it feels like my world is caving in. I am no longer the naïve girl wanting to better the ocean. I wish she was still here, but she has left. She has been gone since the harpies attacked. With their attack my innocence of this world was stripped. The blindfold is ripped away and here I am standing in a glass box. The walls of that outer world are coming closer and closer. I bang against that wall to no avail. I'm trapped, never able to break free. My cries and pleas for freedom go unanswered. Until finally these walls will finish closing in and shape me, and I am left with this mold of myself that is not truly me. Will I be me if I accept this new version of me by allowing this world to morph me into what it wants? A queen? Amphitrite?

Percy grabs my shaking hands, pulling me into a hug. My head crashes against his chest as one hand tangles in my hair and the other one presses against the middle of my back. I stiffen because I hadn't realized that I was shaking. I relax in his hold because the security that Percy offers feels too damn good. He melts my doubts away but I still hold stubbornly to the dregs of them. My shaking stops and my breathing goes back to normal as the steady beat of his heart brings me down from my panic.

"Let's go sit down and I'll explain everything."

"Everything?" I ask it so softly it's a wonder he even hears me. I always feel weak after letting my panic take over. The shame of it weighs me down into heavy melancholy. I wish I wasn't like this. I wish I was stronger than my thoughts.

"Yes, everything." I can feel his lips against my hair as he speaks. I stiffen, waiting for what he'll do. His lips are there for a moment and then they're gone as if he thinks better of it. I'm glad he decides against a kiss and that he respects my boundaries. A hug for comfort is one thing but a kiss for his own needs is another. I'm being greedy allowing this hug. It gives false hope. *I* could never be *her.*

Pushing out of Percy's hold I look around and notice the little path looks similar to the one I took last night to the grove. I nod in that direction, indicating the earthy path. "We could find a place to sit through there."

Percy sees the direction of my nod and shakes his no, a sneer on his lips. "Not unless you want to piss off the sprites. Those paths lead to areas that are sacred to them."

The feeling of something tickling my nose crosses my mind. "Do these sprites, by chance, fly?"

"Yes. They're more like lesser nymphs but since they are far older and more one with this realm, they are their own species. They look exactly like a nymph but with wings and only about this big." He holds his hand out, his pointer finger and thumb inches apart. "Nasty little things, really."

Oh ... that sounds exactly like what I encountered. "Well, they must not be that bad since I was in one of their groves."

His eyes bulge in shock which is followed by a playful smirk. "Didn't anyone tell you not to follow those paths? Even us immortals leave them alone." He chuckles, the sound of it sends flutters to my core. "Only you would come across one and survive."

"Apparently I'm now immortal. I can't die." Or so I thought.

"Yes ... true. But there are far worse things than death. Their personal favorites are curses. In the human realm, if their grove is destroyed they unleash famine and pestilence upon the area." Percy looks me over. "Thankfully, it seems that they liked you."

"Thankfully." I can't even imagine how something so small could be that destructive. A shiver goes down me at how close I had been.

Percy runs his hand through his hair. "Let's go to our ... your room to talk. We're less likely to be overheard there."

"Why does it matter?"

"A lot of what I have to discuss is not for prying ears." His voice is grave and so I follow him as he leads us down to my room.

Chapter Sixteen

I pick at the armrest of the Victorian chair situated in the corner of the room, while my eyes follow Percy as he paces back and forth, gathering his thoughts. I stay silent, giving him all the time he needs to tell me his tale. One that better justify his reluctance to share information.

I don't wait for very long before he's on his knees before me. I stop my picking as I move my full attention toward him. The unexpected proximity of him leaves me breathless. He's the epitome of a beach boy. His wavy, chestnut hair brushes his shoulders, and strands of sun-kissed blonde peek around each curl.

I resist the urge to rub my thumb against the center of his worried brows. If I allow myself to touch him so delicately, I will lose all the restraint that I so desperately cling to. My fingers will turn needy and begin their hungry tracing of his smooth, strong jawline and down his neck to his broad, muscular shoulders.

That is something that I really don't want to happen, so I will my arms to stay put. It's turning out to be more of an effort than it should be.

"I want to start by saying that yes, you have the soul of Amphitrite but you have been reborn. You are a completely different person now. Hell, you are so much more. And I know this is selfish of me to say this. Especially after everything you have been through but ..." He rakes his hand through his hair and he looks so bloody broken when he does it, as if he's laying his heart out on a platter for me and he expects that with his next words I'll stab it.

"I love you. I love *you*, Amy. Dammit, I love you for who you are *now*, not for who you once *were*. Okay? I love your fierceness and anger, something that Amphitrite never had. And I know it's bad of me to compare. I'm terrible for it, but it's true.

"You are mighty and courageous and intelligent. You are so strong, and I don't mean in muscles—although you give a fantastic right hook." He laughs. "No, you are strong mentally. It is a strength that not many wield. Most would have walked away from all of this and not asked for answers or even considered this world. It would be easier to walk away from it all and to just go back to a normal life. But not you, my love, no. You walked right into this with your head held high. And *fuck*, seeing that strength behind your eyes and rippling down your body, it makes me love you even more."

I shake my head as tears stream down my cheeks. His affirmation leaves me elated. He sees *us* as separate, that I am separate from Amphitrite. But I still don't understand. How can he go from Amphitrite to me? They were married. He loved her enough that he found a way for her to be reborn.

I want to laugh at myself. I'm being jealous of my own past life. It's petty, I know. But before he goes on any further, I have to ask. "Why did you have me reborn if you weren't expecting us to be the same?"

He looks down, and a blush of shame coats his cheeks. "At first I did expect that. I loved Amphitrite so much that I could not let her go. Even as her life was slipping away, I begged Hades to save her. There was only one way it could be done and a possibility it would fail. Her soul could not be reborn so we had to turn it mortal. To do so, Hades tore her soul in half. No longer whole, its power faded. The mortal half to be saved for your rebirth, the nymph half tied to the trident. The trident is the only thing that can hold that type of essence in its purest form." His thumb traces circles on the inside of my knee and I allow it. He sees me leaning into his touch but he continues, clearly not wanting any misunderstandings to go between us any longer.

"For you to gain back your other half, the trident had to find you worthy. Only the worthy can wield her. If you failed her test, you would have perished. No one can survive too long with only half a soul. That is why I kept you in the dark. I knew your heart and knew that the trident would accept you so I was not worried." He rakes his hand through his hair again. This time his hair stays standing up at the base. It's boyish and I ache to run my own hand through it but I control myself. He isn't finished explaining, and I need to know more because he admitted that he expected us to be the same. I have to know what changed.

"Okay, I was a little bit worried, but I had faith in you. I was with you while growing up and I also was once the master of the trident. I knew you and I knew her and I believed, no I *knew,* that you would succeed even if my fear was gnawing at me like a little demon whispering that you wouldn't."

He sighs. "I couldn't tell you anything because then the trident would know that your choice wasn't entirely yours. So please, please believe me when I tell you that I love you." Percy's eyes find mine again and specks of violet have overtaken his blues completely, leaving his stare intense and so breathtakingly beautiful. "I love you for you, Amy. Yes, the first time we met I expected you to be Amphitrite. And I'm sorry, that was wrong of me on so many levels. But you know what? I'm glad that I did that."

Before I can get any words out at the blasphemy, he rushes on, holding me firmly against the chair so I don't get up. "I was able to spend those years getting to know you. And over the years as I watched your brilliant mind and fierce anger I realized that you are not Amphitrite. You are you and because of that I was able to fall in love with *you.* You ignite this *need* in me, something Amphitrite never could do. I loved her but never with the intensity that I love you with.

"It's sick of me to even think it, let alone speak it, but if I could go back to stop Amphitrite from dying, I wouldn't. I would gladly allow her to. I would choose the same choices all over again if it were to bring me you."

He lets out a heavy breath as he searches for any sign that I accept his explanation and declaration of love. Tears flow from his deep blue eyes that are now no longer overtaken with violet but are instead speckled with it. The vulnerability in them tears down the already cracking mental wall I have in place to shield myself from being hurt. I came into this conversation expecting it to be the end of our relationship. But this ...

My own tears are no longer the few stragglers that escape but are now pouring down my face as fat droplets accumulate at the bottom of my chin. His silence tells me that he is done, that he doesn't have anything else to say and he doesn't need to. I now see that the betrayal never really was a betrayal. He also views me as separate. In a way, Amphitrite and I are the same but we are entirely different and he sees that. He loves me for me. What I view as faults he views as strengths. And with that, Percy has pulverized the mental wall separating us.

I choke out a laugh. "Of course you would see anger as wanting. You must be a sadomasochist."

Percy's own strained laugh counters mine. "I may just very well be." There's a pause. Worry etches his face as his brows knit together but before he speaks again, I throw myself at him. My lips collide with his. Like it is second nature, our bodies mold together as our tongues dance. He tastes of citrus and clear water. It's refreshing and all I want to do is drink him in. All of him. This kiss barely satiates my hunger for him. I am starving and this kiss is a mere sip that leaves me craving more. If he were a well, I would be on my knees begging for every last drop. Who was I kidding when I thought I could walk away?

I whimper in pleasure when he tugs on my lower lip. His bite sends a pooling heat to my core and flames ignite throughout my body. With that small noise I make, he loses any restraint he has. He growls, a sound that I would do anything to hear again. He lifts me up by the ass and carries me to bed. Trailing kisses from my hip to my ribs, he pulls the toga I'm wearing up over my body. Tossing the garment to the floor he leans back to take off his own. Like me, he has no underwear beneath. My mouth drops and a little gasp escapes. The girth of him bobs in a hello as it's released. Ever so slowly, I look at every dip and curve of his body. Tracing a vein from his groin to his abdomen, I smile when his body shudders under my touch. I flip my hand over to have the back of my knuckles trace his abs. I begin to count, one. Two. Three. Four.

A set of four bloody, firm abs. Does this Greek god spend his days at the gym? Because holy fuck he is *toned*.

When my hand roams over his chest, my fingers spreading through his hair, I look up to his face. He smirks, heat in his eyes. "You're drooling."

More like the opposite. The sight of him has left me completely parched. I need him. Now. I lick my lips before shifting to have him in my mouth. Quickly he moves out of reach and I groan at the denial.

"Nuh-uh, my love. Let me worship you."

He gently pushes me onto my back, and I willingly oblige. I'm too excited to argue who gets to do what first. My head swims with what's about to happen and goosebumps pepper over my skin as he begins kissing down my neck. His thumb roves over my nipple and it peaks against his touch.

He moans into my neck. "Your breasts are so damn bewitching. I'm going to love watching them bounce while you ride my cock."

I flush from his admission and begin circling my own clit, needing to release this built up tension. My breath hitches when I find the perfect rhythm rubbing against the little bean. Percy stills his kissing and looks down to see what I'm doing.

"As sexy as that is ..." He removes my hand from myself and while making eye contact, he puts my wet fingers into his mouth. His tongue twirls around my two fingers and then he gives them a hard suck before releasing them with a *pop*. "I'll be doing the worshiping. Another time you can play with yourself, and when you do, I will have a front-row seat to watching you come undone from your own touch."

"You'd be so good at torture," I joke.

"Only if whips and chains are involved." He chuckles and I get the distinct feeling that Percy would love nothing more than to tie me up in a sex dungeon. Would I be down for something like that? Honestly, with my current lust-filled brain, yes. After I sober from this feeling, maybe not? I'm not quite sure. Baby steps.

"Now, where was I? Ah, yes. Boobies." I laugh at the way how he said *boobies* but my laughing quickly turns into heady moans when he puts one in his mouth. I feel his hand skating down my stomach. I open my legs when he reaches my clit. I expect him to finish what I started, but he doesn't. Instead, he pushes one finger in me. He does it slowly, *in* and *out*. And then he glides a second finger in, stretching me further.

He stops his suckling of my breasts and begins kissing down my stomach and to my core. The fresh air against my moistened nipple is cold and makes it harden even more, but the feeling is soon forgotten when Percy's hot mouth presses against my clit. His tongue darts out. It's like a struck match lights up and burns throughout my entire body as he flicks his warm tongue back and forth in different rhythms, trying to find which one I like the best. My hips dip and I arch into him when he curls his fingers in me. His fingers work at a slow pace while he devours me.

When he begins doing figure-eight motions, I grip his hair with both of my hands and start riding his mouth. "God, baby. I want your face dripping with my juices." His animalistic growl vibrates over me, becoming my undoing. "Percy! Fuck, I need you inside of me owning this pussy." I scream out as my orgasm ripples through me in waves.

Percy's chuckle is husky as he pulls his fingers out of me and wipes his face. "Every day since you went off to France I'd beat off to the image of you in that tight red dress you wore on your birthday. I'd think of how good you'd feel around me as I come inside of you, doing exactly that, owning your *sweet* pussy."

My chest rapidly rises and falls and under hooded eyes I challenge, "Then what are you waiting for?"

He smirks and covers my body with his. My hands snake up his sides, feeling the corded muscles as he enters me. I hiss at the initial entry but welcome the feeling when my body adjusts. When I relax, Percy slides in further.

"My little goddess, you're better than my dreams." He sighs between suckling and kissing my neck.

"Percy, please." I don't even recognize my own voice. It's husky and strained.

"Please, what?" he asks as he slides his dick back, the head at my entrance. He goes back in slowly and then out again.

"I'm so close," I pant out and beg once more.

He pauses and looks down at me. His eyes darken as they roam over my flushed body and then he pulls out. I groan out in frustration at the emptiness. I almost want to cry at having that wave of pleasure suddenly taken away from me. Going onto my elbows I ask, "What—" But I'm cut off when Percy grabs the back of my thighs and pushes my legs up, causing me to fall back. With my legs up I'm put on full display and holy shit it's hot, being on show for him like this. I revel in the feeling of empowerment it gives me as he stares at me like a piece of art and then he's in me. The different angle gets him in deeper and he rubs perfectly against my g-spot. My nails scratch down his sides and over his hips as I cry out. I close my eyes as I feel myself quickly reaching the peak once again.

"I want you to look at me while you come." Oh, *God.* I swear that is the sexiest thing that has ever spilled from his lips. My eyes snap open, finding his. The intimacy of the act brings me over the edge and I tumble down, coming harder than I did before. My legs jerk and strain against his hands while wave after wave of pleasure makes me convulse around him. Percy groans as he finds his own release shortly after mine. The sound brings on another orgasm, smaller but still there. He feels it and rocks his hips a few more times, riding out the waves with me.

I wake to Percy's fingers skimming up and down my back. I had fallen asleep in his arms, spent and worn out after we went a second round. Fingers spread out through his chest hair, I watch as my hand lifts and falls with his steady breathing. It seems mundane to marvel at this small movement but to me it's a single snow drop that prompts an avalanche. Percy is my *home*, and I want nothing more than to have mornings in his arms and nights with limbs entangled. To be able to share so many life experiences with him is something I look forward to. This little moment marks a new beginning, one where there are no more secrets between us. To me, this type of intimacy is more special than larger memories that others would brag about. I stretch out my body, my breasts pressing against Percy's side. I wince at the ache my movement caused.

"Are you okay?" he asks, his mother hen voice back.

"I'm ..." I don't know why I hesitate, it's nothing to be ashamed about. I take a deep breath before the words rush out. "This was my first time so I'm a little sore. It's nothing a hot bath can't fix." There, I said it. And if he has a problem with it he can shove it, because men don't make a big deal out of this. Only boys do.

"Mmm, shall we?" There's not a hint of disdain, only total lazy ease as he continues to run his hands along my body. The feeling leaves me with shivers that have nothing to do with being naked. It almost tempts me to stay put but I need to get up and clean myself. I shift my body to get out of bed but Percy has other plans. Grabbing my wrist he brings me back to him. The kiss he gives me is intoxicating. I can taste a hint of myself on his tongue. It's ... weirdly a turn-on. I thrust my tongue in farther to get a better taste of the combination that is us.

Not breaking the kiss, he positions me over him. My legs wrap around his torso as he rolls us to the side and positions us vertically. Standing up, our bodies never separate as he carries me to the bathroom.

"Clingy," I mumble between kisses.

"More like a man who can't get enough of his woman." There's that statement again. He bites my lip and I revel in the words, *his woman.*

"Semantics," I say, shrugging my shoulders. He slaps my ass in reply.

"*Ooh,*" I purr. "Clingy and aggressive. If I didn't know better, I'd think you're just the type of man who'd lock me up."

"Now *that* sounds like a wonderfully taunting idea."

I brace myself on his shoulders and lean back to get a good look at his face as I ask, "Why were you never this playful before? Like you were playful, but never more than teasing."

The sparkle in his eyes dims. "Because I'm a coward."

My brow furrows in confusion, and I tilt my head, urging him to explain. He stares back at me for a beat, his eyes searching mine. Finding what he needed to see he then says, "There was a way for you to stay mortal." He waits for my reaction but I remain placid, not giving him any indication of my thoughts. I could've avoided all of this?

With no hint of hostility from me he carries on, more steadily now. "And because I knew there was a chance that you could choose that path, I never got too close. Because if you had chosen that path, then I would have to leave you. And if you were to choose the other path ... Well, I was scared that once you knew everything you would no longer want me in your life. So I drew a line between us, just in case I was no longer in the picture. I'm a coward because I did it for me. So that when it came down to it, I wouldn't be hurt. I hadn't realized until yesterday that it was all in vain. Over the years without me knowing, you kept dusting away at that line until there was nothing left. It was just you standing across from me where that line once was. My heart, already in your palm, waiting to be squashed by a path that didn't involve me. And I would have to live with that as I watched you walk away." He doesn't say it, but I did walk away from him. Even though it was unknowingly that I did something that haunted him since my rebirth, it still tugs at my heart. The pain that I caused him out of my own raging hurt fills me with self-hatred. Instead of pushing away the feeling, I soak it in.

"I don't think that makes you a coward," I say softly, caressing his neck. My hand slides up to cup the side of his face. Percy leans into it and closes his eyes.

"But it does," he whispers. "It's cowardly to not be true to yourself."

"I don't believe that. You were scared of losing me again. Preparing yourself for it to happen does not make you a coward. You being able to let me live my life without you, even if it hurts, is strength."

"I guess." His eyes don't meet mine but instead stare just below my neck. "There are things that I've done ..."

I sternly tug the back of his head, making him look at me. "I love you." There, I said it. But heroics aside, I internally cringe. Nothing like someone proclaiming love after having sex with you for the first time.

The gloom leaves him replaced by a vibrant, ear-splitting grin. "What? I didn't hear you."

I roll my eyes. "Yes, you did."

"I want to hear it again."

"Why?"

"You've never said it before." He's right, I haven't. Not even as kids when we would hug our goodbyes. It's something that I don't say often. I hardly said it to my parents. I believed showing in your actions that you love someone spoke much louder than words but seeing his reaction to hearing it makes me second guess that choice. Maybe I will start saying it more often. But for now, I don't give him the satisfaction of hearing it again, instead I release my legs from around him. This time he doesn't hold on to me as I break away from his arms. I walk over to the small waterfall that I had washed my face with the other day. It was only a day ago, but it feels like a lifetime ago.

"What are you doing?" I can hear the smirk in his voice. That damn smirk.

"Isn't this the bath?"

"No."

I look around dumbfounded. "I don't see anywhere else for bathing." He squints his eyes in mischief as he gets up and walks over. They sparkle like a child's do before they open a gift. But it's not a gift Percy is opening but double doors that I hadn't seen. They're situated between the floor-length mirror and waterfall. I hadn't noticed the doors because ivy cascades down from above them, hiding them from eyes that don't search hard enough. Peering around Percy into the open doors, all I see is rock. He looks over his shoulder and gives me another delicious smirk before walking through the arch of the entrance. He veers left and disappears around the corner.

Chapter Seventeen

"Holy shit," is all I can muster as I'm greeted by an underground hot spring. Steps lead down to a steaming bath that could probably fit twenty people. Next to the steps, clean water flows in at a steady speed and is carried to the far end where it filters out over a ledge. The edges of the pool are smooth and unnatural as if someone had carved it out to be the perfect indent for spring bathing. A few torches line the rock wall. Two at the entrance and one in the back. Their flames are a soft orange and red instead of the pale blue of the torches that light the hall leading to our chamber. They emit a dim light that keeps the waters darkened, the bottom not visible.

A low groan of euphoria rumbles out of me with each achingly good step into the water. The water gliding over my skin feels like a slice of heaven. It's perfectly steamy but not so much that it becomes unbearable with time. My muscles slacken as the warmth and whatever minerals are in the water soak through to my marrow.

I could seriously spend the rest of my days living in this spring.

At the last step, the water only comes to my hips and I'm a bit disappointed. Maybe this experience isn't going to be as heavenly as I thought it would be. I look up to Percy, frowning. He leans down and bites my pouty bottom lip before taking my hand, leading me farther down to where the water is deeper.

Oh, thank god. I was becoming sorely disappointed at the lack of depth and am relieved that this is not some fancy kiddie pool. Although with the way the water feels, I could've totally made it work.

I hum in contentment before giving myself to full relaxation by floating on my back. How good it feels to finally just ... let go. Winter solstice I hadn't truly let go. Once the shadows took over I wasn't really present anymore. And because of that, when the high wore off, I couldn't relax. My mind was still a major wreck, unable to settle. But here—right now—my mind has settled. I've made peace with Percy. I am no longer fighting for my life and to top it off my soul is complete. It's weird to think that only a few days ago I only had half a soul.

There were no more mind games or beating around the bush. I would no longer be kept in the dark. And my daydream of a hot bath with Percy finally comes true. What more could a girl want?

"Come here," Percy says. I realign myself and look over to find him sitting in a makeshift bench carved into the wall. Not knowing what to expect I tread over to him. "Sit," he commands.

I tilt my head in confusion but do what he asks. "Now turn your body and sit cross-legged."

"Okay?" Moving myself to where my back is to him, I bend my legs, criss-cross apple sauce. I wait for whatever is about to happen by mindlessly swishing my hand in and out of the water as it laps around my hips.

His hands clasp my shoulders, and then he begins kneading into them. "Oh, *oooh.*" I groan. "I've actually fantasized about this,"

"Me, naked? I wouldn't doubt it."

I roll my eyes. "Clingy, aggressive and now cocky? You're becoming a walking nightmare." I lean into him as he gently works out a knot in my shoulder and another moan leaves my lips.

"I really doubt I'm any of those things." Percy moves on to the next sore spot. "Well, besides cocky. Because I am most definitely"—his teeth graze my neck, traveling up. Hot air tickles my ear as he whispers—"cocky."

How does Percy manage to make an insult sound so ... appetizing? Tingling shoots down my spine, leaving butterflies on a rampage in my stomach. My toes curl as the coiling sensation between my thighs ramps up. I squirm, trying to ignore what Percy's breath against my skin does to my willing body.

"We'll need to start training."

"Training?" I sound half-asleep. My brain is abuzz as I drift off with each knead of my shoulder.

"We're at war," he simply states.

"War?" I squeak. The statement rocks me out of my lull of relaxation and content horniness. I launch forward only to be quickly pulled back by Percy. He presses my back against his chest and doesn't release his hold on me until he feels me relax. He then continues to rub my shoulders, making his way between the blades and along the spine. Percy said it so calmly like it's no big deal. Like *war* is not something to worry about.

"Yes, war. It has been a very long war. Eons. *Literally.*" Percy's voice drips with disdain. Finally, something to show me that it actually affects him. "It has been stagnant since Amphitrite's death, with bursts every now and then. We are immortal, we can't be killed. The only ones who suffer are the nymphs and other beings." His kneading stops as he lets out a noisy breath. His arms suddenly wrap around me protectively and through that simple act I feel the urgency he feels to keep me close. With a shaky intake of breath he says, "And it will be full-blown war now that you're back."

This confuses me. "Why does it matter if I'm back?"

The hold Percy has on me tightens. "Because the trident has resurfaced." He leaves me with no further explanation, like I have any idea what the significance of that is.

"And? You're holding back." I thought we were past this, keeping secrets.

"As you know the trident is her own being." I nod my head for him to carry on, still not understanding what that has to do with anything. "And ... she is the only thing capable of killing an immortal."

"Oh." Oh shit ... "But that doesn't explain what that has to do with me."

Percy's hold tightens even further, to the point where it's almost suffocating. I feel him looking around, searching. Even though we're still alone he speaks in a low whisper. "Anyone can wield her. Only myself and now you have the knowledge that she only grants her full power to her master. So others may wield her, but only her master can give the killing blow." I can't help but feel the crashing weight of this world once again fall upon me.

"Oh ..." is all I can muster. I'm starting to sound like a broken record. Percy doesn't need to say it. The way the trident sings to my anger—I am her master, and she demands blood.

"Does Hades ..."

"Oceans, no. I trust Hades but only to an extent. It's not common knowledge but a few other immortals knew of the trident's self-awareness. When they came looking for her, I used her to end them. Only a handful of immortals are left and I was never able to figure out who did not care to wield her and who secretly hungered for power." Percy shudders. "The attacks dwindled and became less frequent after Amphitrite's murder. One hasn't happened in decades but that is only because the bond could no longer be scented on me. The trident had disappeared, and with it the need for war. Now, she will be scented again and this time, whoever is behind the bloodshed won't stop. They won't let her slip from their fingers again."

"You're scared."

"Of course I am. The trident is yours as you are hers. It will be obvious that she is bonded to you. Anyone within a thousand-kilometer-radius will be able to smell it. The bond is that strong. If the trident is ever taken from you, the thief will soon realize that they need you for their goal. So yes, I am scared. I'm scared of losing you all over again."

I turn in his arms, cradling his face in my palms. His eyes don't meet mine and I tighten my grip on him, forcing him to look at me. "I will not leave you."

"You don't know that." His eyes are hooded, the agony already claiming him.

I grasp the back of his head, tugging hard. Through closed teeth I hiss, "I. Will. Not. Leave. You." Percy must see the burning rage dancing within me because he only nods his head before giving me a gentle, tentative kiss on the lips. He embraces me once more, nuzzling his face into my neck.

"How did ..." I want to say Amphitrite, but I have to come to terms that in another life I was her. Say it. Accept it. "If I was immortal then how did I die?"

"You weren't immortal. You were a nymph. You had a long life span, but weren't immortal." Percy releases me as he grabs something from behind him. Then his hands are rubbing my scalp, shampoo foaming up. The suds smell of eucalyptus. The combination of the head scratch and aroma is beyond divine, and the sensation leaves me feeling like I'm being sent to another dimension. So much so that I thought I heard him wrong.

"That doesn't make any sense. How am I immortal now?"

"To retain your soul the trident's power had to combine with you. In turn, that power made you immortal. We didn't know for sure that would be the outcome but it was a high probability. At the time, I honestly couldn't have cared less. Just as long as you came back to me."

I am immortal and bonded to the trident. Something that should frighten me, but it no longer does. I have come to terms and accepted that this is my new life. It also eases my mind to know that I have full control over the only thing that can kill me ... and Percy. Blimey. Just the thought of him dying chokes me up.

Percy finishes washing my hair so I use this as an opportunity for some space, to think of what all this entails. I lean my head back to rinse the soap out. Satisfied with the result, I dive into the water. Sinking to the bottom I sit there cross-legged, moving my arms so that I stay down. I hold my breath until stars start dancing behind my eyes. My lungs feel as if they're on fire. I thought maybe breathing wasn't a necessity, being immortal and all. Guess I was wrong. Before I can't hold my lungs any longer an image of Percy swimming down in the ocean comes to mind. He had no air bubble surrounding him. Percy *breathed* the water. Revelation hits. I let go of the breath I had been holding and gulp in water.

I break through to the surface, sputtering and coughing. My eyes bleary, I look to Percy who is still seated where I had left him. He must've washed himself because his own hair is wet. Thick chunks of darkened honey are tousled over his eyebrows. A bead of water drops and falls on his full lips. He turns said lips up into that playful smirk that I once found annoying but now find captivating. "Having fun?"

"How the hell did you breathe underwater?" My voice crackles. The burning remains deep in my throat as it buries itself within my lungs. Percy just looks at me with astonishment. His mouth pops open and close like a fish on dry land.

"Is that what you were doing?" he finally asks.

The pressure of the water against my chest compounds the pain, so I go over to sit on the steps to get out of the water. Percy follows and as he walks up the steps, I can't help but admire him as water slides down his backside. His body is teeming with lean muscle and gleams with droplets of water. He is so perfect that I feel like I'm in a wet dream. Oh gods, don't tell me. Is Hades going to show up and pay homage to my body as well? If I wasn't in so much pain, I would give that coupling some more in-depth thought.

"You could ..." Talking more sends me into a fit of coughs. Talking really hurts. My eyes streaming with tears I start over. "Can't you breathe underwater? I saw you."

There's a clink and then a glass of water in my face. "Drink."

"No, thanks."

Percy sighs. Sitting next to me he says, "It's not regular water."

I raise my eyebrows, eyeing the cup. It looks no different than normal water. "What did you do?"

"I have healing abilities through water. But"—he shrugs—"you said no." He lifts the glass to his lips.

"No, no, no." I reach out for the glass and he lets me take it from his hand.

The water tastes no different, except for an extra thickness to it. It didn't look different, but it feels like I'm swallowing pudding. The cold, unnaturally thick liquid slides down my throat. I would complain about the disgusting feeling if it wasn't for the fact that it immediately makes my pain go away. Lifting up to the top step I lay back on the floor with my arms spread out and knees bent, my feet flat against the second step.

I don't think Percy can help himself. My body is displayed like a meal for him so it's no shock when he starts trailing his fingers in swirls across my thighs all the way to my neck. "To answer your question, yes. I can breathe underwater and so can you."

I snort. "Such bullshit. Clearly, I can not." I wave my hand around, dismissing his statement.

"All immortals can, Amy. It's extremely painful but it can be done." He doesn't explain further.

"I'm listening." I have to remind Percy to give me the details because touching me has clearly distracted him.

"When under duress our bodies are constantly trying to compensate. So we can breathe underwater but it will feel like we're drowning the whole time. We don't die because our body works at a fast enough rate that it takes the oxygen from the water and feeds it into our lungs. It's really a wonder. Same goes if a limb got cut off, our body will eventually regenerate it." I can't even comprehend the pain that Percy went through to get me here. How long was he drowning before we made it to the Underworld? It seemed unnecessary when he made a bubble of air around me, why didn't he do the same for himself?

"Percy?"

"Hmmm?" His distracted reply tells me he's done with talking but I need to know.

"Did the others have to experience that to get here?"

"No, they took a different entrance. It's a more preferable route. It's on one of the islands we were heading to but your condition had worsened." His hand glides down my backside before his touch disappears.

Pouting, I ask, "Why did you stop?"

"As much as I'd enjoy spending the rest of the day being ravished by you, we have lots to work on."

"Meaning?"

"Practice." He gives my butt a smack and then grabs a towel, walking out of the room. I toss my head back down, making a dull *thud* when my forehead hits against the floor. Practice? For what?

Chapter Eighteen

"**F**ocus."

"If you tell me to focus one more time, I'm going to stab you. I *have* been focusing." I really have been and Percy telling me to is not going to make me focus any more than I already am.

"If you were actually focusing then you would have moved the water. Even a little bit."

Seething with frustration, it takes everything in me not to toss the bowl of water at him. I spent the morning in our chamber practicing with the trident. I easily learned that with only a thought the trident will shape itself into any weapon of my choosing. Percy also informs me that within a certain radius the trident will still listen to me, that I don't have to be touching her for her to change into what I wish. But I do need to be touching her for her to end an immortal life. Her thirst for blood still sings to me but it isn't as strong. This morning when I held her, she didn't thrum through my veins demanding a kill like she did during my argument with Percy. She seems to respond strongly to the anger, like she knows it is the emotion most likely to give her blood.

Done with the trident, Percy has me "training." He has it in his head that since I'm now immortal, I have some hidden talent. Specifically, one that has to do with manipulating water. Apparently Amphitrite was on his level when it came to water manipulation, but like I told Percy this whole afternoon: in this life, I was human. Humans don't wield the elements like it's nothing. But he is convinced that I have something because every immortal does, whether it's water like himself or the weather like Zeus. He explains that immortals are tied to this planet, that we are meant to serve and that the earth wouldn't let us exist unless we have something to offer.

I first try water, then fire, air, and then earth. I feel absolutely nothing. None of them bend to my will. The only thing I manage to gain from all of this is a headache. So here we are, with a bowl of water *again* and Percy's annoyingly calm voice. It's beginning to lose its whiskey-like tone and starting to sound like an old monk.

"Reach out your hand and imagine the thousands of atoms crawling out of the bowl. Each one their own being but combined as a whole. Fused together in perfect harmony. Feel the energy flow from you." Percy elongates his speech, trying to make all of my senses think of water. But all it's doing is having me imagine him in an orange robe.

It's not working, clearly.

"Hello, gorgeous!" Alice's cheery voice rings out clear across the field. One moment she's a kilometer away and then the next I'm taken to the ground. She giggles like she's having the most fun of times.

"I just love a good sprint!" she cheerily exclaims.

I lay there flat on my back, stunned. I merely look up at her, blinking slowly. "Whoa."

What just happened? She was like a dart of light as she flashed toward me. I didn't even have time to react besides a flinch to put my hands up. Her inhumane speed also clarifies any questions I have about her being human. Humans most definitely do not move that fast.

"It's the wind, baby," she says in an Austin Powers voice and blows me a kiss before getting off of me.

"She's a mountain nymph, the wind grants them aid." Percy gives a better explanation than Alice's playful reply.

I nod thanks to Percy for the information and then turn to Alice. "Have you come to watch me fail?" My right brow is raised in question.

"As fun as that sounds, I have actually come to rescue you."

"No." Percy's tone is final, causing my hand to twitch toward the bowl. Alice sticks her tongue at him but before they can interact anymore I throw the bowl up in the air.

"Freedom, freedom, freedom," I chant.

Percy admonishes, "You can't be serious. You need to practice."

This is followed by Alice's hushed, "Goblin dick."

I look at her in exasperation over the term that she's still intent on using, and then back at Percy. Coating my eyes and voice in steel, I roll back my shoulders and say, "I *have* been. I need a break." I link arms with Alice and look back to Percy. "You're not my keeper." My eyes meet his, unwavering.

Percy walks up to me, pushing a strand of hair behind my ear. "You're right. I'm just worried. It shouldn't be this long of *nothing* happening."

"Maybe I don't have a connection with any of them." It's a depressing thought that I'm pretty much a crippled immortal, but since I was born human, I'm lucky to even have gotten this far.

"No, I don't think it's that. Maybe it has something to do with your soul needing more time to adjust," he contemplates. I don't think that's it but I don't disagree with him. At this point it would just be a waste of breath. Percy leans in to kiss me goodbye, and as I open myself to him the kiss deepens.

"Blah. I'm right here, guys." Alice gags. Percy doesn't stop kissing me, instead he gives her the finger.

"Classy." She huffs.

I withdraw from the kiss, feeling embarrassed. I tend to forget about the world around me when Percy is involved. He pulls me back, lightly licking the outline of my bottom lip. "Delicious."

"Bastard," Alice says through clenched teeth while tugging me away from him. Bowing to Percy, she says dramatically, "Your majesty."

I give Percy one last look of promise for tonight before I'm giggling, being tugged away. Arm in arm we skip to our next adventure because honestly, it's always an adventure with Alice. There's never a dull moment with her and I really need a break after the mental exhaustion of staring at the elements. I swear, mental training is more tiresome than physically training your muscles.

Alice snags a basket of fruit on our way to the orchard. One of the kitchen wisps gave her a bottle of champagne to take with us. I eyed the bottle in Alice's hand. Her knowing smile gave way to laughter as she promised that it was not ambrosia. When we sit here beneath the rows of bearing pomegranate trees, I cautiously sip from the bottle. For once, Alice is telling the truth.

"I've missed these moments with you," I admit. After Paul's death and then his revival, everything happened in a whirlwind. I no longer have any quality one-on-one with Alice. She's the sister I never had. Her absence has left a hole in my heart. I never knew how much I wanted that bond until I had it, and now I never want to let her go.

Laying on my back I stare up at the canopy of green accented by hues of red and purple. There are wisps a few rows down silently harvesting the ripened fruit. Alice lays next to me, stomach against the ground. She holds herself up with her elbows for easy mobility to feed me. She insists that food tastes best when someone else feeds it to you. I don't mind though, it's nice to be cared for. Her actions make me feel comfortable. That sisterly bond of love that borders on maternal. I know she would lay down her own life to protect mine and I would gladly do the same.

"Me too, babe," she replies before bringing the bunch of grapes to my mouth.

I reach my hand out, twirling it around through the rays of light that break through the canopy of leaves. I marvel at the way dust sparkles in the light and how the shadows an inch over shift along my fingers. "It's weird how it feels exactly like sunlight," I muse. The false sun leaves a faint warmness that soaks into me.

"That would be Persephone's doing. Before she came along, it did not exist. Neither did the plants. The stories say that Hades was a stern ruler who reveled in darkness. What you see during the night hours is what it was like constantly here before Persephone walked into Hades' life. She has him by the balls." She cradles two grapes in the palm of her hands, eyes twinkling in amusement as she continues, "And I believe they are also this size."

She pops them in her mouth. "But I bet these taste better than that old fart."

I snort. "Just how old is he?"

"Hades is one of the oldest. It's believed that he was around when Nyx still walked this earth."

"Nyx? I've never heard of him."

"Her," Alice corrects. She puts another grape in my mouth before carrying on. "No one knows much about her, only that she was darkness incarnate and mother to those born under the shroud of the moon. She is mostly forgotten. Only the oldest remember her."

"That's sad."

Alice shrugs. "With time all are forgotten."

I look at her. "Humans have forgotten all of you."

"That is true, but that is our doing."

"How so?"

Alice contemplates her next words and then says, "Humans fear what they cannot control. We tried to get along. We did, for a short period. We were worshiped, but it was out of fear, not love. A war broke out eventually between us and the humans. Their fear was too strong. In the end they had scouted where our nurseries were, all nymphs alike. Simultaneously, they slaughtered our young. Not one human showed mercy. So we returned the favor and then vanished, leaving behind destroyed coliseums and great cities buried. I laughed as I watched Pompeii turn to ruin." And then, eyes glazed in the memory, Alice laughs. The maniacal sound of it raises the hairs on my arms. In that split second as Alice loses herself to the memory I get a glimpse of a cold-hearted monster.

The sweet grape turns sour in my mouth as Alice shows no trace of remorse for the human children murdered. To go that far, simply for revenge? Hate is such an ugly thing. Let it drive you and it consumes you, always hungry for more. I can't even imagine the devastation. I know the pain of losing someone you love but for innocents to be murdered solely for existing? Their lives had just begun. So many joys that they will never get to experience that got wiped out all because they were in the wrong place at the wrong time. Caught in the middle of a war that they had no part in. I weep for them and for the nymphs who were also caught in the crossfire.

"Why are you crying?"

My laugh is bitter as I wipe away my tears. "Percy said war will start again. Many will die, and all for what?"

"The only thing that would spark this war again is knowledge of the trident."

"Yes, and now it is in my possession."

At that admission, Alice goes completely still. I realize my mistake, no one is supposed to know. Her nostrils flare as she finally sniffs the bond. Her gaze slowly meets mine. Her head tilts as if listening, her eyes becoming distant as a breeze plays with her hair, curling around her chin.

"Where is it, Amy?" I strain to hear her low whisper.

"It's in my room." I'm confused by her question. Why does it matter? It makes sense why she'd have an interest, everyone wants to know about it and why lie when the cat is already out of the bag? My bad for being careless with that information, but if you're going to dig your own grave, at least make it deep enough.

The fog leaves her eyes. Before I have time to react she's up and running, already out of my eyesight. The direction of her departure is, of course, the same as my chambers. I shout to the nearby wisps to get help before I run after her. I trip over the hem of my toga and fall to the ground.

Shit. Shit. Shit.

I want to rip this dress off of me but instead I pull it up to my hips. As I sprint to my room, thoughts of Alice being a spy swirls around in my head. This can't be happening, not Alice. God, I hope this is some sort of misunderstanding.

Halfway there, Percy and Hades are by my side. I don't give them time to ask questions. I only fill them in on my conversation with Alice, never stopping my sprint. Lungs burning, we reach my open door. Hades enters first. There's grunting and then Percy enters, followed by me. The room is a mess. Drawers thrown open, bedding tossed apart. Even the mattress is thrown against a wall. Broken glass from the vase that was on top of the dresser covers the floor. In the center of all the chaos is Hades astride Alice, with her face pressed against the glass shards. Blood trickles from her swollen cheek.

"You know how I love this position, darling, but you're misunderstanding the situation." Only Alice could make light of her current predicament.

Hades doesn't loosen his grip on Alice as he nods to Percy and I. "Go get it."

Hands shaking, I walk to the bathroom. It's just as much of a disaster as the bedroom. How Alice had enough time to do all of this is beyond me. I search for the box hidden behind a stone next to the running water. Gone. The box with the trident hidden inside it is gone. I frantically search the surrounding area, thinking maybe it fell into the water. But all of my searching is in vain.

I storm into the room. Boiling with betrayal. "She has it."

Hades feels up Alice, searching for the trident. "Move your fingers a little to the left, big boy," Alice says as she wiggles her bosom.

Hades chuckles but it doesn't reach his eyes. The trident not found on her, he gets up and pours himself a glass of whiskey. He knocks it back before saying, "Explain yourself."

Before talking Alice brushes the debris off and holds her hand out to Hades, expectantly. Hades pours more into his glass, filling it to the brim before placing it in Alice's waiting hand. She sighs as she smells the amber liquid. She sips it slowly, enjoying the flavor on her tongue. I stand next to Percy, confused at the ease Hades is now displaying. Percy is crouched, blocking the door and ready to lunge at Alice if she tries to escape.

"I'm hurt that you have so little trust in me," Alice muses, her voice more of a thought to be considered than true feelings of hurt.

"What else am I supposed to think when you run here straight after what I told you?" My mood has gone from angry to incredulous in a matter of seconds.

"Babe ..."

"Carry on, Alice," Hades drawls, interrupting her. "We don't have all day. The trident is neither here nor on you. So please, some enlightenment."

Alice looks to me and no one else as she says, "When we were talking the wind whispered to me of someone nearby who was listening to our conversation. I asked you where it was because I wanted to flush him out but I was too late. He had used a passage stone before I was able to get to him." Her eyes plead for me to believe her.

I release my breath in relief. "I believe you." Alice visibly relaxes at my words. I pull the string that calls for a servant and ask for a cloth, ointment and a bowl of clean water. A moment later I'm leaning over Alice as I clean her wounds.

"How did a passage stone come through the barrier?" Percy questions Hades, no longer guarding the door.

Hades rubs his chin, pondering before answering, "That is a very good question. Absolutely nothing has gotten past Cerberus, so for this to happen ... a good question, indeed."

"What's a passage stone?" I chime in.

"Think of it as a portal, but unlike a portal it can only be used once and can take you anywhere. Portals need a beacon on the other end to guide it. For passage stones the guide is your mind. Give the stone a clear picture of your destination and within a blink"—Percy snaps his fingers—"you're there." His explanation has me reeling in another question.

"How do we get the trident back when we don't even know who took it?" Alice winces. I wasn't paying attention to her due to my conversation and cleaned an abrasion a little too aggressively.

"Sorry," I mouth. She sticks her tongue out as an acceptance.

"Alice, is it wrong of me to assume that the spy you saw was a sylph?"

Alice turns to Hades. "I only saw the back of him but only a sylph can manipulate air faster than I can."

"Hmm." Hades nods. "He has finally shown his hand. Poseidon, you are not going to like what I'm about to suggest."

"I've already come to the same conclusion, brother."

"Have you? Interesting." Hades' middle finger traces the top of the decanter. "There is a chance of it failing and him realizing that he needs her for the trident."

"I will not allow that. Wait, how do you know he'll need her for the trident? Who told you?" Percy looks to me as if that knowledge had come from me. I did slip with Alice but I hadn't told her that bit of information. But now the most important key to the trident was being shared in front of her, straight out of their mouths. If anything, I should be the one glowering at him.

"Who do you think forged her?" Hades says in a bored tone, eyebrows raised.

"I ... had no idea. And you never wanted her for yourself?"

Hades ignores the question. Instead, he removes the lid that he had been fumbling with. I watch as he brings the decanter to his full lips. Eyes closed, he drinks the rest of the contents, slowly and deliberately. It is beyond me how he's drinking it like water instead of wincing from the burn.

With the last drop gone Hades says, "Shall I let Hermes know of his daughter's whereabouts or should we just pop in and say hi?"

This discussion has been all over the place. I wonder who and what they're talking about. I've just been standing here, finished cleaning Alice's cuts, watching the two of them converse and feeling a little put out.

Percy quickly glances at me then back to Hades. "She doesn't know ... that Hermes is her father."

Me. That last bit is definitely about me. That glance says it all. I step between them, waving my hand out in a curt wave. "Hello, I'm here."

Hades' brow raises. "Hello." His drink has made his voice smoother, and a quick image of his mouth on me while Percy holds me open and exposed to him plays through my mind. I mentally wave away the horny fog these two men cast over me. Now is seriously not the time to be fantasizing.

"I'm right here. You're literally having a conversation about me without me. Stop with all this vague BS. I'm not a child to be coddled, *explain*."

"Yaaas, queen," Alice all but worships. Everyone ignores her. Now is not the time to give her theatrics acknowledgment.

It's Percy that answers. Running his fingers through his hair he takes a deep breath, agitation oozing from every pore. "Sylphs are loyal to Zeus. It's safe to say he's the one who's behind all of this. Things have been strained with Zeus since we gave his two daughters protection from him, but we had no idea he was after the trident until now. Well, at one point we assumed, but he later proved us wrong."

Percy's eyes find mine. Not breaking contact, he continues, "It will not take long before he realizes that trident only listens to you. You ... you will essentially be bait to lure him to us to get the trident back."

I gulp. I never wanted to meet Zeus. The man—no not even a man—you're no longer a man after doing such appalling things ... My blood boils at the thought of what he did to Clio. How many nights of hers are haunted by her friends' screams? The way he tore them apart as he had his daughter held down and forced her to watch was inhuman. I can't even comprehend, and can only imagine what that sort of sorrow feels like.

Jaw tightening, I say, "I'll do it."

Percy must see the fear in my eyes turning to hot, steely anger because he doesn't question my quick decision. Instead, his mouth opens to say something, but then closes.

"Spit it out, Percy." My foot taps impatiently.

"Your father is also Hermes."

And, there it is. My tapping halts. I had gathered that but also thought I had heard him wrong. "What?"

"It's true. We had to make sure your soul ..."

"No, no, no. Stop." I wave my hands at him. "I don't want to hear this from you. Why am I even surprised at this point?"

I think of my mother's favorite cologne that my father would wear. The laughter bubbles out of me verging on hysteria. My father, Hermes. My father, a freaking god. I can't stop laughing. I'm having a hard time dealing with that fact, but I should have known after everything that has happened. He never aged, and neither did the house staff. They must've been some sort of mythical creatures as well. I should've been able to piece it all together, but he never crossed my mind. Not even once. My laughter cuts off. How could I not have thought about him? Guilt rids my body, coming at me like a tidal wave and I fold in on myself. Percy embraces me while Hades and Alice discreetly leave the room.

"How could I forget about him?"

"Is that what you're upset about? Not that he's Hermes?"

"Blimey, no. I'm actually happy. That means he won't die. How could I bear losing another parent? I didn't think I'd miss him so much when I left but the phone calls were not good enough. The agony it would be to never see him again ..." Tears sting my eyes. "I miss him and yet I forgot about him. What kind of daughter does that?"

Percy's gentle circles along my back do little to soothe me, but his words do. "You had a life-altering experience. Your dad will forgive you for not being at the forefront of your mind. Nothing you do could ever change the love he has for you."

"You think so?" I look to him, waiting for an honest answer.

"I know so. You have no idea the lectures he would give me for hanging out with you." He rolls his eyes in annoyance at the memory.

"I had no idea you two conversed that often. I thought my recent birthday was the only time." And my father knew that I was always out hanging with Percy?

Percy laughs out a bark. "If only. Who knew fatherhood would turn him into such a pain in the ass. There was a time when he was nothing but jokes, but when he became a father ..." His voice lowers, trying to mimic my father's. "*Don't you dare touch her. This wasn't part of the deal. She's my baby. I will wring your neck and hang you upside down if you touch her.*" His voice reverts back to normal. "And yada, yada, yada. He was always going on about the *touching.*" Another eye roll. "What a headache fatherhood made him."

I smile into Percy's chest. The thought of my father being so protective warms my heart. "I miss him."

"I know." Percy kisses the top of my head. "You'll get to see him soon."

I lean back to look at him. "How soon is soon?"

"I believe we leave in a few hours. Time is of the essence."

My heart skips a beat. Soon.

Chapter Nineteen

I feel little remorse for the article of clothing pooled at my feet. I don't know how everyone else can go gallivanting around all the time in a toga, but I surely can't. It's such an impractical piece of clothing.

I happily don black leggings with a matching cotton shirt that a wisp brings shortly after Hades and Alice leave. As I'm fastening the ankle-length boots, Percy catches my eye as he walks past wearing something similar. Our attire is meant to give us easy movement if trouble finds us along our way to my father's villa. Although I really hope that won't be the case, I don't know if I can mentally handle anything more thrown my way. I know as soon as we leave the Underworld though, that this perfect bubble Percy and I have created will be popped.

Percy smirks at my ogling of how he looks in his fitted shirt. "I know, I look good in black."

"You're okay-looking." A half truth. He looks absolutely decadent with his sun-kissed skin against black. He's just so damn cocky that I refuse to admit it fully. Like I said, half truth.

"My heart." With his hand on his chest he feigns being insulted.

I chuckle. "Your heart is just fine."

"Do you need help?" Percy eyes me and then the boots.

"No."

"Are you sure?"

"I'm. Fine," I grind out. These boots are really starting to make me mad. They won't get as tight as I want them. Last thing I need is to be tripping over myself during a fight because they are too loose. A slew of curses leave my mouth, putting any sailor to shame.

"Did I ever tell you how beautiful you are when dirty things come out of your mouth?"

"What?" I sit back, stunned. That was unexpected.

Percy uses my moment of shock to finish my boots for me. Hand behind my knee his thumb rubs in a circular motion. Glass crunches under his feet as he shifts his hip, positioning himself at a different angle. He wraps his arms around my waist and holds me as the weight of him melts into me. I lean down and curl my body inward around him with my cheek resting against the back of his head. We stay like this, breathing each other in. And I swear as we enjoy this small moment of peace together, our heartbeats align.

"Why don't you call me Dove anymore?"

Percy's breathing stills before resuming. "That was random."

"I was just thinking about how when I used to get mad you would call me Dove to calm me down but ever since I became whole, you haven't." Percy stays quiet so I carry on. "I know it's what you used to call Amphitrite."

His head whips back as his hands splay out back on my knees. "Your memories came back?" Why does he seem so eager and invested in my past memories? Could it be that he possibly knew Amphitrite was a spy? That's all I know, though, because when I was in that memory she never thought hard enough about who their enemy was. If my memories ever did come back, I wonder if I would be able to handle that influx of extra memories and if I'd be able to look at Percy the same way. Amphitrite had hated him for a reason, but why?

I wait for a heartbeat before replying. "No ... I was just given her last memory, and in it you called her Dove."

The excitement leaves his eyes before he gives a curt nod. "Yes, I did call her that."

"And?"

Eyes finding mine, he says, "And that is why I don't anymore. I realized too late that even though your soul is the same you are two different people. Different personalities. The pet name stuck but after your completion it felt wrong to keep calling you that."

"Hmm."

"Am I wrong? I can if you want me to. D—"

I shoot my hand up to stop him. "No. You're correct. The thought of you using that endearment now makes my skin crawl. You're right in thinking not to use it. I was just curious."

Percy leans his face into my palm, nuzzling it. "I'm sorry."

"I know." I knew that he was sorry. I could see his true feelings playing out in his eyes. I kiss him then. "I'm yours, Percy." I whisper against his lips.

"I love you," he whispers back before deepening the kiss. I smile against him. My stomach flutters over that one word and I begin to dream of our peaceful days spent together as we get lost in eachother.

Chapter Twenty

I should've expected nothing less from the Underworld, but standing atop a cliff that overlooks the realm in its entirety, I am still amazed. If I ever got the chance, it would take me years to explore every inch of this domain, maybe even centuries. The sheer magnitude of it takes your breath away and leaves you in complete wonder. I don't think anything else I'll ever experience can compare to what the Underworld has to offer.

The dense foliage stretches as far as the eye can see, turning into fields of rolling hills. Off in the far distance I can spot the orchard where I spent the afternoon with Alice. It's nothing but a dot, a grain of sand that can be blotted out and engulfed by my pinky. The distance of it all is so incomprehensible that it's dizzying.

To the west, north and east of me are rivers that flow through the landscape. Each one finding their way to the very cliff that I stand upon, roaring over the side into an endless lake. It appears that the Underworld stretches out underneath the crust of the Earth, but if that is true then I'm sure there would be more entrances than just the few I'm aware of. Something tells me that in actuality the Underworld does not cover the length of Earth but is instead similar to the backpack Clio had on the boat that she pulled my jian out of. Where somehow, with magic that I do not yet comprehend, you can fit things into a space that is much too small to contain it.

Internally saying goodbye to the landscape, I turn to continue our journey and follow Thalia, Clio, Alice, Hades, and Percy down the steep steps that are carved into the side of the cliff. The steps are slick from the spray of the nearby waterfalls that cascade over the cliff. The force of the falls is so fierce that their roar is deafening.

We traverse the steps in silence, focusing intently on our every movement. One wrong move and I would go tumbling down, taking along everyone in front of me. For most of us it would be painful, but we would survive. But Alice, who is not immortal, would most likely die. I press my side flush against the wall and cling tightly to the rope that acts as a safety net. It's worn out, corroded from the water, and I doubt that it would hold if I did end up falling. I'm sure that if I tugged on it just a little harder the beaten down fibers would rip apart as easily as paper. So with every ounce of willpower that I have, I make sure that each step down is precise and steady. I will my frazzled nerves to be calm and to not display the bundled up anxiety over the long fall that would ensue with the wrong footwork.

It was decided that we would all go to my father's villa. That would be our base while we figure out Zeus' routines, where he can "stumble" across me. It's a plan Percy loathes and one that I myself am not too keen on either, but it's the fastest way to achieve our goal without spilling too much blood. We have no idea where Zeus is keeping the trident, so it's not like we can waltz into his home and find it hanging over his mantel. The trident is the key to this war and Zeus will more than likely have it hidden well.

With my limited options laid out before me, it was then explained to me what will most likely occur under Zeus' reign. He will want to use me, to control me, since I'm the only one able to give the killing blow. The plan is to allow him to capture me, then I will willingly follow his commands only to kill him myself once I get the chance. The plan is risky and very dangerous. Zeus could torture me into submission if I'm not convincing enough, or merely due to him being bored. A shiver of fear runs through me that shakes me to my core. The thought of willingly going into the lion's den is terrifying, but it's a risk I'm willing to take. For everything that Zeus has done and what he will continue to do, he needs to be killed. And a small amount of suffering on my part, if that's what it takes, will be worth it.

By the time we arrive at the bottom, my legs are shaking from the stress and it takes everything in me not to crumble to the pebbled ground. I may have been able to survive a fall but the thought of my body hitting the jagged rocks that line the cliff's wall has me sweating with fear. No one else seems to be phased by it though, as their composed bodies follow Hades down the shore.

Percy's hand brushes the back of my arm, and leaning into me he grumbles, "I hate those stairs." I stare up at him, one eyebrow raised in doubt.

His eyebrows mimic my own. "No, seriously. I fell once."

A smile tugs at my lips. "You did not."

"Hades! Remember that time I fell down the stairs?" Percy calls, his chin raised, waiting for an answer.

A boom of a laugh comes out of Hades. It's a laugh that leaves me surprised. I never pegged Hades for boisterous. He calls over his shoulder, a gleam of pure amusement in his eyes. "He made a bet on who could reach the bottom first. Suffice to say, Poseidon won that bet." Another laugh comes from Hades. "The idiot."

"What was the reward?" Clio asks, not at all surprised by Percy's actions, like they were a daily occurrence that didn't even need to be acknowledged.

Hades rubs his chin. "I don't quite remember."

"It was Cerberus," Percy answered.

"Ah, yes. If I recall it hadn't even been a full day before you no longer wanted him."

I look at Percy, confused. "Who's Cerberus?"

"He's the guard to the entrance of the Underworld. He's a three-headed dog. Huge fella."

Oh, a three-headed dog sounds ... grotesque. "Is he so bad that you couldn't handle him for a day?"

"Yes." Percy shudders. "He slobbers an insane amount."

"You're scared of slobber?"

"Cerberus' saliva is acidic."

Oh ... I blanch. "Hades is right, you are an idiot." The whole group breaks out in fits of laughter. Each one trading off insults aimed at Percy. I can't help but laugh along with them and make my own jibes at him. He makes it too easy to tease him. Like a champ, Percy shrugs, a smile tugging at the corner of his lips at each teasing comment towards his intelligence until he's finally beaming. He's not at all abashed by his younger self.

Down here is vastly different from what lies over the cliff. It's cold and drab. Exactly what one would expect of the Underworld. None of Persephone's touch lies down here. No sweet-smelling flowers or lush, green moss, just the bleak tones of gray and the black of the pebbles that make up the shore. Thick fog covers the lake, its waters a constant lap against the shore. I wonder how far it goes, so I voice my question.

It's Hades who answers me. "It's actually a river that wraps around the entirety of my domain. Her name is Styx. She was once her own being, but certain circumstances led her into a deep sleep which turned her into a river. How wide she is, no one knows. Not even me. She tends to change her width often, so maybe she's not as asleep as we assume."

Hades walks onto a dock that I swear wasn't there a moment ago. A hooded figure stands on a boat, his face and body blanketed by cloth. "Evening, Charon," Hades says before stepping onto the boat and taking a seat. The boat barely wobbles at the intrusion.

The figure, Charon, only nods his head in acknowledgement. Alice, Thalia and Clio follow suit, each finding their seat within the boat. When it is my turn the figure blocks me from boarding with his oar. Percy's grip on my arm tightens as the figure towers over me. Bloody hell, he is tall. He has to be two of me combined. His skeletal hand holding the oar wraps tightly around it as he leans down to be eye level with me. His topaz eyes shine through the little holes of the cloth. I feel a brush of familiarity as his eyes bore into mine.

I hold still as he leans in closer. I don't know what is happening, but I dare not move. I feel like a mouse trapped in a corner with Charon being the cat. Percy goes to jerk me away but I slip out of his hold. Never breaking eye contact with Charon, my hand jerks out to command Percy to stop. Whatever is happening, I fear there will be consequences if I don't hold my ground.

The figure sniffs the air around me. There's pressure against my head and then a gravelly voice speaks.

"*Mother.*" The voice has a slight echo as it speaks in my mind.

I instinctively find the thread that connects us and reply, "*I am not your mother.*"

"*You smell like Mother.*"

"*I am Amethyst, Queen of the Sea and Keeper of the Trident. I am all those things but I am not your mother.*" I say my titles so easily, and with that I realize not only is it true but I accept those titles. *I am* Queen of the Sea and I will show my subjects only loyalty and devotion because isn't this what I've always wanted? To serve the ocean? Maybe never in this way, but this is even better. As an immortal queen I can do so much more than I ever could as a human.

The figure tilts his head before slinking back into the boat. "*You're right. Mother has been dead for a long, long time.*" He lets out a heavy sigh before breaking the link that connects us. I wait a moment before entering the boat and find an open space next to Alice.

"What was that all about?" she whispers.

"I don't know." An odd sensation tickles the back of my brain like I'm forgetting something. It's right there, attainable but out of reach no matter how hard I try to grasp it.

I turn behind me to look at Hades. He raises his brow, looking at me with a bored expression. "Yes?"

I open my mouth to ask him about my conversation with Charon but then close it.

"Good choice," he says. I look at him, questioning. Now I really want to ask him, but refrain. Something in the way his jaw tightens tells me to keep silent.

As Percy takes his seat next to Hades, the boat starts gliding through the water. Charon is at the head, rowing slowly. We travel at an insanely slow speed; it makes me wonder if we'll ever reach the other side, especially since it's nowhere in sight. Even if we were close to the shore, I would have no idea because the fog is that thick.

Thalia and Clio's heads are pressed together as they speak in quiet conversation. Alice is busy sharpening her twin blades, so I look out at the fog, trying to see through it. Time passes and the thick whiteness of it has given me a headache, so I turn my attention back to Hades.

"Why does he row so slowly?" I whisper the question. Everyone is keeping quiet throughout this journey so I figure it must be for a reason.

Hades looks at me, slowly blinking his light brown eyes. With each blink the gold specks in them move around. Before my interruption he was having a conversation with Percy. I wanted to wait until they were finished, but they had been talking for so long about the players in this game of chess called war. My question would go unanswered if I waited any longer, and I was very curious. Scratch that, I was very bored and rightly so. My jian between my shoulder blades was already sharpened, sharpening it anymore would be pointless. I was growing impatient. I needed a reprieve, so I interrupted their conversation, not caring in the least about being impolite.

"He does it so as not to wake the dead," he says and then turns back to Percy.

Hades opens his mouth to say something to Percy, but before he can speak the words I ask, "The dead?"

At a painstakingly slow pace, Hades turns his attention back to me. Irritation in his eyes, he tilts his head and then jerks it outward, encouraging me to look into the water. I look over into the water blanketed in fog. As if the fog senses what I wanted, it parts so that I can see what it hides. It takes everything in me not to let out a shout. Instead, I opt for a slight intake of breath. We are surrounded by what could possibly be hundreds of ghosts. All of them are white as fresh bone, their bodies elongated unnaturally as they drift with the current. Granting me only a glimpse, the fog closes once more over the water.

"Why?" It's all I can think to ask as my mind tries to catch up with what I just witnessed.

"They are simply the souls who carried too much hate in them to ever be rebirthed."

"That's sad."

Hades' voice is stern, as one would use to reprimand a child. "When a soul filled with hate is reborn, they go out into the world gaining more hate from life's experiences. That amount of hate in a soul morphs them into something so foul that the corruption of their soul leaks out, turning them into vrykolakas." He leans in closer. "Before you ask, vrykolakas are what is left of a human who no longer knows who they are. All they know is their hunger. They prey on anything, tearing their bodies apart to get to the liver. So, my dear *queen,*" Hades spits the title as an insult. "Before you look at me with ignorant disgust in your eyes, do not feel sorry for the dead, for they are the ones who allowed their hate to control their lives, earning them a place in this river."

The hairs on the back of my neck stand at attention as Hades' eyes harden. The hold he has on me leaves me immobilized. I want to give a witty retort, but my mouth won't obey. My lips remain sealed, no matter how hard I strain to open them. It feels like my lips are cemented closed.

A growl erupts from Percy. "Back down, Hades. She didn't know."

Whatever hold Hades has on me disappears as he moves his focus to Percy. "Precisely my point. To judge without even knowing the full picture is foolish."

My face reddens at that. He's right, but he's wrong about what I was thinking. It's sad that one can hold so much hate, not sad that they're stuck there never to experience life again.

"Ass," I mutter before turning back around. There's static at my back that quickly evaporates when Percy gives another warning growl. I resist the urge to rub the area where I felt the static, it would only give Hades satisfaction that he unnerved me.

Alice lets out a low whistle. "Those are some big balls, babe"

"Big indeed," Thalia says under her breath. So low I almost didn't hear it. Clio nods her head in agreement.

My head held high and my back straight, I look ahead to show how little Hades' words affect me. They did affect me, though. It is shameful that he would think that's what I thought. How terribly he must view me if he automatically concludes my worldview is that small. I want to correct him but when his words turned cold, I held back. Like a wounded animal, I bared my teeth instead of simply saying sorry. Maybe it was my stupid pride stopping me but I didn't care.

The rest of the way is spent in utter silence. Everyone senses the boiling tension between Hades and me. None dare to interrupt the inferno rolling off of us in thick waves for fear that one of us might burn them instead.

Hours seem to tick by until finally the fog breaks, showing a dock similar to the one we boarded from. My relief is short-lived though, because many of the dead aimlessly walk the shore. Back and forth, back and forth. It's zombie-like, the way they move. Dead and yet, undead. They have a more gaunt look to them than the servant ghosts I saw catering to Hades' and Persephone's whims. Apparently the more fresh from life you are, the less hollow you look. Their clothes vary in style, but one thing remained the same: they look tired, as if once their eyes closed they would sleep for eternity.

As the boat docks we clamor out one by one. Not waiting for us to completely exit, the ghosts form a line to the dock, each eager for a chance to get on the boat. I step aside, not wanting to walk through them. The last ghost I stepped through is still fresh in my mind and I do not want that skin-crawling icy feeling again.

I watch the line of ghosts, wondering how hundreds of them will all fit on such a small boat. Instead of going in the boat like I thought would be the case, each ghost contorts into a wisp of light and gets sucked into Charon's oar. One by one at a speed I can't keep up with, the ghosts disappear into the oar. The oar doesn't change in size but I do notice tick marks that weren't there a second ago covering it from tip to base. My guess is the marks are the number of new souls being brought over to the Underworld. Poor Charon must get lonely with no one to ever interact with.

Once the shore is devoid of all ghosts, Charon carries on making his way back across the river at a snail-like pace. I watch him disappear into the fog. A sense of melancholy tugs at me when I can no longer see him. The feeling is peculiar, but I quickly brush it aside.

Percy's presence warms up my side, that burning feeling there once again. This is the first time I've felt it since the original shock of our hands touching, and I wonder why that is. When we're alone I'll have to ask him about it, but right now I have questions for Hades.

My fingers lace with Percy's. "I need to speak with Hades, alone."

His eyebrows furrow but he nods his head. "Okay. I'll hold the girls back. You go on."

"Thank you." I kiss him on the cheek before running off to catch up with Hades, who is already near the entryway of the cave. At Percy's whistle the girls fall back, giving Hades and I space.

Hades raises his brows but says nothing. We stand there for a moment while I try to set my pride aside. "I'm sorry." I say the two words slowly instead of huffing them out so that he knows I mean them.

He raises his eyebrows even further. Geez, just how big is his forehead? I want to ask him but I stop myself before the question flies. *No, no,* I chide, *now is not the time for jokes.*

My fists curl in determination. "I'm sorry for earlier. It was a misunderstanding. I was not judging you—" Hades lips tighten. "Okay maybe I was judging a little bit at first, but then I quickly understood and I agreed with it. I am young but I've seen what hate can do to people. I can't even imagine what kind of atrocity would walk the world if that hate were to be magnified in the next life."

Hades eyes me like he's seeing me in a new light, and then holds out his arm and says, "Walk with me."

I blink before taking his arm. I swear Hades has got to be the moodiest person I've ever met. One second he's hot and then the next he's cold. His moods are like a summer storm, you never know when the skies will break and rain down on you.

"Your apology is accepted." He takes a deep breath. "I also have to apologize. My domain and how I rule can be a touchy subject. I have been judged quite harshly. It has never bothered me but it did with you. I like you. You are more yourself this time around."

"I'm glad you like me because I actually like you too."

He squeezes my arm. "That is good to hear."

The pebbled ground turns to sand as we near the rays of sun shining into the entrance. "I actually have a question about Charon."

"Ah yes, he's not one for speech but I should've expected he'd be intrigued by you."

"He said I smelled like his mother. I was thinking maybe the trident being her own being, is it possible that she is his mother? We're connected, so I figured maybe that's what he was smelling."

"Hmm." He looks ahead, thinking.

I ramble on. "I mean I know it sounds stupid, but it's the only thing I could think of that makes sense to me."

"Amethyst, it is no coincidence that the trident found its way to you. Poseidon was never meant to be her keeper."

"What do you—" blood splatters across the side of my face, burning my right eye as it soaks into my socket. A curdling scream of shock erupts from me as I watch Hades' head tumble to the ground. Hades' body pulls me down with him as the rest of him follows suit. His arm still holding me tightly, I land on top of his warm corpse. To my horror, blood gushes out of his severed neck. The sound of the liquid sloshing onto the sand makes me want to vomit.

A roar of laughter vaguely distracts me from Hades' pumping blood. I look up at the noise. A man with bleached hair and bronze skin stands off to the side, twirling a metal chain with a scythe-like sword attached to it. My brain doesn't seem to compute that I need to get up and move.

"Feels so good to finally behead that fucker!" The man's voice is a rumble and I swear it crackles with thunder.

My gaze flickers to his weapon. Around and around it goes. The buzzing in my ears grows louder, but even I barely notice that. Shock. That's what I'm in. The signs are all there and I can think clearly enough to know I should move, but I can't. My brain seems to be detached from my body. The only thing my legs are capable of doing right now is shaking with tremors as what just happens plays before my mind on repeat. Hades was there, talking to me.

Alive. And now he's not. The white sand around us turns a reddish brown as it soaks up the blood. So, so much blood. Once the blood stops pumping would this whole alcove be drenched in Hades' blood?

The man's smile broadens, finding enjoyment at the state I'm in. "Have you seen my daughters?"

I stare at him, still unable to move. My mind cycles through a thousand thoughts at once and yet here I am. *Move, damnit.*

"No? Well that's a pity."

Is it though? His expression says otherwise as he swings his weapon around, his arms making a giant arc. I faintly raise my arms as he brings the weapon down. There's a clash of metal as the chain that was meant for me wraps around Clio's sword.

"Get yourself together!" Thalia yells as she runs out of the cave.

"Ah, there you are. I've been looking for my lovely daughters." His smile turns feline. Clio frees her sword from the chain. Pulling a gun from her holster strapped to her thigh she shoots it at the man I'm vaguely realizing is Zeus.

He ducks behind a rock and his voice echoes around it. "Now that wasn't very nice." Blinded by revenge, Clio takes off around the bend of rocks. Not at all considering the danger of facing Zeus one on one.

"Clio, wait!" Thalia tries to chase after Clio but doesn't get very far as the beach and sky darken with harpies.

"My love, get up." Percy's voice breaks my stupor. His hands are firm as he tries to release my hold on Hades. I was still *gripping* him.

"It's okay, breathe. Yes, just like that." Percy's voice is soft and tender. I think how alien his voice is against the gory scene. I choke on the laugh I try to squash down.

"He's dead." I look down at his body. *Oh god,* so much blood. His neck is still pumping out blood, but it has slowed down. My lungs begin to burn. No matter how many gulps of air I take I just can't *breathe.*

"Shit. Alice, stay with her."

His presence is replaced by Alice's as he takes off. My eyes dart everywhere and yet I can't see. All I see is Hades' head toppling down, hitting the ground with a hard thud. I don't understand how this is happening. Immortals can't die, and yet there Hades is, his eyes blankly staring back at me. Just like the ghosts of his realm with their dead fish eyes. The light within them gone, never to return again. I claw at my throat as the burning worsens.

"Damnit, Amy!" Alice's hands hold mine down. I don't fight her as she climbs on top of me. She presses her cheek against mine. "Listen to my breath. Breathe in ... out ... in ... out. Yes, there you go. That's it. You're doing good. You're safe."

"But Hades—"

"Don't you think about Hades. You just focus on your breathing. In ... out ... in ... out. Yes, just like that. Are you good?"

There's only a faint ache left in my lungs from the burning but my breathing has steadily come back to normal. I nod my head yes.

"Good. I'm going to help our pals with the harpies. If you feel like joining, then be my guest. If not, none of us will hold it against you. If you do decide to stay put, *do not* look at Hades."

I gulp as Alice gets up. She gives me one last look before running off to help Thalia and Percy. A scream of rage comes from Alice as she slices through harpies. One by one, they are felled by her sword. I keep my eyes pinned to them and not the lifeless body of Hades at my feet.

There are so many harpies. Too many. Their talons and beaks are still as sharp as I remember. Their feathers remind me of a falcon's, in that they are regal. The way they hold themselves as they try to rip my friends to shreds is full of pride. Their chests are puffed out as if their opponents are a waste of their time. If they weren't trying to kill my friends, I would probably be admiring them. But they are trying to kill them. Some of them had come very close to accomplishing just that. I can't sit here any longer in my pathetic shock, I need to help them. If Hades can die, then so can they.

Unsheathing my jian, I walk around Hades, avoiding looking down. Resolve and fury wraps around me as my sword cuts off the foot of a harpie that was meant for Thalia. Its shriek of pain gurgles as my next swing slices its belly open. Its guts spill out and the bird falls to the ground, twitching and then stilling.

I guard Thalia's back while she does the same for me, allowing us to focus on what is in front of us. An endless swarm of harpies descends upon us, blotting out any space for movement. There's so many of them that the evening sky looks more like night.

"Why are there so many of these bird brains?" I yell to Thalia as my jian severs a wing, hoping that my insult would distract one of them.

"I wouldn't call this a lot. There's actually not that many harpies left in the world. This is probably one of the last few colonies." Thalia explains it so easily, showing that this fight is not hindering her in the least.

"This is an entire colony?" There have to be at least a hundred of them. I wonder if this would be considered a small or big colony. I also find it comical that we are discussing them as we are also killing them. I hope our indifference hurts their pride, anger always makes one sloppy. Even if they don't understand us, by our tones they can probably tell that we are talking about them.

"Are we really having this conversation right now?" Her back bumps into mine. "Give me a little push, will ya?"

I look over my shoulder to see that she's struggling with a harpie that has her weapon grasped in its mouth. All she needs is a little push into the creature to gain an advantage. I oblige her request, unable to do more due to my own set of harpies to contend with.

"Why are these stupid birds even helping Zeus?"

"Seriously, more questions?" she huffs out in exasperation.

"It helps me focus." I shrug my shoulders before yanking my jian from a face I had impaled.

Thalia grunts before answering. "I don't know why they're helping him. They're prideful and *intelligent* beings who don't take orders from anyone."

I frown at that. They obviously take orders from Zeus. If that's out of character for them then why? What changed? I tuck that question away to think about later as one harpie lunges for my right arm. I swing to block it, my jian slicing off its beak. Blood gushes out as its screams become gargled from choking on its own blood. The sound is sickening and makes me cringe like one would when hearing chalk screeching against a chalkboard. I realize too late that the lunge was meant to distract me from another harpie flanking my left who was looking for the perfect opening that I left for it.

Shit.

I swing anyway knowing that it will be futile. Shards of ice pelt into the harpie just as it is about to rip open my torso.

Good gods, that was close.

The ice couldn't stop the harpie's momentum though, and its body collides with mine. The force of it throws me back. There's a sharp pain against the back of my head as it smashes into a nearby rock. My vision blurs, the fight in front of me beginning to look like a haze of fuzzy shapes. I try to keep my eyes open but it's becoming more difficult with each second that passes by. With my next blink my vision clears up along with the pain at the back of my head. My first experience of near death regeneration has me reeling at the insane speed of healing.

I quickly scan the area, my jian at the ready. No more harpies flood the sky. Instead, they litter the ground. Many of them have ice shards sticking out of them, courtesy of Percy. A thread of jealousy tugs at me. I wish I could manipulate water, or anything really. At least then I'd barely have to lift a finger to help out and be able to kill many at a time.

My eyes follow Percy as he walks toward me. Not a drop of blood made it on him. I've really got to stop being jealous of him, but he's too perfect. I can't help but feel not good enough. Like I'm lacking in so many areas making me not fit to be by his side. How can I be a good enough queen when I'm not as powerful as he?

"What are you sitting around for?" he jests as he holds out his hand.

I take it, letting him help me up. "You seemed to have everything under control."

He rolls his eyes and tips my head back to drink me in before bringing our mouths together. His lips are hot and filled with fervent urgency. Breaking the kiss, his voice is coated with emotion. "Even though you're immortal, it damn near broke me seeing you crumpled there drenched in blood."

I touch my hair. There's a chunk matted in my sodden hair and I try not to think too hard about what it could be. Or more importantly, *whose* it could be. I pull my hand back, inspecting the red covering my fingertips. I'm sure my blood is mixed in there, I had hit my head pretty hard—I'd be surprised if I hadn't split my skull.

An animalistic scream breaks me from my thoughts. Thalia is not in the area and neither is Alice. Percy and I bolt, our shoes kicking up sand as we run around the bend of rocks where the screaming is coming from. The mound of rocks where I had last seen Zeus ...

Only heartbreak could cause a scream like that, meaning Zeus surely killed one of my friends. Alice is a nymph, if she dies then that's it. But Thalia and Clio's mother was mortal, from what I understand. So would they still be just as indestructible as Percy or even me? I pray that the soul-wrenching screams mean anything other than what I'm thinking.

There are only two silhouettes in the sunset, their knees bent on the sand. There should at least be four if Zeus is still around, but he isn't and neither is Clio. Thalia clings to Alice as her screams become hoarse. Waves from the Caribbean Sea soak into their clothes. None of it is being paid any heed when Clio is nowhere to be seen. As Thalia's screams die down, she tells us what we already assume: *he* took her.

Chapter Twenty-One

"What'd I miss?" the masculine voice behind me asks. It's a voice that I thought I would never hear again. Everyone besides Thalia, who is unfazed, staring blankly up at the sky as she leans into Alice's shoulder, jumps. They all look at me in confusion as a startled scream of petrified shock bursts from my throat.

I whirl around to the familiar voice. I can't seem to process the tall, broad male standing before me. With his head of waist length dreads perfectly attached to his torso, stands before me none other than Hades himself.

"What in the bloody hell are you doing here?" I demand, my voice cracking at the end.

"Uhm ... I came with you guys, remember?" Hades rubs the back of his neck as if his new head didn't get put on correctly.

"Your head got chopped off." Why is there a need for me to even elaborate on that fact?

He squints his eyes and reels his head back like he is affronted. "I'm immortal."

"And your head got chopped off."

"And I'm immortal."

"I need to sit down." My own head is covered in this man's blood and tissue and yet here he stands, head perfectly attached. "What the fuck," I whisper on an exhale.

"Are you that upset that I'm not dead?"

"No." Tears sting my eyes. "I just ..." I strain for words as my hands rub up and down my face. "I thought we lost you," I choke out.

Not asking for permission, Hades envelopes me in a hug and awkwardly pats the top of my head. I don't push him away. I really needed to feel this. His solid form, warm and *alive*. I hadn't realized that the regeneration ability could bring you back from something like that. We really are immortal. The complete realization of it all dawns on me and it weighs down on me like a sodden towel. I really need to ask more questions and not be so ignorant about the workings of this world. I am such a fool.

"There, there," he says with another pat. The awkward moment has me squashing down another hysterical laugh. Today has been too much for me to mentally handle and then to top it off, Hades failing compassion is comical. The two just seem impossible to exist on the same plane of reality.

"I hate to ruin this reunion but where is Cerberus?" Alice questions.

Hades sighs before letting go of me. As if this question is one that he's not looking forward to finding the answer to. "That is a very good question. I can only assume he's dead, since this ambush wouldn't have been possible otherwise." He scouts the beach. "Ah, there he is." He frowns and then walks off to the mound in the distance. The rest of us follow.

Birds circle around the three-headed dog, some already making a meal out of him. The dog is carved up like a roasted chicken, ebony fur matted in his own blood. It looks like it had a very slow, painful death, because the wounds are many but appear to not be too deep. Tortured to death. I feel sad for the animal who was brutally murdered for no reason other than having the job to protect the entrance to the Underworld.

Hades rests his palm on its middle head and begins to sing,

"Walk the path of death,

the tracks you tread are cold,

so cold,

standing at the gate of death,

I will follow you and break you from your bond."

The words Hades recites are a watered-down version of what was sung for Paul. It must be something that helps one's soul find their way home, or maybe it's just a tradition that merely helps the living cope with loss. Either way, it's a lovely hymn.

Light shines from Hades' palm causing Cerberus' body to cave in. Like a whisper on the wind, Cerberus' body flakes off into tendrils of silky smoke. The smoke twirls around Hades and I swear I hear yipping from the smoke before it shoots off to the cave.

Hades turns to us, his body slumps in sadness for only the briefest of moments that I almost didn't catch. "I'll meet you at Hermes' in ..." He looks down at his wrist, checking a watch that isn't there. "Five days? Yes, five days."

"What do you mean?" I ask.

"It will take me five days to breed a new watchdog. I can't leave the Underworld unprotected."

"Better not have Persephone hear you say that." Percy laughs.

"Yes, I don't doubt my fiery little flower's capabilities but she can't create another Cerberus. Not only was Cerberus meant to fight off intruders but also to scare away any curious humans. She'll understand."

"Wouldn't humans spread the word of a three-headed dog?" I butt in, curiosity always getting the better of me.

"My watchdog is made up of shadows and death who can shift into anyone's nightmare. When word is spread, most humans chalk it up to this place being haunted. Other more foolish humans who seek to rid the place of Cerberus find themselves dead."

"So their curiosity murders them. That's so wrong."

Hades looks at me coldly. "It is what it is."

Before waiting for a reply Hades walks back to the entrance of the Underworld, his long shadow from the low sun chasing after him. Not looking back he twirls his fingers back to us. "Toodles."

"Five days, brother," Percy says as his arm wraps around my shoulder, pulling me against him. Hades tilts his head in response before he vanishes into nothing.

"Uh." I look at the empty space Hades was just in.

Percy squeezes my shoulder before letting go. "He can warp."

"Warp?"

"Teleport. We call it warping."

I ponder that new information before asking, "Can you warp?"

"No, although that would be pretty cool. Only those who walk with darkness can warp."

"Who else is able to do that?"

"Hades is the only being who walks with darkness. Well, him and Charon."

Hmm, that was good information to know. I would be on edge if the enemy was capable of such a thing. I'd never get any sleep, always being on alert in case someone just popping in. *Hey, how you doing? Just going to give you a nice little stabby.* I shudder at the thought and shake myself. And I get the distinct feeling that I don't have to worry about Charon trying to oust me. But I note to myself to never get on Hades' bad side. He would not make for a light enemy.

Percy walks over to the water. Ankle deep in the ocean, it dawns on me that he isn't wearing shoes.

"Do you ever wear shoes?" I ask.

He glances over his shoulder, giving a, *did you seriously just ask that,* kind of snort. "Of course."

Looking back at the rippling tides, Percy kneels down, playing with the water. Except he isn't playing. The water curdles and foams as each splash of wave shifts over each other to form a boat.

Percy smirks at my astonished face. "Your carriage awaits, my lady." I roll my eyes at him. He's always been playful, making light of any situation. Especially now that my soul is complete.

I inspect the boat, curious if it'll get me wet. The water swirls around within the structure of the boat, splashing around like it wants to escape its makeshift fortress. I scrub my hands in the water to wash them clean before I place them against the boat, feeling it out. Where my hand touches, the water stills, becoming solid. My hand meets what feels like glass, and doesn't dip in. I bring my dry hand back before tossing my shoes aboard. Climbing in using the ladder Percy had thought to include, I find myself awestruck by the detail. It looks exactly like a ski boat.

Talking to no one I say, "Brilliant."

"I know I am." I roll my eyes *again* at Percy. I ignore him, and instead I pay attention to Alice and Thalia as they take their seats. Alice moves to sit in the front while Thalia chooses the farthest seat from everyone. Her face is blotchy, with red-rimmed eyes from crying so hard. I can only imagine where her dark thoughts are taking her. I don't know what terrors she faced herself before she left Zeus' side but it doesn't take a genius to know that she most likely faced similar experiences to Clio's. And the way Zeus mutilated Cerberus is a good indication of what the man is capable of, and the lengths he will go to for entertainment. I force myself not to go down that road of thinking. It will only lead me into a pit of sorrow I don't wish to venture into.

Scooting across to Thalia, I take her hand into my lap and give it a warm squeeze. "We will get her back."

Her blank eyes flicker with rage. "Make him suffer." It's the first emotion she has shown since the loss of her sister.

"I plan to do just that." I search her eyes, willing her to see the truth in my words. I will make him suffer. If all else fails, that is one thing I will make sure happens.

"Come here." I coax her to place her head on my lap.

Brushing through her hair, I sing to her the lullaby my mother once sang to me,

"*Didada, dida dida.*
Laoshu pashang da zhong.
Yi dian zhong.
Ta pao xialai.
Didada dida dida."

Her body softens at my touch as my voice glides over her skin. With the help of the boat speeding off she drifts into a fitful sleep that I'm sure is plagued by nightmares of Zeus.

Chapter Twenty-Two

The villa is exactly how I left it five months ago. The burnt orange of the clay roofing and cream walls remain untouched by this year's hurricane. The windows that make up the ocean-facing side of the villa reflect the water in a beckoning glimmer of moonbeams. *Enter me and all will go back to the way it was. Home, home, home ...*

The villa remains a quiet, unchanged paradise. As if it is trapped in its own timeless bubble, the world still ticking forward without it while my own has flipped. And because of that, this villa is no longer home. Too much has changed for me to still call this place home. So I whisper back to its calling, *no*.

A sense of yearning follows me as I walk the wooden path leading from the beach to the villa. The feeling is of innocence, of nostalgic memories of a childhood that is over. The sand dusted across the path is rough against the pads of my feet. I hadn't bothered with putting my shoes back on, finding it pointless with the villa so near. The breeze dances across the wide green leaves, causing light rustling as they leisurely dip to and fro. The breeze finds me next and in its tango it wraps around me. The warm night air tickles my calves and twirls upward. It brushes past my hair and I breathe in that wonderful sandalwood scent.

Ahh, I've missed this.

Percy doesn't walk with me. None of them do. They trail behind me, sensing that I need this moment to live in my childhood memories. To say hello and to also say goodbye. I remember those sweet sunsets when mother would chase me along this very walkway. My giggles mingled with her lyrical laughter as she'd catch me at the back door, tickling me all the way to the bathtub. I wonder what she would think of me now. Would she be proud of what I've become or would she view me as a monster simply because I am no longer mortal? I hope she'd be proud. No, I know she would. A mother's love is unwavering. Even if I were to become a monster, she would still be blinded by that maternal love.

Setting my boots outside of the mud room I don't make it very far inside before the steady voice of my father welcomes me. "Amy?"

The house may no longer feel like home, but his voice does. It sends a shuddering wave of longing through me. I missed my father, but I didn't realize how much until I hear his voice. He holds me at arm's length, giving me a once-over before crashing me into his chest. He holds me tight, not in the least repulsed that I reek of death. That the dried blood is crinkling off of me, falling to the floor with each tight squeeze he gives me.

"I am relieved that your soul was able to complete itself."

"How did you know?" I ask, and then I answer my own question. "Wait, duh. They must have told you."

"Alas, I was not told of your health, merely that a base was needed. But on your birthday you broke the binding I helped place on your broken soul, so I knew it was only a short period of time until you became complete or simply ..." He doesn't finish his sentence, unable to say that if the trident hadn't accepted me, I would not be here right now. My incomplete soul would've destroyed me. By the time I had made it to the trident I was already feeling myself fade. Looking back, I see that I probably only had a handful of hours left. So close ...

This whole time my father knew there was a possibility that I wouldn't make it. That before I left for France could've been the last time he'd ever see me. Instead of holding on to me tightly so that he might get those last few months with me, he let me go. It is the most unselfish thing anyone has ever done for me. He allowed me to live my life how I wanted, even though he knew that the last few months could've been my last. The weight of his love sits heavy on my heart. My father—kind, selfless and the best dad anyone could ever ask for. I am so lucky.

Tears for the profound love he has for me well up at the corners of my eyes, and I open my mouth to further question my father about what he means when he mentions the binding of my soul, but his body stiffens, which stops my unspoken question. As he releases his hold on me I follow his gaze tracking behind me to the rest of the party strolling in.

"We have much to discuss, and I'm sure you would like to wash up first," he says as he gives us all a once-over. I nod my head. He had no idea. Or I guess he did since he could see all the grime on me. His lips tighten as he looks beyond me. "It seems the journey here was eventful. Rose will show you to your rooms." His stare turns searching, and I see him mentally count our numbers. "Although, I was expecting two more?"

My flinch did not go unnoticed by my father's watchful eyes. To my relief, it is Percy who speaks. "Zeus ambushed us, hence the blood. Hades has to re-secure his realm and Clio ... Zeus took her."

I've never seen my father display any amount of hate but there it is. His lips contort into a sneer of disgust at the mention of Zeus, and his hands curl into tight fists. "Apparently we have more to discuss than I thought." His jaw ticks, and I wonder if Zeus had done anything to my father or that his display of animosity comes only from the things my father has heard about him.

"Zeus also has the trident," I inform him.

His nose flares and his eyes flicker to the rest of the party. Whatever he is about to say is interrupted by the housekeeper, Rosa, as she appears by his side. Her footsteps are so silent that I didn't even know she was there until my father moves to the side to allow her access to us.

Looking at her now with a new perspective, I can see that she is not a mortal. Not a wrinkle graces her plump face. I always thought it was great genetics that kept her looking young, but she has been with the family for far too long for age not to have marked her.

"Hello, Amy," she says, tilting her head up to look at me. When I look back at her I am greeted by a wholesome smile and warm eyes.

"Hello, Rosa."

Like my father, she embraces me in a tight hug, also not caring about the blood. Her head reaches my chest. "I swear you've grown since last I've seen you."

"And I swear you've shrunk," I counter.

She ends the hug with a smoky chuckle. "It seems that it wasn't that long ago that you were below my waist making off with baked goods in the middle of the night."

My mouth drops open. "You knew about that?"

"Little star, we all knew." Little star. A name she started calling me when I brought home a bucket of sea stars. Now I wonder if that's the true reason behind the name or if she's known all along what I was to become.

"All? Why was I never reprimanded?" I look between her and my father.

She smiles, and her face softens like melted butter. "Because children must be allowed to be children. Now, let me take your weapons and get you into a hot shower."

Rosa reaches to help with taking off my weapons. When she goes for my jian I flinch away. "No. It stays with me."

Rosa says nothing at the tone of my voice, only nods her head in understanding and steps back, but father looks at me with concern. I can feel the stares of the others tingling up my spine. If anyone asks why I want it with me, I wouldn't care enough to explain to them the reason. I may be at my childhood home, but that doesn't mean I feel safe. Not after today. If anything happens, I want to be prepared. I *need* a weapon accessible to me, always. When I least expected, Zeus attacked. I never want to feel that helpless again.

"I'll be in my room," I say, walking around my father to go through the kitchen.

"Dinner will be waiting," my father calls. It's past midnight and he plans on feeding us? Food is the furthest thing from my mind. I honestly just want to curl up into a ball and drift into nothingness. Today was too much and my mental walls are crashing down, taking all of my energy with them.

I expect Percy to follow me but he doesn't. A part of me is disappointed, although the majority of me didn't want him to. My father may be Hermes, a Greek god, but he's still my father. It just feels too awkward to be intimate with Percy right now when I haven't spoken with my father about anything. Not to mention extremely embarrassing for my father to know that I'm doing that stuff. I've only dated once and my father never met the guy. To me, this is all a whole new ball game, and I'm sure for my father as well. I assume I'm his only child, but I could be wrong. My father has been alive for an amount of time that I can't even fathom. He's probably has lots of children.

Going straight to my room I immediately strip my clothes. The shirt and sweatpants come off like a dried scab. The feeling and sound is repulsive and has me cringing. I toss them into the fireplace, pleased to be rid of them. Grabbing a lighter on the mantel I set the clothes on fire and head to my bathroom. I never want to wear those clothes again. Not only are they stained with blood, but they will always be a reminder of what happened today. Hades and Clio ...

Stepping into the shower I leave my blade on the lip of the tub situated between the fabric and plastic curtains. Out of sight if someone were to come in, but close enough for me to grab. Having it within arm's reach is a great comfort, one that I wish I didn't feel the need to have. I'm slowly coming to realize that I will always want a weapon next to me. Zeus took away my security, and it feels like he also took a part of me with him. A piece of my happiness that I'm not sure I'll ever get back.

The water at my feet turns a rusty orange, nowhere near the color of my darkened, grim thoughts. At first, the hot water heightens the smell of blood and I bite down on my fist to hold back a gag. Swallowing the bile that still made its way up my throat, I start the process of washing my hair, hoping that it will distract me from the smell. The blood in my hair is so thick that I have to triple wash it. After the second wash, the smell of blood disappears and I can finally smell the strawberry notes of my shampoo.

Finished with cleaning every inch of myself, I stand under the water with my face upturned and try to drown out my roaring thoughts. I imagine rolling waves and humid summers. Clear blue skies and then those amazing rainfalls that last only a few minutes but fall so heavily that they leave everything soaked. I imagine my toes curling in pristine, soft sand ... pristine, soft sand soaked in blood. Hades' head rolling. Eyes gone distant, blanketed in death. His body falling, me being taken down with him. *Blood, blood, and blood.* My thoughts are soaked in it, and even though he's alive, I can't stop thinking about today. He died. Even though he came back, he still died, and that is something I can't quite cope with right now. I sit down and curl into myself. The water pelts against my back in unforgiving blows as I sob out all of my hurt.

The sound of seagulls wakes me. I never went downstairs for dinner. Instead, I had sat in my papasan out on my veranda, staring up at the waning moon. Someone must have carried me to bed when I dozed off, because I don't remember walking here.

A muscled arm curves around me that brings my hips closer to him. My butt presses against something hard. Is he naked? Even though I wasn't expecting Percy to be in my bed, I am glad to wake in his arms. If I'm being honest with myself it is better this way. Him being here distracts me from my bleak thoughts, and the comfort his presence brings casts away any shadows that cling to me.

His hand glides under my silken camisole. He makes teasing circles up to my breasts, around my hardening nipples and then back down to my navel. His touch brings wet heat between my thighs and my body strains against him. I lay there feigning sleep to further bask in his touch. Percy must know that I'm awake, and if he doesn't, then he doesn't care, because either way his hand goes under my shorts. My legs willingly move open as he parts me with a finger.

"Perfect." His breath tickles the back of my neck. I lean into his finger, wanting more.

"Perfect and demanding." He takes his finger out and puts it in his mouth. "You taste just like ambrosia." His eyes roll back as he licks his top lip. "The sweetest honey."

Bringing his hand back down to me again he places two fingers inside me. His fingers curve with each withdrawal, hitting against my sweet spot. I let out a heady moan and answer his stroking with my own relentless thrusts into his hand.

"Yes, my love. Anything for you." The sound of his voice coated in lust is everything. I never want to stop hearing him sound this way—raw and unrestrained. It's empowering to hear the hunger in his voice, that I am able to elicit that reaction. I'm loving this one-sided conversation we're having. Just him communicating with my body, no words needed on my part, but he knows exactly what I want from him.

His fingers become more fervent making the heated sensation in my core spasm in tight coils. My nails dig into his bicep for support as his pumping becomes faster. Fast enough that I have given up matching his pace and instead focus my attention on each time he rubs against my g-spot. I grip the edge of my mattress and stifle my moaning with my pillow.

"Percy." My voice hitches an octave, coming so close to going over the edge.

Just when I'm about to topple over, Percy moves at such a speed that I don't even have time to cry out at the absence of his fingers. He flips me onto my back and raises my hips to remove my shorts. My hips in the air and legs over his shoulders he places his mouth on me and devours me like it is his last meal. My body clenches right before that final step to the peak. So achingly close. His wicked licks bring me closer to the edge, each one firm and soft. The wetness and strength of his tongue fills me with euphoric ecstasy and I finally topple over that cliff. I wonder if Jesus enjoyed his last meal as much as Percy just did.

I try to slip away from under Percy, but he grips my hips and holds me in place. My legs twitch uncontrollably in pleasure as he drinks me in, not letting any of my orgasm escape his mouth. Percy's moans are deep and guttural, each one sending a vibration across my already over-sensitive area. The feeling of warm liquid splashes across my back. He places me gently on my side and gets up to go to the bathroom.

"Did you just ..." After that amazing trip I can't properly formulate a sentence or think coherently, apparently.

He grins like a wolf who just finished eating all three pigs. "Cum? All over that beautiful back of yours? Yes, and honestly"—he shrugs his shoulders—"that's never happened before." He goes into the bathroom and then comes out with a dampened towel. Really? Never?

While he wipes the towel on my back, cleaning up his mess, I ask, "How?" I can't wrap my mind around it. How is it possible for that to happen when I didn't even touch him? And I know he didn't touch himself because both of his hands were on me. Having that effect on him makes me feel powerful, like the sexiest being on this planet.

Bringing the towel between my thighs to clean there also he says, "Because I am too damn enraptured by you."

"That makes sense." Not. But I still take it and twitch slightly when the towel rubs down my sensitive clit.

He chuckles against my skin, hearing the sarcasm in my voice. He pays homage to my nipples by giving each a light bite followed by a flick of his tongue. "If you keep this up, then I'll never want to leave this bed."

"If *I* keep this up?" I stare at him in disbelief. "You're the one who keeps touching me."

"It's your fault that you're irresistible."

"Uh-huh. Well, you can watch my irresistible self walk out the door. I'm starving." A rumble erupts from my stomach acknowledging my statement.

Percy frowns. "You went to bed hungry." It isn't a question, but a disapproving statement.

"I was tired," I say flippantly. My eyes never leave Percy's as I get up to pull up my shorts and fix my top. There's a predatory glint in his eyes. The way he looks at me is so carnal that I debate crawling back into bed with him, and he knows it. He smirks, knowing how the curve of his lips like that drives me wild. I flip him the bird before turning and walking out of my room, not giving him the satisfaction of his desires.

"Aw, come on," he grumbles, disappointed by my dismissal of him. But if I look back once more to see his disheveled self in my bed, I will be the one who'll never want to leave these sheets.

Chapter Twenty-Three

"I see you two slept well," my father states right after Percy takes a seat next to me. He stares at the both of us like a little kid about to tell an inappropriate joke. I've never seen this side of my father and I don't know if I like it.

The bacon I was eating catches in my throat. Between coughs I say, "What?" God, I need water.

My father hands me a glass of orange juice. "You both look well rested," he repeats. His lips are downturned, but not in a frown. They slightly curve upward at the corner while the fuller part of his lips try to restrain the smile. It looks like a failed rendition of duck lips.

"Mhm." Gulping down the juice I curtly nod my head while my face turns beet-red. He can't seriously be implying what I think he is.

My father sighs heavily. "My little girl is not so little anymore." Now I'm really choking as juice comes out of my nose. Fuck me, this is just too embarrassing.

Percy looks at me, concerned as he hands me a napkin to wipe the orange juice dribbling down my nose. "Are you okay?"

"Do I look okay?" My eyes tear up with the burning of my sinuses. Thank God I don't wear makeup, my face would look like a nightmare if I did. Did my father seriously insinuate what I think he did?

"Honey," my father says, looking genuinely unperturbed. "It's only natural." He reaches over the table and pats my hand.

"Oh my god, no. Stop. We are not having this conversation." Oh fuck, he is insinuating.

"Whatever conversation we're having I would love to join," Alice chimes in as she takes a seat, filling her plate with an assortment of food. She's piling it so high it's a wonder how her tiny frame can stomach all of it.

"Amy is embarrassed that her dad knows—"

I clamp my hands over Percy's mouth, stifling the rest of what he was about to say. "Speak another word about this and I will stab you."

"Now I really want to know," Alice says through mouthfuls of bacon and eggs.

"I may be your father but I'm not a prude. I understand that you're an adult who's going to do adult things." He makes a motion with his hands, one in the shape of a circle and the other hand pointed, going into the circle.

"For crying out loud!" I exclaim at the same time Alice beams and says, "Sex!"

"I would like some sex," Thalia says, rubbing sleep out of her eyes. She's disheveled from just rolling out of bed but I am happy to see that the haunted expression no longer shadows her, instead it is replaced by resolve.

"Me too." Percy snickers.

I punch him in the arm lightly. "Bunch of animals."

Pinching my thigh, Percy replies, "You love these animals." I really do, but I don't voice my agreement. I only roll my eyes and continue to try not to choke while eating my remaining breakfast.

With everyone at the breakfast patio, all traces of embarrassment leave me as easy laughter and lively conversation fills the area. My father tosses a croissant at Thalia, aiming for her head. It hits her on her crown with a dull smack. Why my father randomly did that, I have no idea. I can only guess maybe to distract her from her thoughts.

Her nose scrunching, she sticks her tongue out and playfully throws a piece of bacon at him. My father catches it in his mouth, chewing and smiling as he throws another croissant her way. The gesture is childish, but the scene it portrays is wholesome. They remind me of siblings who even as adults still find enjoyment in pushing each other's buttons.

I lean into Percy and ask, "They're pretty familiar. Have they known each other long before this?"

"Hermes and Thalia?"

"Yes."

He takes a bite of his own bacon before clearing his throat and saying, "Hermes has known Thalia since her breakage from Zeus. Same as Clio. And then with Alice, he's known her since she was a babe."

"Is... Alice my sister?"

Percy chokes on his food. His face red from coughing he laughs, "No. Alice is a mountain nymph and all mountain nymphs fall under Hermes' jurisdiction. Therefore he's present usually a week after every nymph's birth to give them a blessing."

"So he's a king?" My eyebrows shoot up.

He coughs again. "No. More like a protector but he doesn't have control over their lives. But the mountain nymphs respect him enough that they're loyal to him first above everyone else. Plus the blessing he gives them is the reason why they're able to manipulate air."

I watch as another piece of food flies across the table and ask, "How is it that my entire crew was not mortal?" It's been a burning question, one that I've been trying to find the answer to.

Percy flattens his lips, debating if he should divulge to me whatever he's about to say but then he lets out a sigh. "We knew you were dying and that you would need guidance to bring you to the Underworld. Literally, a day before the harpies' attack I was planning on coming to see you, to tell you what was happening to you. But then the harpies happened and everything spilled out in a not so gentle way."

"So my father sent a fake crew to take care of me?" I ask, putting the pieces together.

"Yes and no. Hermes sent Alice, I sent Paul and then the girls tagged along because they got wind of it since they live in the Underworld."

"Huh." Is all I can say. It feels like a violation and yet at the same time it also sends a warm feeling in my chest at their concern for my safety.

More food flies back and forth across the table. Thalia bats away another croissant and it lands in a bowl of oatmeal that splatters onto Percy. The patio goes silent as Percy's attention shifts from me to my father and then to Thalia, whose face is a bright red from trying to hold in her amusement. I can feel the change in the atmosphere and I dread what is to come next.

My father notices the change too. He grabs food the same moment Percy does and at the same time their fistfuls of food are released in the air. Food flies every which way as Alice and Thalia join in the food fight. Shrieking, I duck under the table, not at all wanting to be a part of this insanity.

"That was my face," someone yells, sounding a lot like a frenzied Alice, followed by a roar of delight from Percy.

An apple falls to the ground in front of me, and I reach to pick it up. I am still hungry, after all. Glancing around to make sure no one will notice me, I shift to ready myself to run inside. I momentarily stop when I notice Rosa standing in the doorway. Her hands are curled into fists on her robust hips and a look of fury shines in her eyes. If looks could kill we all would be dead, but Rosa surprises me and instead of shouting at them she turns around, marching back into the house.

More food splatters across the floor and oatmeal mingled with juice drips off of the table. In my inspection of the surrounding mess I glimpse Rosa standing off to the side with the garden hose in hand, pointing it straight at us. I see her before anyone else does and scramble out of the way, trying to avoid the unwanted shower. But my efforts are futile because as soon as I get up to run, Rosa unleashes the water. I should've just stayed hidden under the table, I see now that was the safest spot, from both the food fight and from Rosa's spray of revenge.

Startled yelps and squeals erupt from the group at the unexpected ambush. My father stands there with his hands up, laughing and says, "Truce! White flag!" His pleas go ignored while Rosa continues to drench him. "Rosa, please, mercy!" But Rosa does not show mercy when food is involved.

"You've *wasted* all of this food," Rosa grits out, hosing down everyone in the face who tries to leave, even me. Acknowledging defeat we sit there, our heads tilted back in pure enjoyment as Rosa soaks us to the bone. Giving a satisfied harumph, Rosa throws down the hose and marches off but not before staring each of us down, daring us to make a move.

These are truly my people, and I really do love them. All we need now is Clio to complete the gang and then everything will be perfect. I will do whatever it takes to get her back, no matter the consequence.

As we clean up the disaster of a breakfast, talk quickly switches over to this upcoming week. Four days from now Hades will join us to infiltrate Zeus' domain which is located in the easternmost part of the Alps—Slovenia. Specifically, the Dinaric Alps is where his lodgings are. After yesterday the plan changed. No longer is it a suicide mission for me, but instead a rescue for Clio. The trident is only second priority.

"Their nests are north of Slovenia," Alice informs us.

"We would have to get rid of them first," my father says, leaning his soaked torso back into his chair. Beads of water drip off of our clothes and splash onto the sandstone patio. Puddles sporadically mark the stones, not yet dried out from the morning sun. "They'll become a nuisance once Zeus alerts them of our arrival."

Percy reaches his arm over my shoulder and pulls me to him before saying, "Knowing Zeus, I bet he has a unit of them dwelling at the lodge. We'd be wasting time going north to take care of the colonies that aren't already accessible."

"Yes, but," Father counters, "*if* he has a unit there then by the time we're finished fending them off, the backup will have arrived. We'd be overwhelmed. Too many things can go wrong if we don't take care of the northern colonies first."

I don't like the slaughtering of a whole species, but it is something that can't be avoided. And I also didn't want to waste any more time with Clio being in Zeus' clutches. Who knew what all was being done to her.

Also, the harpies chose to listen to Zeus, that was their choice. What Thalia said about them though keeps brushing against the back of my mind. I can't grasp why the harpies would follow Zeus if they were such proud beings, who not too long ago didn't follow orders from anyone. He has to have something that he's using to control them or at least something to hold over their heads, but what?

I turn to Thalia and ask, "You mentioned they are intelligent. How intelligent is intelligent?"

It's Alice who answers my question. "They have their own caste system and language. If one learns the language, then they could easily communicate with them, although they don't tend to be kind to outsiders. Even though there are different colonies, they live peacefully neighboring each other throughout the Alps. They're smart enough not to fight for territory." I hear the unsaid jab, *unlike humans.*

"How does one not fight for territory as a colony grows?" I want to believe that if it's something humans could accomplish as well, they would do it. That humans don't only care about control over the well-being of others. I want to prove that they aren't as bad as Alice makes them out to be.

"Simple, a neighboring colony will merge with them."

"You said they have a caste system, so then when colonies merge how is it determined who will govern?"

"The top of the caste is the chief, if the chief has no mate then they will mate with the neighboring chief's daughter. If the neighboring chief has no daughter, then his niece will be next in line. It's quite—"

"Brilliant?" I cut her off. It truly was, and now I know that Alice was right, that it is something humans could never accomplish. In a way something similar had been done in the past. Austria would marry off her daughters and even so, when it came down to it, alliances crumbled and bloodshed found its way to her doorstep.

"Yes, brilliant is a good term." She nods her head.

The harpies were much smarter than I originally thought. To be able to create a system where war is never waged. They seemed to go above and beyond to avoid conflict. Knowing this, I doubt they would easily go along with Zeus' commands, especially with their colonies dwindling. And then like a lightbulb, it dawns on me.

"I think I know why they follow Zeus, and it has nothing to do with respect and more to do with being controlled." Conversation between my father and Percy over tactics becomes hushed, their focus turned to me, waiting for my unspoken revelation. "Zeus has their children."

"Holy shit." Alice's jaw drops.

"That does make perfect sense," my father muses, rubbing his jaw. "When you're on the verge of extinction, your young are what matter most."

Thalia interjects, "Harpies are extremely protective of their chicks, there's no way Zeus got ahold of them. Plus, how could he have possibly got them all without the others warning each other?"

That is a good question. One I don't have the answer to. I shrug my shoulders, letting my idea drop. "I guess I am wrong."

Alice turns to Thalia. "Valid skepticism, but you did not live among them. I did. They would do anything for their chicks. Their pride is too strong for anything else to bring them to their knees. Zeus has got them by their damn *goblin balls*. I don't know how, but he has to have their chicks."

Well, that's a new one. Goblin balls? Really? I want to shoot an incredulous look at Alice but she's turned to Thalia, unable to see my eyes bulging.

"Gods, I love that brain of yours," Percy says, bringing a kiss to my temple.

"It was a simple deduction," I say. "One that I'm not sure is correct. Thalia does have a point."

Percy shakes his head and specks of violet accumulate around his pupils. "If it was truly simple, then any one of us would've thought of that." His voice turns husky, and I can't help but blush at what the change in his eyes implies.

"He's right," my father agrees. "Because of your *simple deduction* you just saved us from unnecessarily wiping out a species."

Percy moves his hand from my shoulder and sits it on my thigh. His thumb hitches underneath my top and grazes against my skin. Whispering into my ear he says, "And because of that I am so turned on right now that it's taking everything in me not to bend you over this table and fuck you right here. Right now. In front of everyone."

Oh my ... WHY? Who the fuck says that? And my father is RIGHT THERE.

I glance at my father to see if he heard what Percy said. He's engrossed in discussion with Alice and Thalia, now talking about the logistics of our new plan. Thank the actual abyss that no one heard Percy. It is embarrassing enough that anyone can tell what he is thinking by looking at his eyes but to hear him speak it out loud? Gods, if my father heard him I would've happily rolled into a ditch to live for the rest of my life. That sounds much better than the predicament I currently find myself in.

"You are so inappropriate," I say through clenched teeth. Percy nips my ear which causes me to yelp. Everyone stares at me, I'm sure they can tell that inappropriate things just occurred by my flushed cheeks.

The chair screeches as I abruptly stand up. "I need fresh air."

"We're outside?" Thalia says.

"I need beach air. Fresh air. Water air. Yes. Yes, that's it. Air is the best next to the water. Nothing beats fresh water air." Blimey this was awkward, but I wasn't going to wait for anyone to reply. I shot out to the beach at a steady pace, not stopping until I got to mine and Percy's driftwood. It's empty of any birds, with only sand dusted over it. The pelagic birds no longer swarm the beach. They must have migrated somewhere else or merely don't feel a need to be here with Paul not around. That thought sends a pang of sorrow through me. Paul was undoubtedly happy. Instead of dying and having his essence flow back into the cycle of life, he became a Guardian. It was a great honor for him. I'm happy that he's alive, but it hurts because in a way he is no longer with us. He was with Percy much longer than me, so I can only imagine Paul's absence affects Percy even more.

The steady sigh I exhale calms my rattled thoughts. I needed to stop thinking and start doing. If I want to not lose another loved one I need to become better. I need to become more powerful, and to do so I have to practice. Percy thinks that I have some dormant ability that I somehow can awaken. And he strongly believes that it's water. All I need to do is practice, and try harder, because I clearly am not trying hard enough if I keep failing.

I came out here to get away from Percy's illicit words, but watching the peaceful waves breathing in and out against the shore gives me an idea. I'm the Queen of the Sea, so maybe I will have better luck practicing with actual ocean water.

My toes curl into the sand with each step that I take into the ocean, only stopping when the water reaches my knees. Closing my eyes, I empty my mind, thinking of only the salty air and water as it laps against me. I envision my will seeping out of my fingertips, reaching out to the water, grabbing onto it and then bringing it to my hands.

I look down, feeling good about it this time.

Aaaand nothing. Of course.

You know what, screw it. I dive into the water not caring about drenching my pajamas that were just beginning to dry. If I'm going to do this I'm going all in. What's that saying, *go big or go home?*

I lay on the shore where the waves are still able to rush to my head. Each tug and pull of the waves surrounds my stretched out form, encircling me in a sandy lover's embrace.

Can't get any more *one with the element* than this, right?

Finding my place of emptiness once again, I allow only thoughts of water. This time I envision a solid wall of water hovering over my prone body to block the waves crashing against me. I thought maybe this time if I kept my eyes closed that it would help me focus better. I will surely feel the waves stop, signaling that I have accomplished what I sought to do. Seconds turn into minutes until eventually time holds no meaning. The only indication of how much time has passed is that the sun now stands at high noon.

A sigh of defeat deflates out of me. I scowl up at the cloudy sky. I have been concentrating for *hours* and have nothing to show. Maybe water isn't my ability. But what is? It should come naturally, be easy for me to manipulate, but it isn't. I think that it's time to give up on mastering something that I so obviously can't wield.

Tears sting my eyes and my throat burns while trying to hold them back. I so bloody wish that I could manipulate water. That I could do something as amazing as the others but I especially want it to be water because I want to share something with Percy.

"*My Queen?*"

I jerk to a sitting position and look around. "Who's there?"

"*Why are you sad, My Queen?*"

The beach is empty. Not a soul in sight, but that tiny voice sounded like it was right next to me. And yet there is no one. Something scaly glides over my ankle. Letting out an undignified yelp I launch myself up and out of the water.

"*I am sorry, I didn't mean to frighten you.*"

What grazed me is a lone fish. A fish that is ... talking to me? No way. It's the same way Charon had communicated with me. Now knowing what is happening, I instinctively know how to find the mental cord that connects myself to the fish. "*I was merely startled, I had not realized that I had company.*"

"*I felt you as I was swimming by. I couldn't help but to say hello.*" A beat passes before the fish shyly says, "*Hello.*" His voice is higher, reminding me of a young child, and just like Charon's, the voice sounds like it is speaking to me through a tunnel.

Smiling, I reply, "*Hello.*"

"*I ... I wish to stay but I am growing tired from the waves.*"

"Oh! Well I—it was nice to meet you!"

"*The pleasure was all mine. I shall tell my brothers and sisters that our queen has awoken. Goodbye, My Queen.*"

I let go of the link as I watch the fish's shadow under the water swim away. Oh my god, I just talked to a fish. Was this really happening?

By the time I make it back to the house I am panting and don't have a care in the world as my sand-ridden body runs through the house screaming into every room. "Family meeting! Family meeting in the living room!"

Taking a seat on the leather sofa, my father only raises his eyebrows at my disheveled self. He's followed by Thalia and Percy, who I usher to sit.

"I've never had a family meeting," Thalia states, a little intrigued.

"Alice!" I yell down the hall. "Family meet ... oh ..." Alice comes around the corner with a loaf of bread in her mouth, a bottle of wine in each hand and a plate of steak balanced on top of her head. Like a true hungry acrobat.

"Alice, dear," Father groans in exasperation. "Is that my aged wine?"

I grab the plate from her head, setting it on the coffee table. Alice plops down, ripping a chunk out of the bread with her teeth. Between mouthfuls she says, "It sure is, Daddy." *Oh my god she did not just say that.* "One hundred years I believe." She looks at the other bottle. "Ah, and this little prize is one hundred and fifty!"

Another groan from my father. "I was saving that for a special occasion."

"I'll take that." Thalia says, grabbing the older bottle from Alice and uncorking it with her mouth.

I glance at Percy who takes this opportunity to ask as he takes in my wet and sandy self, "What happened to you?"

"Ah yes, the reason for this family meeting." I clasp my hands together in a prayer and then release them. "I can communicate with fish." Chatter between Thalia and Alice about which wine tastes better ceases as their attention turns to me.

"That's what I was doing," I continue cheerily, "I was out in the ocean trying to manipulate it. Complete fail by the way." I pointedly look at Percy. "And then a fish started speaking to me."

"Fish don't speak, babe," Alice soothes.

"Let me rephrase, he spoke to me telepathically. He sensed I was near and wanted to say hello and then he said that he'll tell the others that I have awoken." I raise my hand to my head and make an explosion motion. I slowly lower my hand, becoming uncertain as all of them show varying signs of concern. All besides my father, who seems to be mulling over this new information.

"Why don't any of you look happy?" I ask, trying not to sound hurt.

Percy leans over to take my hand into his. "It's not that we're not happy, it's just that no one can communicate with sea life, not even the water nymphs. At least not on that level."

"What do you mean?"

"I, as well as the water nymphs, am able to direct our will onto what we want from them. We can kind of get a sense of how they feel but it's basic emotions. Not complex enough to understand the reason behind what they are conveying and to have a conversation." Turning my hand over Percy kisses each of my fingertips before finishing, "Just another thing about you that amazes me."

His words send a flush through me and then I feel shock as the loaf of bread Alice was eating hits Percy upside the head. "Not the time for that," she scolds.

"That's rich coming from you," Percy says as he throws the bread back at Alice. Like an animal she catches it with her mouth. Oh, for the love of everything, this better not turn into another food fight.

"Thanks for returning it."

"I'll throw it harder next time, hopefully knock out some teeth."

Thalia cackles, legit *cackles*. Alice looks at her, more concerned than when I said I spoke with a fish. Maybe the alcohol is already getting to her. Gosh, between Alice and Percy I already feel like I need some at this point as well.

"Okay guys, reel it back in." I snap my fingers around to regain their focus. "Is this why I'm getting nowhere with the elements, because my power lies with telepathy? And does that mean I can communicate like that with other animals, or is it just aquatic animals because I'm their queen?"

My father, silent in his bubble of contemplation, finally speaks. "I have a feeling that skill doesn't only pertain to animals."

"You mean humans, or even us, advanced species," Percy states, awe coating his voice.

"Only one way to find out," my father says and then turns to me. "Go on, test my theory." I gulp. Nervous now with the pressure and plagued with doubt. What if I'm not good at this either? "If it helps, nymphs tend to be pretty scatterbrained, so Alice would be an easier mind to enter," my father suggests.

"No." The immediate no from Alice leaves me a little hurt. The darkness from her voice and facial expression lightens as she says, "I'd just prefer my thoughts to myself. Wouldn't want to scare you with all my naughty thoughts of you naked." She winks.

"Thank ... you? I don't think that's how this works but okay ... uhm." I look between the others, not knowing who I should do this with.

"I'll volunteer." Percy grabs both my hands, bringing me down to the floor with him.

Not letting go of my hands he gently says, "Close your eyes, it helps in the beginning."

My eyelids close. Everyone around me is silent, as if they're holding their breaths. Alice's obnoxious eating has even stopped. I think about the thread that I used with Charon and the fish. Floating in the darkness is a bright thread of thick gold. The moment I latch onto it I feel Percy flinch.

"Hello?" I ask. Not at all thinking that I'll get a reply.

"You are amazing."

"How am I even doing this?"

"I don't know but would it be weird if I told you that it's turning me on?" I end the connection but not before I give the thread a slight tug, envisioning punching him in the shoulder.

"Ow." Percy looks down at his arm, rubbing it. "How did you ..." he trails off. "Freaking amazing."

"What is?" Thalia is now at the edge of the couch, totally transfixed by what's going on.

The smirk that Percy gives me is a promise for tonight. Not looking away from me he says, "Not only did she speak with me but she also punched me with her mind."

"That's ... I for once have no words," Alice says.

"The word you're looking for, Alice," my father notes, "is powerful." He clenches his jaw like he has more to say, but decides against it. Knowing my father, he won't voice anything that's speculation, which piques my interest. Just what exactly does he think I'm capable of?

Chapter Twenty-Four

After dinner and a long shower, I spend the rest of the evening practicing telepathy with Percy. Talking with him through the mind link is as easy as breathing. By the end of our session, I don't even need to find the string to be able to communicate with him. I associate the feeling with an extra muscle. A small focus on that muscle and I can speak with Percy as simply as if I were using my mouth. It's a weight off of my shoulders to finally be able to do something special. To have an extra ability like the others. Telepathy isn't as cool as manipulating water, but I can work with this. Even though I couldn't use it in battle it could come in handy for something else. You never know what the world will throw at you next. I understood a fish, meaning I could probably communicate with any species and understand them and vice versa when I used the mind link.

I try punching Percy again through the link but nothing happens. I don't know why I'm finding it harder to cause anything physical with the string. I try again and again but by the fourth time the effort it's taking me to give him a mental punch is creating a migraine that only grows worse with each attempt. I rub my temples, trying to ease the tension.

"That's enough for today," Percy says tenderly.

"No, I can keep going." I tug more firmly on the link, trying my hardest not to wince at the amount of pain it's causing me.

"Good gods, woman!" Percy puts a shield up around his mind, shutting me out. The shield is a thick wall of ice with no vulnerabilities I come across as I mentally try to find an opening.

My eyes fly open. "How did you do that?"

"I've been practicing too. I honestly didn't know if it would work. By your reaction it seems to have and I'm glad that I did, because you've had enough."

I have. I am past my breaking point, but I don't want to give up. I want my gift to be more useful and for that to happen I need to practice. We are to face Zeus in three days. *Three days;* there is no time to waste.

"Come here." Percy entwines his fingers with mine and pulls me down onto the bed. His arm slips around me, holding me tight against him while his right hand massages my forehead and scalp. I cocoon myself against his chest, savoring his gentle touch.

In moments like these when I fit so perfectly against him, I have to wonder if there's a god out there who molds souls and bodies to be fated together. Because this feeling with him is beyond perfection.

"What am I doing wrong?" I say, barely audible. It's a wonder if he heard me.

"It could be harder to master simply due to you once being mortal."

"That's what you said when I was struggling with the elements and we now know that wasn't the case."

"It won't be long, you'll become adept soon enough."

"You truly believe that?"

The back of Percy's fingers trail from my temple down to my jaw. He lifts my face up, initiating the softest kiss he has ever given me. His tongue traces the outline of my lips, grazing over my teeth and then in gentle circles he says hello to my tongue. He tastes faintly of the sangria he had earlier. It's a delicious combination mixed in with his usual taste of fresh water and citrus. If my headache wasn't splitting me apart, I would deepen the kiss and ask for more.

"I truly do." He sighs. The sound is what one might think they would hear when a succubus takes a soul. When a succubus takes you, you die a happy man locked in ecstasy. I feel smug that I have this effect on him, and savor the thought of being his personal drug of choice. He certainly is mine, and I know that I will never tire of his clever lips and hard body pressed against me. The way his eyebrows arch and his turquoise eyes are set below them in feline hunger sets me aflame every time he looks at me. He is intoxicating. He lets go of my jaw and continues rubbing my temple and surrounding scalp. The sensation brings out a delightful moan before my eyelids grow heavy and I succumb to sleep.

Chapter Twenty-Five

*T*hree figures form before me, shrouded in shadow. Smoky wisps of a dream twirl around them. Being pulled to the trio, their conversation grows clearer the closer I get.

"Nyx, please. There has to be another way to end this madness." The figure that speaks is on his knees before Nyx. I can't yet fully see his face. Nyx is still a blurred shadow and her cloaked back is turned to me, leaving me with only the view of the other two. Which isn't much, considering they're still in shadow.

"The Demis have become few and far between. We have to stop the Genesis before their next move," she replies, detached, as if she has already accepted and moved on from whatever decision she has made. Her voice sounds familiar, as if I've heard it before.

The third figure clasps the shoulder of the one kneeling. "She is right, Hades. They are the only thing that can kill us. Who will protect the mortals from their crazed bloodlust when we are gone? Who will take care of this planet? The others have already been doomed along with their civilizations."

As soon as he says Hades' name, the shadows surrounding Hades and him disappear. The recognition of them both jolts through me. Standing before Nyx is not only Hades but my father. I try to see what Nyx looks like, but the shadows around her twist and become thicker, obscuring her and making it impossible to see.

Hades brushes my father's hand off of him. "Gaia sacrificed herself and it was meaningless. Her bones were not enough. How would Nyx's death be any different? This is a chance, a chance we must not take." He turns back to Nyx, clutching onto the front of her. "Please, Nyx, I'm begging you. If not for me then for our son. Charon needs you."

"Do not speak to me of our son. I know what I am sacrificing and it is especially for him that I am doing this." The words are venom, every syllable a tight pinch. Her shoulders visibly relax and her voice softens as she says, "Hades, whatever you do, do not bring me back. The Genesis' time in this universe has come to an end. You must promise me. Only suffering will happen if you bring me back."

"I can't ..."

"Promise me! You know this is the only way."

A rumble sounds in the distance. It shakes the ground, and then there's an earsplitting roar followed by a gaping crack in the earth. Water shoots out, forming a geyser of rock and water.

"We don't have time for this! They have found us, it must be done now!" my father screams in panic. His eyes are filled with dread as he looks out beyond. Three large shapes walk in the distance toward them. What I thought were explosions that alerted the trio of nearby foes are actually the footsteps of three giants. Their roars create chasms, destroying the ground around them. They are the size of mountains. Even though they are in shadow, when I look upon them I am consumed with a crushing forlornness that leaves me wrecked and weak beyond comprehension.

Nyx goes to her knees. Her forehead pressed against Hades' and hands clasped to the sides of his head she says, "Don't miss."

Crying out in anguish, Hades thrusts a weapon upward into her chest. Rivulets of blood trickle out of her mouth, puddling on the earth between them. Words not yet garbled with blood she recites, "I, Nyx, Daughter of Chaos and Bringer of Darkness, willingly give you the essence of a Genesis." The light goes out in her eyes as her neck slackens and her body slumps forward. Pressed into Hades, he releases the blade from below her ribs and tenderly lays her

down. A ball of yellow light protrudes through her chest. Hades coaxes the
rest of it to leave her body, speaking soft words of encouragement. In his palm
he forces the ball apart, peeling it like you would an orange. He then places a
fair portion of Nyx's essence in his robe, while the other part he then stabs with
his blade. The same blade he sacrificed Nyx with. The moment that part of her
soul is stabbed, a blinding light so white that it leaves me blind encompasses
them.

When the light no longer shines so brightly against my closed eyelids, I open
them to see Hades standing over the empty space where Nyx's body once was.
In Hades hand is the trident, pulsing in hungry vibrations with Nyx's essence.

Heart pounding, I wake to my sweat-drenched cameo sticking to me. Sweat
drips from my brow, and I wipe away the slickness. Percy's limbs cling around
me, our bodies creating an inferno of heat. Trying to escape but not wake him, I
carefully unlatch him from me and slide out of bed. Out from under the covers,
I shiver when the maxed air conditioning blows down on my dampened skin.
I grab my house robe and slip it on, trying to recall the nightmare. I vaguely
remember. It's at the forefront of my mind and yet it's foggy. No matter how
much I sift through the fog it won't dissipate. I see my father's face etched in
fear and Hades torn and in tears but why, I do not know. For the life of me I
can't remember.

The house is silent as I walk the halls. The soles of my feet pad along the icy,
wooden floors and I wish I had put on slippers to protect them from the cold.
The first beams of sunrise kiss the horizon, bringing in soft shades of orange
and red through the floor-to-ceiling windows in the remembrance room. The
fish in the tank start to come to life as the morning sunbeams find them. They
lazily swim about, starting whatever morning routines fish have. Curling up in
a blanket I sit in a high-backed chair placed near the window. From this part
of the room the air conditioning doesn't beat down on me but I can still feel
remnants of it permeating from the corners of the room where the vents are
located.

"It's a beautiful morning."

"Father!" Bollocks, he scared me. Like a wraith, I hadn't heard him enter.

My father's smile is playful as he looks down at me from behind my chair. "I was about to enjoy some tea, would you like a cup?"

"Tea sounds wonderful."

I wait, staring at the sun as it makes its journey over the horizon. Father is only gone for a heartbeat before he's handing me a fresh cup of steaming tea and taking his place to the right of me in an identical chair. The tea tastes of chai, leaving my body warm and content, chasing away the chill in my bones.

"I always wondered if you ever slept," I muse as I breathe in the wafting aroma of my tea.

Snorting, Father replies, "Of course I sleep. Given that I am a second generation *god,* I only need a few hours to be well rested."

"Why do you say it like that?"

"Say what?" he asks.

"*God.* You say it as if it's not what you are."

Leaning forward, he says like it's obvious, "Because I'm not."

"I don't understand."

"Would you like the short or long version of history?"

Before taking a deep sip I say, "Long. You know me, I'd end up asking too many questions when given a short explanation." He snorts at that.

Father looks out to the ocean as he thinks, pondering where he should start. "Thalia and Clio are third generation, their elementals are weaker and they rest the average amount a mortal does, yet they are essentially immortal. Then there's Poseidon, me, Hades, Hera and Zeus who are second generation: Demi. We are stronger than them but nowhere near as strong as the first generation, the Genesis."

My eyes flicker when father says Genesis. I feel like I've heard that term before, but don't remember exactly from where. Father carries on, not noticing my recognition, "And unlike the Genesis, we need sleep, just not that much. It is said that the Genesis came to be by the one called Chaos. It's ..." He sighs. "This part can be a little tricky to explain. Chaos is an entity, essentially the true god who created this universe and all its living things. He then created the Genesis who symbolize certain aspects of the world. He created them to become caretakers of this universe. Gaia cared for nature, Uranus the sky, Nyx for night, Hemera for day and Oceanus for bodies of water. They represented what they cared for, being energy themselves."

Father chuckles, his eyes distant as if recalling a memory. "Hemera personified day. Light would ooze from her skin, sparkling as if she carried a thousand rainbows within her. And when she smiled"—the corners of my father's eyes crinkle as he himself smiles—"the whole room would flash with rays of sunlight." My father shakes his head out of the fond memory. "I'm getting side-tracked."

"It's okay, I would've probably asked anyway. Besides, it's wholesome to see you reminiscing. I hope to meet her."

The type of grief that takes years to control contorts my fathers face into soft sadness as he says, "The Genesis no longer live."

That information shocks me. "But they were immortal weren't they? I mean we are, and we're what, third and second generation. How can they be dead?"

"Yes, we are all essentially immortal. There are things that can kill us, though rare and kept secret. I believe Poseidon only knows of the trident, but there are other ways."

I open my mouth to ask what the other ways are but he raises his mug to me. "That knowledge is meant to be buried, I will not divulge it to you or anyone else."

"That's ... understandable." It totally is, but I still would like to know. There are other things that can kill us and I would very much like to know what, and if anyone else knows of them.

"Anyway," he carries on, "the Genesis were tasked with taking care of this universe, but they grew tired. They found that when they birthed children, their offspring carried that same energy as them. Not as strong, but just the same. Once the second generation grew into their abilities they then would help the Genesis with the caretaking. Unlike Chaos, we are not gods, simply because we cannot create from nothing. So you see? We are simply caretakers of this world."

"Not the universe?"

Father looks upon me approvingly. "Is there not one thing you don't catch?"

"You praise me now for my intelligence, Father, but I must not accept it. Even being educated on mythology I was still blind to who Percy actually is."

Solemnly, he says, "Sometimes we choose to ignore the uncomfortable so that we may live in a state of comfort."

"I can't stand ignorant people and yet there I was, living in ignorant bliss." I purse my lips at my own ignorance.

"In different times of our lives we all are guilty of just that. Don't view it as a fault but rather a stepping stone, for when you face what you willingly ignore you then grow as a person."

"Ever the scholar," I tease.

"I am old," he agrees, toasting to the compliment.

I snort. "I've no doubt about that."

My mind wanders to Percy, where was he in the midst of all this if the second generation was birthed from the first? "How could Percy only know about the trident and not the other ways to cease immortality?"

"Poseidon was the last of us to be born. He was but a babe when the war started. And the other few Demis were young, kept away from the war."

"I take it that is the reason the Genesis no longer live. What happened?"

Leaning back, my father closes his eyes. "These are hard memories to live through once again."

"I'm sorry, Father, you don't have to tell me." Even though I am very curious. The questions of this unfinished conversation will burn me alive.

"Ah, but I feel that I must. If one does not know the past how can they prevent the same mistake from occurring in the future?"

"Here you go again with your wise words."

A smile tugs at his lips. "Chaos once spoke to the Genesis. They would call and Chaos would answer. When the Genesis started procreating with the species of this universe, Chaos stopped answering their calls. At first it did not bother the Genesis, but then a few grew angry, spiteful. I was only three hundred when it began. The slaughter ..." His eyes flutter close as he recalls the images of the dead; of the masses that were undoubtedly murdered. War killed in the thousands, not the few.

"Whole planets were wiped out. The sea of carnage that was left behind ..." He winces. "Each planet once thrived with life and out of spite they were no more." When Father's eyes look to me they are plagued with all the ones he once loved, lost.

"What of the others who were up against that magnitude of anger? They exist I presume, so why didn't they stop them?"

"They tried, my dear. It was three against two, Gaia and Nyx. The odds were not in our favor. In the end we won and that is all that matters."

"How?" I prod.

"The only information you should know is that the trident gave the killing blow."

"You're really not going to tell me the other ways we can be killed, huh?" Father looks at me pointedly and then gets up. My eyes follow him as he makes his way over to Mother's statue. Father is just too good for me to sneak unwilling answers from him.

"I love her fiercely," he says. "Every time she's reborn I find her, for I can not bear to ever share her."

I know Father loves my deceased mother but to find her after every rebirth? "How many times has she been reborn?"

"Four. Of those four only once she was a man. People weren't so open-minded during that time period, but that couldn't be helped. I was lucky enough that in that lifetime he felt the same as me."

"You laid with him?" The thought doesn't repulse me, it's just that my father has only ever shown any interest in my mother who is a female.

"I did. I told you, my love for your mother is that fierce." I think about my situation and how Percy at first expected me to be Amphitrite and how I am not. We share the same soul but I am not her.

"She's not the same though," I argue. "I can guarantee you that." And if I were to meet her in her next life, she wouldn't be my mother, just another stranger. My mother is dead and I will not entertain the idea of finding her again once she is reborn. It would be too difficult to see the woman who loved me and raised me be someone completely different. The encounter would only end in heartbreak.

The unexpected laughter that barks forth from my father is boisterous and it leaves me stunned. "Of that you are correct," he says, wiping away tears, a sign of how hard he was laughing. "She was different in every lifetime and yet my heart still recognized her."

Doubt replaced by venom, I seethe, my anger getting the best of me. "How is that even possible?"

"Because we are soulmates," he says simply, ignoring my tone. "When you find yours, you'll know what I mean."

"You're saying Percy is not my soulmate?" I don't want to believe that there's someone out there who I would love more than Percy. Before now I didn't even know soulmates were a thing. A soul made for you ... The idea seems blasphemous when thinking there was someone out there other than Percy who is destined for me.

"He would've demanded the rite if you were."

Rubbing my temples, I try to take all this new information in. "That's fine. Screw the rite, whatever that is. Percy probably didn't want to do it or he was waiting until I was ready."

"Doubtful."

I glare up at him. "How can you be so sure?"

"When an immortal connects with their soulmate it goes against instinct not to claim them. The rite is a *blood claiming* where your souls fuse."

As father dips his hands into the fountain, I ponder what he said. I finally admit more to myself than to him. "I don't have that with Percy."

"It appears not, but do not fret over it. It is rare when we do find our soulmate. It will be a long time before you or him encounter your mate. If ever." His words were meant for comfort but for once my father's words left me with no comfort at all, only dread for a future without Percy.

Chapter Twenty-Six

It feels like an eternity has passed since I last played the cello, but when I hold the bow at my fingertips, that eternity vanishes to yesterday. I have so many songs memorized over years of daily practice that the song I play now comes easily to me. As the conversation I had with my father from yesterday morning replays through my mind on constant repeat, the upbeat music becomes melancholy. My eyes catch those of Percy, who sits on the chaise lounge that Miss Justine would sit upon during my lessons.

He tilts his head, listening. Concentration furrows his thick eyebrows creating a crease between them. He looks sensual and poised, like one of those Greek statues. His tousled hair playfully sits atop his eyebrows, still damp from a recent shower.

"I love you," he mouths, knowing that I wouldn't hear him if he had spoken it. His full lips are enticing and with his whispers of endearment he chases away those sad thoughts that were beginning to consume me.

Changing the tune to a romantic lilt, I close my eyes. My lips curve up into a soft smile as my body hums with the passion that I feel for him. I don't speak the words back to him but instead I convey my feelings through the cello, each string echoing that love, a pure love built on friendship. Not something fluffy and forced like soulmates.

Right here, right now. I choose to live in this moment, loving Percy with my whole being because *this* is what matters. I won't let a future of a *what if* possibility dictate how I feel now. If I were to do that, I would be accepting a life without Percy, which would slowly destroy the relationship currently between us.

A sense of being watched by someone other than Percy has me opening my eyes. Hades stands in the entryway, his arms relaxed with his head and shoulder leaning to his left against the wall. With his finger he motions for me to be quiet and then points to Percy who has fallen asleep on the lounge. Even in slumber he's handsome. I don't think I'll ever get over the shape of his jaw or the line of his straight nose.

Quietly ending the melody, I walk over to Percy to admire him for a moment. His thick eyelashes brushing against his cheeks would make any woman jealous. My eyes stray to his full lips that are parted slightly. How can someone look this perfect? I watch him for a little longer before tearing my attention from him.

Hades follows me from the room. I lead him to the gardens where I take a seat on a bench placed between two blooming rose bushes. Hades stares down at me, choosing to stand rather than sit. When I look at him all I see is red. His head is no longer atop his shoulders but instead is staring at me from the ground. I close my eyes, concentrating on my breathing. *He's alive. He's alive. He's alive.* The ringing in my ears subsides as my heart slows down.

"You haven't been getting much sleep," he states.

"I didn't think I cared all that much for you," I acknowledge, barely above a whisper.

At that confession, Hades finally sits. We sit there in peaceful silence while birds in a nearby bath chirp in merriment. The silence is not awkward, but one of mutual content. I haven't known Hades for long and yet I care so much for him. I don't know when I started to consider him someone I could confide in. With that thought it took everything in me not to hold him against me. To feel his warm body pulsing with life, just to assure myself that he is indeed here. That he is alive seems to be a miracle, one that I have a hard time comprehending.

"I'm having a hard time wrapping my head around you coming back from getting ..." The image of his head tumbling flashes before me and I gulp for words that I can't bring myself to say. The images keep assaulting me at a rate I can't block out. My chest tightens and feels heavy as my breathing becomes a struggle.

He must see the control that I have lost as the panic sets in, because he places a soothing hand between my shoulder blades and says gently, "Breathe with me." I listen and follow his steady breathing. My own gradually calms down, matching his.

"Talk to me," he suggests, not demanding, but in a way that gives me a choice not to if I don't wish to.

I exhale a long breath, emptying any negative reserves before saying, "I find it too much at times. Watching what happened to you. Then there's Paul. I think that if I wasn't in the picture that he would still be here, he would still be laughing with Alice. Why is this new life filled with violence? Is this how it's always going to be? Watching my loved ones die over and over? How can anyone get used to this? I surely can't. Every night I'm haunted by what's transpired. Harpies chasing me, Paul's entrails hanging from their beaks. Zeus' maniacal laugh. And it's not just your head. It's Percy's, Alice, my father. Sometimes it's even me. I just ... I feel like I'm the only one losing my mind."

My body feels constricted, like a snake is wrapped around my chest, tightening with each breath I take. My chest burns for release and so I give it just that. I cry. I cry for everyone I've lost and for everyone I haven't but surely will. All the while Hades hand remains a steady presence against my back as the rest of me is wracked with sobs.

"I'm sorry I'm such a blubbering mess." I sniffle at the end of my crying. Hades removes his hand as I sit back, wiping away my snot and tears.

"Do you feel better?"

"A little bit," I croak.

"Then it's okay to be a blubbering mess."

Staring off, not focusing on anything I ask, "Will it ever get better?"

"Death is grim. No matter how many we see pass we never truly know how to say goodbye. How we handle it, though, determines whether death will haunt us. Accepting and coming to terms with your emotions is a healthy start. In times of war, revenge can help; but when revenge is the only thing keeping you up, that's when death haunts you." Nodding my head I accept his words. Hades adds as an afterthought. "Time. It will always hurt but time will help dull what death brings."

"And now I have eternity." I can only imagine the extent of Hades' age. The prospect of one day becoming that old leaves an unsettling feeling in the pit of my stomach.

"That, you do," he agrees.

"I'm still perplexed by how you're—" I wave in his general direction, still unable to voice what happened to him.

"Alive after the big slice?" He makes a cutting motion across his neck.

Closing my eyes, I say tersely, "Yes. That."

"It's quite simple, really. We have regenerative abilities. When one has a fatal wound like I did, my soul won't leave but stays tethered to my body, and then when my body is once again livable my soul finds its way back."

"How is the trident capable of killing you then?"

"Because it has the ability to sever that line between body and immortal soul."

Slowly blinking, I ask, "If I were to kill Zeus with it, where would his soul go?"

"The trident would have a meal, of course. Similar to the river, Styx."

"The river ... how?" This revelation is heading in the opposite direction I thought it would.

Hades laughs at the perplexity in my voice. "She's not just a river but an entity. There long before I was born. When she's feeling lonely, she'll come from the waters for a chat but she mainly finds enjoyment in feeding off the souls I send her way."

"She sounds ... pleasant." The side-eye that Hades gives me says that he thinks otherwise but he doesn't voice it.

"What's that look for?" I question.

Shaking his head, Hades says, "You'll meet her eventually and when you do, you'll see just how *pleasant* Styx can be."

Well, I was being sarcastic but I guess Hades didn't catch that in my tone.

The shuffle of footsteps against brick alerts us of company. Strands of red glisten in Thalia's chestnut hair as the afternoon sun shines down on her. She stares at us, looking both of us over. Her lips turn downward as she takes in my swollen eyes. I know what she sees, I've seen it many times when I've looked in the mirror after a good cry. The whites of my eyes awash in a pink hue which makes my moss-colored irises turn a grassy green. I can only imagine how puffed up my clogged sinuses make me look right now. I wonder if she knows why I have these tears. Does her sister walk through her dreams like she does mine? Does she dream over and over of Zeus hacking away at everyone she holds dear? She must, for the same bags under my eyes from sleepless nights also plague hers. They're so dark and I wonder if maybe she's getting even less sleep than me.

"Rosa saw you heading this way, lunch is ready." Her arms are loose at her sides. She goes to step forward but stops. Her hands turning into fists she clenches them once before nodding her head to us and then turns around walking back to the villa.

"She needs help," I deduce. Maybe I'll try to talk with her after lunch. No one should suffer alone.

"She's been through a lot. Out of all his children, Zeus was the most wicked to her."

"What happened?"

"It's not my story to tell." The finality in his voice says that if I prod I'll come up empty-handed, and I'm fine with that. When Thalia trusts me with her story I will listen but in the meantime I will shower her with love and compassion.

Plates of sliced, air-fried duck line the table with dishes of hoisin sauce, cucumbers, and carrots. Rosa has been spoiling me these past five days by cooking up all of my favorite dishes. Peking duck is served with a crunchy tortilla that's sprinkled with fresh cilantro. It's one of my childhood favorites. Waiting for the rest of the clan to be seated my mouth waters in anticipation as the divine smells waft up my nose. I literally have to swallow down my drool before it has a chance to find its way out of my mouth.

Before taking a seat to my right, Percy places a kiss atop my head. "I've never seen such bliss upon your face."

"Rosa's cooking does make one blissful, does it not?"

Placing duck first on my fried tortilla and then his own he replies, "It does. I'll have to steal her from Hermes to be my chef." It's weird to hear Percy call my father that. To me he is still just Father. I have to remind myself that my father has lived thousands of years which to me is still incomprehensible. I can't seem to wrap my mind around the extent of someone's knowledge who has lived that long. I guess Percy may as well be just as old but it's hard for me to view Percy that way. To me he is the boy who I grew up with who just happened to end up being an immortal. I can't seem to put two and two together.

"Rosa is loyal to me," Father cuts in, serving his own duck with vegetables. "But for Amy she might visit every now and then."

That's right, I had forgotten that once we get Clio back, I will be living with Percy. There, in Atlantis, I will formally be crowned. It's something that we only vaguely talked about due to more important matters that needed to take place first. It's ironic how politics repulses me and yet here I am, soon to be crowned. The duty thrust upon me leaves my mouth dry in apprehension. Will I make a good enough queen? I know nothing about leading people.

Sensing my doubts, Percy places his hand over my knee. The calming circles his thumb makes soothe my rattled thoughts. With everyone in attendance, talk switches to the rescue. My father enlightens Hades on what we had discussed earlier about the harpies.

"The only thing," Hades adds, "is we have no idea where he has the chicks. If it were that easy then the harpies themselves would have already done so."

I hadn't thought about that, none of us had.

"Fuck." I run my hands through my hair, frustrated with our lack of knowledge. "Clio is going through hell I can't even fathom. We don't have time to search out the chicks."

"We will make do," my father assures me.

Not having enough time to figure out where the chicks are being held our plan to rescue them is scrapped and we revert back to our original plan. Or one of the originals, at least. We are not going to take out the colonies before heading to Zeus' but will instead infiltrate and try to rescue Clio unnoticed. With that decided, we plan to leave when the sun has risen. The Himalayas are on the other side of the world, meaning when it is day here it is night there. Harpies are diurnal so striking when it is their time of sleep is a perfect opportunity to lessen their interference at Zeus' lodge. What confuses me is how we are going to get there in time.

"Seconds," Alice said.

Seconds? I can't think of how that is possible, but I don't ask because soon I will find out.

Naked in my bathroom, I stare at myself in the mirror. My hair, the color of ravens, is stark against my pale skin. I notice that after the renewal of my soul into immortality my tan has disappeared. I thought it was due to being in the Underworld, but since then I've spent every day out in the sun and not a hint of that marks my skin. I'm just as pale as the day I was born. The only markings that are the same are the random beauty marks. One on the corner of my cheekbone, under my right eye, and the other in the hollow of my left cheek.

My mother's side of the family bickered about my tan skin but praised my almond-shaped eyes. My skin color was not deemed beautiful by their Chinese standards. *Ha, if they saw me now I would finally be seen as perfect.* For that was their only problem, I was never white enough. When my mother got sick the visits to China stopped and when she died her funeral was the last time I saw my mother's parents and sister. My memories of them are fond, but I was never close to them. While dealing with the loss of my mother I had no energy to keep in touch with them, and so as with any relationship where you stop trying, our communication ceased.

My eyes follow Percy as he comes up behind me. His own eyes are hungry as he takes me in. I don't shrink from his stare but instead I stand there, shoulders drawn and chin tilted. My body sears where I feel his eyes roam.

As his fingers trail down my spine curving around my backside I wonder if he too has noticed a change in how I appear. His hand roams back up, cupping my left breast. Pinching my nipple, he pulls me against him. His eyes find mine and they never stray as his other hand caresses down my navel.

"Why am I so white?" I blurt out.

"That's random, but because that's your natural skin tone." His lips find my neck, kissing and sucking while his hand reaches further down.

"But I haven't been able to tan," I carry on.

Percy stops his groping and stares at me, giving me his full undivided attention. "My love, you're immortal. You won't tan because your body is constantly healing you."

"You're tan."

He smirks. "I was born naturally tan."

"Hades said that a mortal body can't contain an immortal soul."

"Your body is no longer mortal."

"*How?*" I stress the word.

Percy looks at me for a moment as if he were looking deep within my soul. "I don't think you realize that you were in that cave for weeks and during that time your body went through a change."

"Oh." *Weeks.* My mind reels at that information. I was down there for that long? This seemed like a joke, but what else could explain my body being different? It would also explain why the Winter Solstice was being celebrated the night I left the cave. No wonder it hurt like a bitch. It felt like my insides were being shredded and clearly that was what exactly was happening. It reminds me of what one might go through if they were turned into a vampire. Their entire cells are replaced by new, stronger ones. Time must have moved differently in the cave because for me it had seemed I had only been in there for a few hours.

My interrogation ceases as I ponder all of this, which Percy takes as a green light. A moan of pleasure escapes me as Percy's hands become more purposeful with their squeezing and tugging. Closing my eyes, I let go of my thoughts and instead savor his touch. Wanting nothing more than to get lost in him.

"Look at yourself," Percy commands. "Look at how your body reacts to my touch." I obey him. My back is flush against him and my hips move into his firm fingers.

"Beautiful." His voice is guttural.

It brings out my desire even further and it takes all that I have to contain the muscles spasming at my core. "Please, Percy," I beg.

"You never have to beg. Never."

Oh god, that statement is intoxicating. "I want ..." His touch is making it hard to think as the coils in my stomach almost find their release, but I want all of him. "I want you to take me to bed."

"Yes, My Queen." He stops his fervent rubbing to pick me up and take me to bed. There we find release and lose ourselves, arms and legs entangled, our breaths mingled, calling to each other's souls.

Chapter Twenty-Seven

Even with my hair tied back I'm dying in my puffer jacket and knee-high winter socks. I can feel beads of sweat accumulating under my clothes, congregating at the middle of my back and underarms. Everyone else looks just as hot and uncomfortable as me dressed in their own winter clothing.

"Remember the plan, in and out," Hades says as he makes eye contact with everyone. "Let's make this quick and easy." I want nothing more than to lodge the trident into Zeus' neck, but Clio's rescue is more important, so I nod my head in agreement.

From out of his inner jacket pocket, Hades withdraws a rock. Grinning, he holds it up between his thumb and pointer finger. "Passage stone." His words are for me only since the rest of them have been involved in this world for far longer than I have.

Without warning, he throws the rock on the ground. Upon contact it explodes, whirling in a thousand circular sparks. Eventually it stops, leaving a portal rimmed with red that mirrors a field of night-shined snow reflecting from the moon and dark snow-tipped mountains that tower in the distance.

First my father and then Alice step through. Percy leans down, his head against mine, "Once we're through, don't stop walking." Giving me a kiss, he takes my hand to urge me through with him. I squeeze back for him to wait. Nodding to Hades I say, "You go first."

"The one who opens it has to close it. The door is here, therefore I shall go last." His palm out, he gestures to the portal. *"After you."* He speaks in the forgotten language, which I now know to be the first—and once the only—language spoken throughout the universe.

Shrugging my shoulders, I walk through. It's a dizzying experience as scenery passes before me at a speed my eyes can't keep up with. With each step, the images flash by faster and with each image comes their own smell. Fresh grass, dirt, fish, human sweat, and so much more invade my senses. The experience reminds me of the spinning teacup ride at fairs. The combination of the different smells and speed of our walk is enough to make me stop to vomit.

Feeling my hand loosen from his, Percy holds onto it tighter, forcing me to keep walking instead of stopping to throw up. It takes ten steps until I am standing in an icy field of snow. The images no longer spin past me, but my equilibrium doesn't understand that.

I vomit and then roll over, pressing my face into the cold, hard snow. I try to distract myself from the aftereffects of using a portal by hoping my face will freeze off. It always helps after a sickening ride to apply a cold water bottle to my face, so why not try the method out with some snow? My face against the snow turns out to produce a much better result than the water bottle ever did.

Hearing the crunch of snow under shoes, I turn my head to see my father crouching beside me. Sympathy marks his face as he says, "The first jump is always the worst."

Laying there, too sick to do anything, I watch him as he rolls up both of my sleeves. Placing his thumbs on my inner wrists, he presses down on them. The pressure is hard enough that I tug away from him. "What the bloody hell was that for?" I fume.

"Thank you would suffice."

I'm no longer nauseous. The incessant spinning stopped after the pressure he applied. "Thanks." I mutter my gratitude, still a little put off that it had hurt.

"What?" My father cups his ear, feigning he didn't hear me.

To my relief, no sentries are posted at the entrance of a hedge maze that marks the only entrance to the palace. Thalia steps forward and we follow her lead until we're standing before an arched opening of stone that leads into an outside foyer. I wonder what's going through her mind as she traverses where she was once caged. You had to have considerable courage to walk right back into hell. If she is frightened of being captured again, she does not show it. A rage burns within her. I can see it with how she is poised like a caged animal. Her grip on her own swords is tight and her back is hunched, ready to spring at any slight movement. I can only hope that she does not let the rage push her into losing her sense if we run into trouble.

We do not know exactly where Clio is kept and decided that to cover more ground and be less noticeable, it would be better to split up. I don't feel comfortable with that idea. In every horror movie, bad things result from splitting up. I fret over the possibility that Zeus knows of the other ways to kill an immortal. But if that is the case, then why did he steal the trident? Maybe my father was right about it being a tightly held secret. If very few immortals left knew of the other ways, then the war would not have ended when the trident disappeared. Would it?

In the foyer, there is a door on each wall. I clasp my father's arm in farewell before he and Alice go through the door on the left. Hades and Thalia choose the door to the front, while Percy and I go to the right. It's quiet, not a sound to be heard other than our breathing and the snow swirling across the stone floor.

The calm before the storm.

With no lights on, it's even darker inside. A sea of drapes are drawn closed, allowing no light from the moon to shine through the windows. We walk slowly and purposefully so as to not trip in the darkness and alert others of our presence.

All the doors in the hall are closed, and every time we open one my heart pounds with undiluted fear. Will we find Clio or Zeus? Or maybe we'll find some monster that I'm sure Zeus will have lurking behind one of these doors, either slumbering or devouring some unwilling victim. The thought chills me to the bone. When you have lived as long as Zeus and became sadistic from boredom—I never want to find out what would amuse someone like him.

There's faint relief when each room turns up empty, but a nagging anxiety pulls at me. *Where is she? Is she even here?* With every door we open, that anxiety tugs at me. Something feels very wrong, but I can't put my finger on what. It could just be nerves. I so want to believe it to be nerves.

At the end of the hall is another set of doors. Through them is a hall similar to the one we just came from, lined with more doors, but this time no windows. At the end of the hall is yet another set of doors. Only these doors are massive and seem to be meant for a giant. It's a door that I imagine a viking would dream of entering to their banquet in Valhalla. Zeus' demeanor reminds me of what a viking would be like when they're off in battle, slaying their enemies, drunk on killing. Knowing his abilities, I have to wonder if Zeus was once known as Odin. In a way, it would make sense. He does fit the bill.

Unlike the other doors, this one is loud as we push it open. I flinch while it groans in protest, as if alerting its master of company. Sword drawn, I survey the area. It seems to be a theater. Rows of seats flow downward to a stage that is lit with candles at its base. The flickering of the candles gives enough light to vaguely make out what's on the stage.

No.

Nailed to a wall is the bloody form of Clio. Percy calls for me to wait, but I ignore him and run to Clio, not checking if anyone else is in the room. She doesn't flinch as I call out her name. Her pearlescent skin has taken on an ashy pallor. Markings of blues, purples and reds tinge her battered body. Closer to the stage I can see that wrought iron nails hold her up by the wrists and, *oh god,* my trident is embedded into her stomach.

"Clio, Clio," I beg. My hands flutter around her naked body that's covered in bruises and fresh blood. Zeus must have recently done this to her for her wounds to be this fresh. She moans in pain, but her eyes still stay closed. Dammit, I don't know what to do. Do I remove the trident or the nails first? After a quick debate, I opt to remove the nails first. Gripping the nails, I pray that they will be easily removed. For once, my prayers are answered as a sickening wet sound occurs at the release of the nails. With both nails gone, her body sags. I catch her, already anticipating what was going to happen. She feels like nothing but bones, as if she hasn't eaten since I last saw her. Blimey, if he abused her like this, she probably hasn't. Zeus has no qualms about torturing his daughter. A daughter that he sees as property. The bastard. He will burn for this.

"I got you," I chant to her, but it's more to reassure myself and to calm my fraying nerves at the state of her.

"No, don't!" Percy yells at me. He should be closer and yet he sounds so far away. If he is yelling for me to not remove the trident, then he's too late; the moment he yelled I had already taken the trident from her body. The trident warms in my hand, buzzing with satisfaction. The feeling reminds me of when you go all day without eating and when you finally fill yourself with food you are left ... satisfied.

No ... no no no no no.

Clio's shallow panting goes completely silent as the last of her breath rattles from her mouth. It's the death rattle that everyone fears hearing as they lay next to their dying loved one. The rattle reverberates to my very core, shattering me into a million pieces. I rock back and forth, holding her against me. I clutch her bony body into mine and will for none of this to be true. But it is true, and there is no reversing this terrible mistake.

Through garbled cries, I sing for her soul,

"Who shall bring you
Into the death-sleep sling you.
When you walk on the Path of Death
And the tracks you tread
Are cold, so cold.
When you stand by the Gate of Death
And you have to tear free,
I shall follow you.
With my song,
You shall be free from your bond."

Clapping erupts, followed by, "Well done! That was a marvelous performance!" Zeus hops onto the stage. His mouth is in a full grin, not a trace of sadness over the death of his daughter. I reach for the trident that I dropped after dislodging it.

"Nuh-uh." He wags his finger before my hands are wrapped around the trident. "I wouldn't do that if I were you, or I might just have a little fun with your lover."

I grab it anyway and then frantically look for Percy. A harpie has him pinned to the ground, its beak a hairbreadth away from his neck, waiting for Zeus' order. The room is too poorly lit for me to make out the look on Percy's face. If Zeus thinks I will lose this chance at revenge, then he is sorely mistaken. Percy can easily recover from a harpies bite. My trident on the other hand, is not so forgiving. I don't look Percy's way. I feel guilty for these thoughts and looking at him will only make this decision harder. Zeus is right *here,* and I finally have the trident. This needs to end. No one else has to suffer another minute at the hands of this prick.

Zeus is close enough that I can easily slice him, it doesn't even need to be a killing wound. A small nick will get the job done just fine. The trident reacts to my bloodlust, fueling my rage like an endless cycle. Zeus' triumphant eyes turn fearful as he takes in the grip I have on the trident and the vengeance that seeps from my pores.

He steps back, tripping over himself. "Kill him!" he orders like the coward that he is. The worst always talk a big game and in the end, are the most cowardly.

Before Zeus gets the idea to block me with whatever ability that he possesses, I will the trident to morph into a dagger and throw it at him. I've never trained with knives but the trident flys true through the air, knowing where I want it to land. It finds contact with his left eye. I hear the distinct popping of his eye followed by the crumpling of his body to the floor. I don't have time to bask in the frozen look of terror displayed on his face because the harpie that was restraining Percy rams into my side. Its claws rake down me, leaving my side searing like it is dipped in fire.

Screaming in fury and pain, I lunge forward, trying to get the harpie off me at the same time its beak comes down where my head was a moment ago. Pinning me back down with its claws, it goes to peck at my face. Its breath is rancid, smelling of decaying fish. The harpie makes the mistake of not holding down my other shoulder, and as it reels back for the finishing blow, I reach for the dagger at my hip and thrust it into the harpie's throat when it comes down for my face. I twist the blade in its throat, feeling the crunch of it against bone and cartilage. A small part of me revels in the feeling. Blood comes out of the harpie's beak in rivulets and splatters on my chest and neck. As its grip loosens, I slide out from under it. With a thud against the floor, I know the beast won't be getting back up.

I wildly scan the theater, looking for any more attackers. There are none. Zeus had only thought to bring one harpie with him. His ego was his downfall and I relish that he died by my hand. He'll never be able to harm anyone ever again.

I had left my jian near Percy, dropping it as I ran to aid Clio. My aid being a decision that I will regret for my entire life.

"Percy?" I call out, hoping that the bird was unable to follow through with Zeus' order. Only silence greets me and the drip of blood from my soaked clothes landing on the floor. Not wanting to be weaponless in case more harpies show up, I take the trident from Zeus, but not before twisting it and stabbing him once more in the other eye.

"Walk blindly in death, you bastard." I know taking out his eyes is an empty sentiment because the trident ate his soul, leaving nothing to wander any planes of reality that exist in this universe. But I do it to satisfy my own anger at the injustice that was done to Clio.

I cautiously walk to Percy's body. He lies there limply on the ground. I don't dare look at the darkened mass where his head should be. So much blood surrounds him and I don't have the courage to see what I have done to him. Instead, I kneel at his side, praying that he will forgive the pain that I have brought onto him. I hope he knows that if his life was truly at risk I would never jeopardize that. I would have willingly done anything Zeus had asked of me, but I knew his soul would stay tethered and once he was done regenerating he would come back to me, whole and complete. And if he is mad, then I will drown in his anger. Because I do deserve it. What kind of person allows this to happen to the one they love?

The door opens and I whip around. I relax my fierce grip on the trident when Alice's face is lit by the candles. I warily look at her as she scans the theater, inspecting the damage that was done.

Cold eyes turn to me. "You killed her."

"It was an accident," I plead. "The trident was embedded in her and I went to remove it, not knowing that my touch would activate the power. I didn't think it worked like that." And then I was crying. I never meant for that to happen. Clio, who was my stunningly beautiful friend. Who had looked up to me for something my past life had done for her and *I* had killed *her*. I can understand if Thalia will hate me. I killed her sister, and that is all on me.

With a gentle touch, Alice brings me into her arms. My crying and complete trust in her leaves me blind to her following movements. My body tenses and then slackens as I lose consciousness from the knife that she severs my spinal cord with.

Chapter Twenty-Eight

I wake in a dank cell and to the feeling of chains biting into my wrists and ankles. Fear takes over at the knowledge of not knowing where I am and not being able to defend myself. I tug on my restraints, only to cut my wrists. A bead of blood sticks to the edges of the metal manacles. My wound quickly heals and along with it the pain. What should've taken a day to scab over and another four, maybe five, days to fully heal took less than a few seconds.

Light shines through a barred window, illuminating the heart-shaped vines that climb down into my cell. They twist and coil over each other, creating a waterfall of green foliage. The window is too high for me to see anything other than the clear blue sky. A bird flies across my view and I hear its caw as it passes. The familiar sound is that of a raven. I'd recognise their cry anywhere. During my stay at Oxford, a raven was always perched outside my dorm window. It was always the same four ravens who took turns each morning pecking at my window until I opened it and they released a trinket from their talons, dropping it into my palm. Each bird would give one hushed caw in goodbye before taking flight back into the sky. I only knew the raven was different each morning because eventually I was able to discern their different voices. Milo's was higher pitched than Sylo's, and Edgar's had a curl at the end of his caw. I named them all, Ezric being my favorite. He was the largest out of the four and had the gentlest caw. The bird in the sky sounds eerily similar to him, and an ache of sorrow fills my chest at the familiarity.

The cell that I amin appears to have been recently cleaned. The evidence of that is a bucket that sits off to the side, out of my reach. A dirty rag lays over the rim, dripping water onto the floor. A man the size of a boulder appears, his keys clinking against each other as he searches for the correct one. My heart rate increases when he opens the door of my cell. He ducks his head when he enters, and when he stands to his full height, he towers over me. I hold in my breath as he gets closer. The sheer *size* of him is alarming. He looks me up and down and curls his upper lip. He snarls, apparently disgusted by what he sees. I have an inclination to snarl back at him.

Everything in me screams for me to fight, to take up a defensive stance, but I shove down the instinct. I'm in chains, unable to get the upper hand in this situation. For now, I will play the subdued, broken down prisoner until I know where I am and who is holding me. I doubt this brute runs the show around here. Wherever here is.

He doesn't say anything, only grunts for me to move forward after the snarl he gave me. He unhooks the chain attaching me to the wall. I look to him for direction, and he gestures for me to lead the way. He follows me as he holds onto the chain connected to my manacles, like he is my master and I his obedient dog.

There is only one way out of here, up a narrow stone stairway. I climb it and at the top of the stairs I find myself in the middle of an open courtyard, surrounded by tall walls of more gray stone. A tower stands off to the west. The layout of the place reminds me of a castle in medieval times, and I wonder just where I have found myself.

The oaf of a man tugs on the chain, causing the manacles to dig into my wrists and then ankles while I try to balance myself. The cuts are deeper this time from the invasion and it takes longer for them to heal. I grit my teeth, holding back the curses I want to spit at him. His face shows nothing. The tick of a thick vein pumps at his temple, the only indication of his annoyance at having to escort me. I'm sure he has other things he'd rather be doing, but I don't care, let him be annoyed. When one is consumed by their own desires and wants, they pay little attention to what's around them.

He tugs on the chain again, which has me stumbling to my right, and I cry out this time. The recent cut not yet healed, the edges of the manacles slice a tendon, causing my hands to go limp. I'm sure that if it were the tendons at my ankles that were severed, he would not have any patience for me to heal and drag me to wherever he was ordered to take me. Thoughts of wringing this chain around his neck help temper the rage that has begun boiling in my veins, and I regret not at least trying doing that very thing when he first entered my cell.

The crash of nearby waves distracts me from the searing pain. The sound reminds me of Percy, and I hope that whoever is behind this does not have him as well. If he is captured, then it is by my hand, for it would've never occurred if he wasn't decapitated. And what of my father and Thalia? Hades? I pray that they made it out in time and that neither one of them were captured. I say a prayer in my head, but I'm not even sure if that is how you pray. Can Chaos even hear my thoughts? So I pray out loud under my breath, hoping against all odds that the creator of this universe hears my plea. "Please, *please* protect them. Let no harm come to them. You have stayed quiet and ignored your Genesis' prayers. Please don't ignore mine. *Please, I beg of you.*"

No voice resounds in my head, nor do I hear a boom of agreement. The only thing that changes around me is the shift in the wind. It brushes the loose tendrils of my hair, coaxing the strands to tickle the back of my neck. A current of hopelessness washes over me as I am ushered in the opposite direction of the towers. Like an already trained dog who has learned the concept of heel, I constantly check on the chain connecting me to the brute of a man, making sure that I don't get too far away or too close to him. Paying attention to him like this, I am able to walk through the remaining grounds without any more harm caused to my wrists and ankles. My damaged wrists still haven't fully healed yet.

Outside of the grounds, a grassy field of yellow and green greets me. The wind blows again and soft music floats through the field. The blades of grass swishing to and fro remind me of the seagrass that dances with the tides on the ocean floor. Lost in thought, I track the wind. The blades turn this way and that, creating snake-like images slithering in a wave that slowly dies down. The serenity of the moment is too good to be true, which is then confirmed when my eyes land on Alice. She stands in the middle of the field, her arms crossed and her features set in stone. No emotion lies within her eyes, either. Like the very notion of her stabbing me in the back was inevitable. As if the last few months meant nothing to her. I want to scream at her. To cry. To berate. I feel like I could tear out my hair at the frustration and loss that consumes me. *Why? Why? Why? What game are you playing? You are my friend. You were my friend.* All of this I want to shout at her, but I rein in my emotions and try to wear a face just as lifeless as hers, because it's not just her in the field. No, standing next to Alice are a woman and a man, both dressed in white cotton. The man displays a bored look while the woman looks as if she has won. What she has won, I do not know. She beams at me, a mad glint to her eyes. They are strikingly similar to Zeus'. A shiver runs over me, and it isn't from the wind blowing against the beads of sweat forming at the base of my neck. Whoever this woman is, she exudes power.

"Kneel before your queen," my keeper commands when we come to a stop before the group.

"He speaks!" I admonish. Given the situation, I should stay quiet and listen, but that would not be me in the slightest. So I opt for sarcasm and anger instead of the fear that's clawing at my throat. "And here I thought the only thing you knew how to do was grunt and snarl like a pig."

At that, he kicks the back of my knees. I fall down, but not before seeing the unknown man smile in amusement. He shares the same eyes as the woman standing next to him. I want to spit in his face, but instead I groan out in pain when my restraints open my still healing wrists. They numb once more as the tissue and nerves are sawed to the bone. The cutting of nerves doesn't stop the burning lacing through my wrists and cut ankles, though.

Falling to my knees, I finally notice the body on the ground. His breathing is coming in short, shallow pants and his face is swollen to the extent that he couldn't open his eyes if he wanted to. He is beaten to such a pulp that I barely recognize him. But I do recognize him, and a fury runs through me at the cruelty they have shown my father.

"What is the meaning of this?!" I demand. I fight against the chains, not caring in the least about the amount of blood I am losing. The pain doesn't connect with my brain as I try to get to my father's broken form. The man of my life, my childhood hero, reduced to this savagery. I try to get up only for the oaf to push me back down. My chest presses into the ground, his foot digs into my back. "Get off of me, you lump of shit!"

Sighing irritably, the woman says, "Rubeus, leave her be. Can't you see? She's distraught. It's not every day you see the death of your father."

At that, I freeze. "He's not dead." I say it out of determination. He can't be dead, that's impossible. He's still breathing. I can hear it and I can faintly see the rise and fall of his chest.

"Oh, but it is possible." I look up, not realizing that I had voiced that part out loud.

Looking back down to my father, relief floods through me. "You lie, he still breathes."

Liar.

The woman tsks, a sound that I already loathe. "You will speak to me with respect or a lesson will be learned." Her hand reaches out to slap me. I don't flinch and instead watch at the effort it takes her not to follow through with it. She pulls back her hand, dropping it to her side.

"Remove her chains." The oaf named Rubeus does her bidding. The heavy manacles no longer pressing on my healing wounds is a reprieve that I'm thankful to have.

"Be a good puppet and you shall be rewarded." Her tone turns dark with a hint of craving as if she very much would like me to do what she says next. "Be a bad puppet and there will be ..." Gripping my father's hair she tugs his head back, exposing his throat.

"Don't touch him." My voice is weak, not the solid strength I so desperately wish it to be.

She ignores me and presses a knife to his throat. Not able to look away, I watch in disbelief and unrelenting horror as she slices his throat open. His blood does not spray out like I imagined it would, but instead it gushes out in thick rivulets. The woman lets go of my father's head and it smacks against the ground with a wet thud.

And then the woman does the unthinkable; she licks the blood from her knife. My *father's* blood. Her eyes roll back, flickering in euphoric ecstasy. "Ah, how sweet." She moans. "The memories he has of you make me now think of you as my own ... Lovely ... just lovely. I've always wanted a daughter."

She smiles down at me, blood smearing her teeth. The smile is that of love, but all I see is wickedness, and I can't hold back the disgust that bubbles up. She ignores my gag and tauntingly says, "Come, dear." In a whir, my father stands before me. "I'll be your father."

I reel back on my heels, stunned and mortified by what she has done. She somehow has taken the image of my father. She is his likeness in every way. Even the voice and posture are spot on. The only thing that is different are the eyes. They are not the green of my father's, but are clouded over, as if she is blind. The clouding of them eerily reminds me of the shopkeeper in France and I save that thought for later.

Not holding back the hatred I feel for this woman, I spit at her face. The ball of saliva lands perfectly in her left eye. "My father is alive."

A laugh of dark humor reverberates from her as she wipes the spit from her eye. "Foolish puppet. Your father is dead."

Not believing her words, I look at my father's form. His body's too still, with his neck laying at an awkward angle. He should've regained his health by now. His head wasn't severed. He should be healed by now.

"Father?" My voice cracks at the bile that rises up, burning my throat. My world turns upside down and I can't come to terms at what's been laid at my feet. "How?" It's all I can say as I come to terms with the inconceivable. This can't be happening.

Flipping the blade she used on my father, she says, "With this, of course." The disbelief must be written all over my face for she continues, "It's a blade made from the bones of Gaia herself. Therefore, it has the same power that your trident does." She pauses, considering, "Well, not as powerful. The trident accomplished what her bones could not."

I gape at her words. This can't be happening, but my father is still not moving. Instead, he's laying face down in his own blood. And then it hits me: she's speaking the truth. My father did mention there were other ways to kill an immortal.

Hopeless and so painfully broken, I ask, "What do you want?" With my father dead before me and butchered before my very eyes, I feel heavy and so, so lost.

She leans forward, replacing his image with that of her own. "Isn't it obvious? I want you to be my puppet."

Seeing my chance, I lunge for the blade. She laughs and allows me to grab it from her. I plunge it into her chest, very much finding comfort out of the sickening suction as I twist the knife further into her cavity.

"You silly fool. It only works once and then the bones are useless!" She shrieks as her laughter becomes frenzied. Blood drips out of the corners of her mouth and she looks like the devil. She *is* the devil. Her words leave me in a rage. A rage fueled by betrayal and death. My screams are those of a banshee who has lost everything, one who would do anything for revenge. I recover the knife from her to stab her once more, but am hit upside the head. The hit is hard enough that I topple over, landing on my father's body. Touching his corpse leaves me with a hollowness so cold that I begin to shake. *Live, I will. Come back to me.*

"Be my puppet." Her voice is that of a serpent. Hissing softly before the fatal strike.

"Never," I rasp, my unshed tears scorching my throat.

"Wrong choice, puppet."

I look up at her. "Who are you, and why are you doing this?"

Sighing, this time more impatiently, she snaps her fingers. Rubeus picks me up and I scream at the loss of my father's body. Too soon. I am taken from him too soon.

Thrashing against him, I throw my head back in defiance. There's a satisfying crunch as the back of my skull makes contact with his nose. He curses, but not before throwing me on the ground. I bounce like a ragdoll, the blades of grass scratching scissor-like knicks along my exposed skin.

The woman leans down, morphed back to her original skin. No longer does she mask herself as my father. Good. "My name is *Hera,* and I will show you mercy this time, puppet. But don't make me regret that decision."

Mercy? She calls this mercy? If she thinks maiming my father is mercy, then she is more delusional than I originally thought.

Ignoring her warning, I roll away from her honeyed breath. I go to grab her ankle, but her foot makes contact with my face before I have a chance. My last thoughts before succumbing to darkness are the loss of my father and a prayer that she doesn't have anyone else.

Acknowledgments

Honestly, without my editor, this book would've been total crap. Taylor, you're amazing. Thank you for giving The Rise of Amphitrite love and giving me solid advice on how to better it.

Thank you to my beta readers, your feedback helps me – a newbie author – grow as a writer. You guys are *chefs kiss.

And dad, thank you for being my cheerleader. It really means a lot. I hope you enjoyed my first novel. And don't let mom make you feel weird about reading the smut scenes. It's okay.

About Author

Savannah Zherebnenko lives in the PNW with her husband, two kids, and three fur babies. When she's not zombified from her young kids, you can find her in her garden or in the kitchen canning, baking, cooking... slaving. Just kidding about the last one. But really, and if she's not doing any of those things, she's curled up with a book and a full glass of wine.

You can find her on Instagram at https://www.instagram.com/savannahzher.writes/

CPSIA information can be obtained
at www.ICGtesting.com
Printed in the USA
LVHW021217070423
743749LV00008B/327